MURDER ON THE
18TH GREEN

FEDERICO MARIA RIVALTA

MURDER ON THE 18TH GREEN

Translated by Elizabeth Pollard

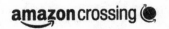

Text copyright © 2013 Federico Maria Rivalta

Translation copyright © 2015 Elizabeth Pollard, Centro Studi Ateneo

Previously published as *Un ristretto in tazza grande* by the author via the Kindle Direct Publishing Platform in Italy in 2013. Translated from Italian by Elizabeth Pollard, Centro Studi Ateneo. First published in English by AmazonCrossing in 2015.

Published by AmazonCrossing, Seattle

www.apub.com

Amazon, the Amazon logo, and AmazonCrossing are trademarks of Amazon.com, Inc., or its affiliates.

ISBN-13: 9781503948679

ISBN-10: 1503948676

Cover design by David Drummond

Printed in the United States of America

MURDER ON THE 18TH GREEN

PROLOGUE

I'm leaning in, perfectly positioned, about to start my back swing. My pelvis rotates right, my left arm is straight, and my right follows, all my weight staying on my right leg. When I reach the peak of the movement, like a slingshot pulled back and aimed, there is a fraction of a second, a moment when everything is still; in that moment, the mind must create a vacuum. It's like a spell: there's no sound, no color, no thought. Your body only exists as an instrument to perform its movements. I feel my hips start turning to the left and the movement forces my arms to lower, bringing the head of the five-iron to the ball. The descent is powerful, and on impact, my body weight, amplified by speed, focuses onto a plastic ball 1.68 inches in diameter. The force is so great that I don't feel the impact; I step through it. My arms continue their movement like the hands of a clock that, having passed six, climb up toward nine o'clock, and finally reach twelve. I turn my head to the left in line with my shoulders. Now I can follow the ball's flight with my gaze. I can see it as it continues to rise, but, because of the sunlight, I lose sight as it slows and begins to fall. I can't see where it lands, but deep inside I know: it is close to the flag.

I could hear my golf buddies congratulating me on the shot. I tried to conceal my satisfaction with the false modesty of someone who's used to making certain shots thanks to years of practice and inborn talent. There were four of us: Massimo Salvioni and I were playing against Arcadio Casati Vitali and Alessandro Ranni, who, true to form, destroyed us. They'd already won the game at the thirteenth hole. Massimo and I played to the end, partly because we just wanted to play, but also to buy time to get over the beating before returning to the Frassanelle clubhouse. It was Saturday afternoon, and I was secretly, irrationally hoping the clubhouse would be empty; it's never fun having to admit defeat to anyone who asks, and they always ask. We reached the green and, just as I had expected, my ball was a few feet from the hole.

In golf, order is determined according to the distance of the ball from the hole. Mine was the closest, meaning that I would be the last to play. I watched and waited, leaning on my putter. By the time my turn came, I was tired and unmotivated, and I botched it: the ball teetered on the edge of the hole, but opted to defy gravity and did not fall in. Arcadio didn't spare me one of his usual tasteless jokes. I looked at Massimo, who shrugged. Finally, it was over, and we were free to seek solace in beer.

Golf is a very competitive game, so good sportsmanship is needed to prevent a relaxing walk with friends from turning into something that resembles a boxing match.

Whenever we played, Arcadio managed to violate all the rules of etiquette—he had even hit Massimo with a small branch after some lively bickering about his constant talking whenever Massimo and I were up. As if that weren't enough, when it was their turn to swing, he demanded reverent silence.

On the way back to the clubhouse, I had the feeling that other members were just waiting to ask how it went.

Arcadio, in his usual style, beat them to it by exclaiming, "OK, who's next?"

If nothing else, his bragging spared us any further questions. Arcadio went straight to the locker room while Massimo, Alessandro, and I stopped at the bar. If we had only imagined the madness our short stop would trigger, we would have hurled ourselves into the showers without even taking our clothes off.

Massimo was irritable and tired, and he didn't bother holding back his anger, saying, "Arcadio would be a good player if he wasn't such an asshole. He just ruined my day, and it isn't the first time."

I was also annoyed about losing the game, which in golf jargon is called "match play." You can play individually or in teams of two. It was great to have Massimo on my team; he never chastised me for making mistakes and, in his joking way, he was almost always able to keep things fun, even while losing. On the other hand, playing with Arcadio was so irritating that, in five hours of play, we'd never once smiled. In contrast, Arcadio's partner Alessandro was a nice guy, polite and reserved, and I asked how he'd come to be paired with Arcadio.

He responded, "Do you want to know the truth? His father asked me to, but it's really a pain. I end up looking like an asshole, too . . ."

Like most of us, I'm rarely shy with my opinions about people— provided they're not present. As there were no other members within earshot, I complained, "Count Alvise has so much class, it seems impossible that Arcadio is his son."

Massimo was one of my favorite golf buddies, not just because he was fun to be with, but because he loved golf as a sport and not as a status symbol. He was about fifty-five years old and well-built, an easygoing, highly social guy. He was a gynecologist at Padua Hospital, but he rarely talked about his work. When he did, it was usually in response to the smutty jokes that were a daily affair in the men's locker room. At the same time, he could be a little touchy, not the type to let things roll off his back. If he felt wronged, he'd make it known, and, unlike me, he'd do it right to the face of the person who had wronged him.

As piqued as I was by the defeat, Massimo gave his thoughts free rein, saying in a tone mixed with irony and anger, "The count's son? I know whose son he really is. Anyway, I want to talk to his father about it when I see him, because I'm really pissed about the whole thing."

It all ended there.

Francesca, the bartender in her late thirties who was on duty that afternoon, took our drink orders, and later, with the weary air of someone who'd had a tough day, mustered up a smile to say good-bye.

CHAPTER ONE

Whenever there's a golf tournament, I always arrive an hour early. For some reason, I'm superstitious about this ritual, even though I can't say that it's brought any measurable success. I'm not a great player; I've got a handicap of thirteen, which puts me close to the best among the three amateur categories. However, unlike some fanatics who practice daily, I can only dedicate two days a week to golf. I compensate with good coordination, which, as in so many sports, can be a decisive factor.

Every Sunday, my routine starts with a walk past the driving range and a stop at the club bar. The bar is the only place in the club where there's no distinction between a bad golfer and a good golfer, but there is a difference between a bad spender and a good spender—and in that regard, I'm on par.

That day, I was greeted from behind the bar by the bright smile of Luisa, the other bartender. Even at forty, the bartenders still consider me a good-looking man, mostly because I leave them a holiday tip at the end of the year. So each time I see Luisa's smile, I tell myself that even if it's not reserved exclusively for me, at least it's just for a select group of members.

I never have to order coffee; Luisa knows my ritual, and she already had some ready for me.

"Riccardo, have you heard about Massimo?"

For a moment, I wondered why sometimes Luisa called me by my first name, and other times we were on strictly last-name basis.

"Massimo? Massimo Salvioni?"

"Yes."

"I haven't heard anything. What happened to him?"

"It seems he's gone missing."

"What do you mean, missing?" I asked, perplexed. "I just played with him yesterday!"

"Yeah . . . but he hasn't been seen since after the game. In fact, Patty waited for him here until nearly midnight."

Patty was Massimo's wife; she was baptized as Roberta, but she'd get really annoyed if someone tried to call her that. Unlike Massimo, Patty wasn't tall or very well-built; her nose was slightly out of proportion, and her small eyes would have kept her from any beauty contest. However, just like her husband, Patty was extremely friendly and kind. When they were both at the club, it brightened everyone's day, and even golf seemed better.

"Maybe there was a misunderstanding and Massimo went straight home. Or maybe he got an emergency call from the hospital."

"But he and Patty came here together yesterday."

I smiled at the idea that Massimo could have driven home to Padua, more than twelve miles from Frassanelle, and forgotten his wife at the club.

Thinking this over, I took a packet of raw sugar from the tray on the bar. Thanks to some sort of cultural heritage, I consider the habit of using raw sugar in coffee a concession to old culinary traditions. To tell the truth, though, it's the only concession I make. Apart from that, I consider myself the prince of processed food—it's even better if it's frozen.

"Where's Patty now?" I asked.

"I don't know. I think she went to the police."

"To the police? Really?"

"Yes, and Patty's mother has already called three times this morning to ask if anyone has seen Massimo."

"But have they looked out on the course? Maybe he felt ill . . ."

"Yes, they already looked and didn't find him anywhere—and his bag's still in the locker room."

"What did they say at his hospital?"

"That no one's seen him since Friday."

"What a mess . . . I wonder where he ended up . . . ," I said, suddenly feeling seriously worried.

I told Luisa to put the coffee on my tab and then headed down the entrance hall stairs that lead to both the reception desk and the locker room.

The Frassanelle Golf Club occupies a nineteenth century villa set on ten acres of woodland in the Euganean Hills Park. Formerly the country residence of the Casati Vitali family—the counts of Nogaredo—it spreads over two floors and a basement. The club is not luxurious, but its elegant simplicity, combined with tasteful decor in keeping with the rural setting, makes it cozy and welcoming.

I hadn't reached the bottom of the stairs when a cluster of people in front of the secretaries' office turned to look at me. The group included the club president, Andrea Galli, the two secretaries who work there, the two match referees, and two police officers—a marshal and a corporal. I got the distinct impression they were all looking at me reproachfully. I paused on the bottom step, feeling a bit uncomfortable.

Of course, the first person to speak was Galli, whose life is built on hierarchy and etiquette. Galli is tall and so thin that I believe his belly grows inward.

"Ranieri! We've been looking for you since yesterday! Don't you ever turn your cell phone on?" asked the president with an annoyed and scolding tone as soon as he saw me.

Shit, my phone! As I tried to remember where I'd left it this time, the two secretaries recounted in sync the exact details of their failed attempts at contacting me.

"I'm sorry, I must have forgotten it somewhere . . . ," I replied sheepishly.

From their looks, I knew that whatever was wrong, they were confident it was my fault.

Before Galli had a chance to start lecturing me, one of the two policemen came over and said, "Good morning, Mr. Ranieri. I'm Marshal Carmine Costanzo from the carabinieri station in Bastia di Rovolon." I held out my hand to him, but the marshal ignored it, bringing his hand up to his beret in a salute, and continued. "Mr. Ranieri, did you know that Dr. Massimo Salvioni has been missing since last night?"

"Yes, Luisa just told me."

As I uttered those words, I tried to recover some of my dignity along with my hand.

"And tell me, were you with Dr. Salvioni yesterday afternoon?"

"Yes, there were four of us, and we played until six o'clock. After the game, we had a beer together, and then I went down to the locker room for a shower before going home."

"And later, perhaps, did you speak to Dr. Salvioni on the phone?"

"No . . . If I had, I would have already told you."

While we were talking, I was still thinking about where the hell I'd left my cell . . . The marshal probably read the concern in my face, because he immediately asked me how long ago I'd lost it.

"Honestly, I can't remember . . . I know I didn't use it yesterday."

The expressions on the officers' faces went from sympathy to conviction without appeal.

Anxiously, I tried to make myself useful by naming the other players who'd been with us the evening before, until the marshal stopped me on Casati Vitali. In the end, all I could do was agree with them and confess that my phone deserved a more attentive owner . . .

As we were talking, other members arrived, and Galli sent Claudia, one of the secretaries, to collect their fifteen-euro tournament fees. Despite my ritual, I'd lost all interest in golf that day.

Marshal Costanzo was still looking at me expectantly, but I had no idea where Massimo was.

"Luisa told me that you've already searched for him on the golf course, right? Because if he felt ill or something . . ."

"The caddies looked for him yesterday evening. And we've already called the hospitals and his close relatives, but nobody knows anything."

With a knowing look on his face, the marshal stepped toward me and took my arm to draw me away from the others before saying, "Look, Ranieri. By chance, you wouldn't happen to know if Dr. Salvioni had any other 'acquaintances,' shall we say? You know . . . another member's wife, maybe a fling?"

I wanted to joke that I'm a reporter by trade and therefore the least likely person someone would confide in, unless they want to hear about it on the evening news. What's more, I wouldn't recognize an affair even if it was happening right under my nose. I was sorry to disappoint the marshal, though, so I firmly told him, "Marshal, apart from the fact that Massimo doesn't seem the type, I'm not aware of any extramarital affairs."

At that point, I expected the marshal to abandon his smug look of conspiracy, but instead he said, "Well, perhaps this whole thing could be a prank. You know, between old friends."

"Perhaps we should clear up a little misunderstanding, Marshal. I'm not that close with Massimo. I mean, we play golf together, but we don't see each other outside of that. I think Patty's the only one who can help you."

"And who is Patty?"

"Sorry, I meant Roberta, Massimo's wife. She goes by Patty."

"And why's that? It's not like her given name is Genevieve," said the marshal with a certain curiosity.

The marshal's logic was impeccable; I couldn't help but enjoy the air of camaraderie and gloss over the question. "Eh . . . you know . . . Women."

Finally, with a sigh that signaled solidarity in the face of inscrutable female creatures, the marshal gave me back my arm and returned his attention to Galli.

"I want all members to be questioned about whether they saw Dr. Salvioni at any point and if they know anything. If you discover any new information, this is the number at the station. At the moment, we really can't do anything more here."

With that, the marshal and the policeman accompanying him left.

I wondered what to do. I definitely didn't want to play anymore. However, I decided to get changed and spend a few minutes on the driving range; just hitting balls without the stress of worrying where they land usually relaxes me and helps me think. I had no doubt there was a good explanation for Massimo's disappearance, but a nagging feeling whispered that I was missing something.

While changing in the locker room, I overheard some other players speculating about Massimo's whereabouts. The most popular idea, expressed in a rather colorful way, was that he had run off with someone. One member, who I couldn't see and whose voice I didn't recognize, suggested that maybe Massimo was running from gambling debts or worse. I rejected these notions because they didn't fit my idea of Massimo. Of course, it's also true that I've been wrong about people plenty of times. I wondered what Patty thought about all this and especially how she was doing.

I tried to block out the worried thoughts and confused theories running through my head. Once I got on the range, I pulled out my pitching wedge, the iron I always started my warm-ups with. My shots only confirmed that I'd made a wise decision not to play in the tournament; my rhythm was off, I was holding the club too tight, and I was stiff. I hit one ball to the right and the next to the left, and, even worse, it was all totally random.

October is my favorite time in the Euganean Hills. The summer heat has eased, but the cold hasn't started biting yet. The woods in the hills surrounding the golf course glow with the fall leaves ranging from yellow to red, as if all the summer heat they absorbed is being returned in the form of color.

I wondered whether I should give it up and hit the showers. I hit one more ball with the seven-iron, but my arms got ahead of my hip rotation, and the ball curved so far to the left that I'd already put the iron back in my bag before it even hit the ground.

I decided to go back to the locker room. It wasn't even ten o'clock yet, so I was the first player to return. It was so early that Carlo Buonafiore, the caddy master, was still collecting the previous day's dirty towels from the baskets. After I'd taken my shower, I was frustrated to find that the bench that usually held the stacked clean towels was desolately empty. *OK, don't panic.* I knew the cleaning lady usually kept the cupboard in front of the sauna well stocked. And so, naked, wet, and hopeful, I headed down the corridor that led to the sauna, only to notice with astonishment that the sauna's porthole window was completely misted up, and I could see a silhouette on the bench inside.

What could drive a man to torture himself in that way at ten in the morning on a warm October day? For me, it was as incomprehensible as striped toothpaste. I saw the cupboard with the towels and was about to walk past the window to get one when I glanced inside to figure out who was in the sauna. I couldn't see very well, but his head seemed to be in an unnatural position, tilted all the way back like he was staring at the ceiling. I stepped in to ask if everything was OK, but there was no answer. As I drew closer, my heart began beating faster; I knew. I propped one foot on the bench so I could lift myself up and see his face. My heart threatened to burst through my chest. What I saw was so horrific that I felt dizzy, like I was plummeting into an abyss. I tried to control my panic, but looking at that face was like an out-of-body experience. His eye sockets were empty; his nose looked like it had exploded and was spread open in an obscene pose; and his lips were sewn together with a nylon thread as if he were blowing a kiss. The empty feeling reached my brain, the image got tangled up with the sauna steam, and in the space of a heartbeat, everything went dark.

I came to sitting on the wet floor of the sauna, with a sharp pain in my neck, but I couldn't tell if it was from the fall or the shock. The man's body was still there in front of me. I couldn't think clearly. I couldn't understand what was happening or what I should do. Eventually, I got up and slowly made my way out, supporting myself against the wall. I reached the row of lockers in the dressing room and heard voices, maybe greeting me.

I found myself standing in front of someone who looked at me with great concern. Finally, I heard the words come out of my mouth: "Massimo is in the sauna. He's dead."

As I sat on a bench and tried to pull my thoughts together, all hell broke loose around me. In the comings and goings of golfers, kids, secretaries, grounds officers, and various relatives and friends, I could only think about two things. The first was that in every American cop show, the crime scene is reserved for the killer, the victim, and police investigators. The second was that I was still naked. With regard to the first, considering everyone who'd run over there when they'd heard, forensics would find more fingerprints in the sauna than in a Milan subway car. With regard to the second, I decided to cover my family jewels with my hands and walk to my locker with ill-concealed embarrassment.

I still hadn't finished dressing when I heard Marshal Costanzo, who had clearly been called back, order everyone to leave the locker room. I quickly finished getting dressed, closed my bag stuffed with dirty clothes, and headed toward the door. I was about to leave when the marshal called me over.

"Ranieri, wait! Tell me what you saw."

"Marshal, please give me a couple minutes to drink a coffee and try to recover."

"Don't worry about it. You stay here with me; I'll have someone bring your coffee from the bar."

While the marshal shouted at Claudia to fetch coffee, despite being close to her, I put down my bag and sat down resignedly on a bench in the locker room.

Standing in front of me, the marshal began the first interrogation of my life.

"So Ranieri . . . What are you up to, eh?"

"What do you mean, what am I up to?" I asked, flabbergasted.

"I mean, all this mess. Salvioni getting murdered, you finding him, all those people contaminating the crime scene in the Turkish bath . . ."

"It's a sauna."

"What?"

"It's a sauna, not a Turkish bath," I replied firmly.

"Ranieri, damn it! There's a murdered man in there, and you're arguing with me about whether it's a Turkish bath?"

"Look, Marshal, just let me out of here for a few moments. I need to recover and get a breath of fresh air."

"Be patient, it'll just be a few minutes. We called the Padua Police Department, and they told us that District Attorney Dal Nero is coming over with the coroner and forensics. You have to be here because you found Dr. Salvioni. Speaking of which, how did you know the body was Salvioni's? Given the mess his face is in . . ."

"Massimo has a Sampdoria tattoo on his arm. As far as I know, he's the only Sampdoria fan in the entire Veneto region."

"I've been doing this job for more than thirty years, seen my share of murders, but I've never seen anything like this. Looks like the killer was sending a message with the mouth sewn shut and the empty eye sockets . . . If he just wanted to kill him, he didn't have to do all that."

In the distance, I heard an ambulance siren or a police car—more likely both.

"There, Ranieri. Hear that? They're on their way."

"But what's going to happen?"

I was worried about being forced back into the sauna to face that gruesome sight again.

"Oh, don't worry! They just want to ask you some questions."

"Of course, but will I have to go back into the sauna?"

"I don't know. Let them decide. They know what they're doing."

We could hear a heated discussion outside the locker room. Just as the marshal moved to see what was going on, a blonde woman came in carrying a tray with our my coffee.

Abruptly, the woman turned to the marshal and asked him, "Who asked for coffee?"

Before the marshal could answer, I cut in and said, "It's for me."

"Ah! Do you also want a few croissants as well? Perhaps an orange juice?"

Under normal circumstances, I would have caught her sarcasm. However, as I was still a little dazed, I asked, "Well, if there were some raw sugar . . ."

Clearly irritated, she slammed the tray down on the bench where I was sitting and glared at me like a pigeon had just crapped on her coat.

With a tone that did not invite an answer, she said, "Haven't you heard the news? This is a crime scene and the bar is upstairs, where you should go as quickly as possible."

I glanced at the marshal, who, from behind the woman, spread out his arms in a sign of resignation.

I still couldn't understand why she was so angry, so I replied in dismay, "I wanted to go to the bar in the first place! Excuse me, but who are you?"

The marshal jumped in and introduced me to her as the man who had discovered Massimo's body.

The woman, in a milder tone, turned her accusations to Costanzo, saying, "Marshal, I really don't understand. Why would you have coffee delivered to the scene of the crime? You of all people . . ."

Perhaps due to adrenaline from the growing tension, I couldn't help but notice that this haughty woman didn't seem to care whether I had the faintest clue what was happening.

By now I was running out of patience, so I blurted out, "Excuse me. But who, madam, *are* you?"

Finally looking me straight in the eye, the woman replied, "I'm Giulia Dal Nero, the district attorney in charge of this investigation."

Great job, Ranieri. If things continue like this . . .

District Attorney Dal Nero, once she'd heard about my reaction to discovering the body, became more sympathetic. She allowed me to leave the locker room and assigned a corporal to take my information.

A few minutes later, I was finally at the bar, holding that much-needed cup of coffee, ready to give my details to the corporal, who introduced himself as Cipolla. I smiled—his name, which meant "onion," really fit his oniony little face.

We were alone with Luisa, who was under orders to close up so the authorities could continue their investigation. The other club members had already left after giving their info to the police.

Before I'd even made it through the list of phone numbers where I could be reached, the district attorney was standing next to me, looking upset and terribly pale, and asked Luisa for a glass of water.

Then, without turning to look at me, she confessed, "They told me it was a terrible scene, but I never could have imagined something like that."

To be honest, I felt a certain satisfaction in seeing how even the district attorney, who had probably been in similar situations in the past, struggled to deal with what she'd seen. I felt a kind of complicity in sharing with her the sense of dizziness the scene had caused me. Encouraged, I placed a hand on her shoulder and smiled to show that I understood.

After looking me in the eye for a moment, she turned to Corporal Cipolla, saying, "It would be a great help if you contacted the Padua station to share all the data we've collected with the state police."

Then she turned to me and added, "Mr. . . . um . . ."

"Riccardo Ranieri."

"Mr. Ranieri, you'll be able to go soon. But please remain available, because I'll need to ask you a few questions as soon as I get the preliminary report from forensics. Also, I'll need a statement from you since you were the first to find Dr. Salvioni's body."

"Of course, I understand, but, well . . . Unfortunately, I don't know where I left my cell phone, and I don't have a landline at home."

"Where do you live?"

"Here, close to Bastia."

"Good. Then don't leave your house; I'll send a police car to pick you up."

I was surprised by how swiftly she'd gotten a grip on the terrible situation.

DA Dal Nero said good-bye and headed back toward the locker room. I found myself looking at her from behind, and I confess that, although it certainly wasn't the best time for such thoughts, I couldn't help but admire her figure.

Once out of the club and past a large crowd of onlookers, I climbed into my car, a Volvo station wagon. I closed the door and waited a few seconds before starting the engine, enjoying the protection and sense of isolation the car gave me.

The trip from the club to my house is no more than three miles, and very beautiful. The rather narrow road climbs over a hill and then goes through a thick wood full of magical colors. It's quite rare to see other vehicles on the road, but when it happens, it irritates me, and I feel almost jealous about having to share this enchanted place. Once out of the wood, the road joins the main road that links Padua to Vicenza; once past Bastia, I only need to go two more miles toward Vicenza.

I live in an old farmhouse set back from the road; to reach it you have to cut through fifty yards of my neighbor Giuseppe's land. The farmhouse is quite isolated, surrounded by a one-and-a-half-acre garden with an orchard, the back of the property bordered by an irrigation canal.

I love this house. When I moved here from Milan five years ago, I fell in love with it immediately. I live alone or rather, with a pair of German shepherds. I'd wanted dogs like them since I was a child. The female's name is Mila, in honor of the city that put up with me for so many years, while the male's name is Newton, from my passion for physics. Mila weighs about sixty pounds and looks like a coyote, while Newton weighs a hundred pounds and looks more like a bear. The curious thing is that they have such distinct personalities: Newton is lazy, calm, and confident, loves to be fussed over, and is sociable with other dogs, as long as nobody touches Mila. If that happens, Newton will bite—and once is deterrent enough. Mila, on the other hand, is tense, nervous, always on alert to report any kind of danger. Unfortunately for me, any cars that pass within fifty yards, my neighbors' voices, and even the chirping of birds in the trees are all threats to be diligently reported each time she hears them. Of the fourteen hours a day Mila spends outside, she spends thirteen leading a cacophonous chorus of all the other dogs within a half-mile radius. This, coupled with my enormous lack of gardening skill, doesn't much endear me to the uptight community of Bastia.

As soon as I stepped through the gate, I was greeted by the joyful wag of the true owners of the house. As usual, Mila jumped up and scratched at the car door in excitement. I suspect she was trained to do this by the owner of the local auto repair shop; his income has certainly spiked since I've moved here. Even though this warm welcome costs me almost a thousand euros a year, I still think it's money well-spent: an enthusiastic greeting from my dogs puts me in a good mood every time I come home.

I got out of the car and, accompanied by the usual displays of affection from Mila and Newton, I opened the door, turned off the security alarm, and went in search of my phone. It isn't easy to look for something in my house. It spans three floors and more than three thousand square feet. Add to this my natural untidiness and you get an idea of the daunting task before me. I couldn't hope to hear it ring, either, because I hadn't charged it for at least five days. Nevertheless, I thought I'd have plenty of time; considering all the forensics findings, statements from witnesses, and drinks they'd need to get over the shock, I figured it would be hours before I heard from the investigators.

It didn't really matter where I started looking, so why not the kitchen? With this excuse, I decided to make myself a salami sandwich, after a brief stop in the bathroom. I didn't even have time to arrange the slices of salami on the bread when, warned by Mila's noisy protests, I heard the police sirens in the distance. From the kitchen window, I saw the car had stopped at the first gate along the drive, the one belonging to my neighbor. He must have opened it because, when I came down, the police car had pulled up in front of mine.

Newton had added his voice to Mila's protests, but I could just make out the cop calling my name. I turned the house alarm back on, closed the door, and went out to meet him.

CHAPTER TWO

"Mr. Ranieri, we're here to escort you to the district attorney's office in Padua."

I opened the rear door, got in the car, and sat next to another police officer.

"I know, but I wasn't expecting you until later."

I didn't have time to close the door or finish my sentence before the officer threw the car into reverse with a screech of tires, and with a shuddering skid, turned the car around and ran over ten feet of my neighbor's plants. I knew I'd get an earful from Giuseppe about how young buds of heaven-knows-what and police car tires just don't go together.

"I understand there is some news in the case, because District Attorney Dal Nero has asked us to take you straight to her in Padua," the police officer next to me explained.

"But isn't she in Frassanelle?"

"She was, but now she's back in Padua."

We flew down the drive at sixty miles an hour, the sirens going full blast. I prayed to God that my neighbor's chickens were safely in their coop, otherwise I'd have to put up with a lecture about that, as well, and it would cost me in hard cash.

As we drove past Giuseppe's house, I could see the entire family watching from the window. I realized they must assume I'd done something sinister. The look on their faces confirmed my fears: Giuseppe's wife and daughter were both shaking their heads as if to say they'd always known that, sooner or later, someone like me was bound to get into trouble. This was the death knell for my hopes of any friendly relationship with them.

We barreled out onto the main road and accelerated to ninety miles an hour. I was holding on for dear life, scared to death, and tried to explain to the driver that I really didn't think we had to go so fast—after all, I wasn't the murderer. The officers just replied that the DA had told them to be quick. I couldn't understand why, but it didn't matter because all I could think about was my stomach: I've always suffered from really bad carsickness, and in Milan, I even felt sick on the tram. I rolled down the window, hoping the fresh air would help, but the noise of the siren was intolerable. The road to Padua is quite straight, so I managed to keep my sickness under control, but as soon as we reached the city the road began to snake all over the place. If it weren't for the fact that I hadn't eaten since the day before, I'm sure I would have improved the situation further by barfing all over the police car.

We stopped in front of the district attorney's office with the umpteenth screech of tires. I managed to get out of the car under my own power, not needing to look in the mirror to realize how pale I must have been. I felt so ill that I swore to myself that I would never commit a crime, just for the simple reason that I never wanted to go through that barbaric torture again. The two officers virtually carried me into the elevator, which took us to the third, and top, floor. The old elevator was slow as a snail, and the door opened onto a green linoleum corridor with about ten doors off it. The two officers marched me to a door with a plaque bearing the DA's name and knocked. I must confess that I was quite pleased at the prospect of seeing her again. The officer who had driven the car opened the door and put his head in to tell her I was there. I stepped forward, but bumped into the officer who was stepping back out, followed by the DA.

The DA told me that we were going to Salvioni's house and would be able to talk on the way. So we got back into the elevator, and when we got outside, I realized with dismay that we were taking the police car again. It goes without saying that we set off with a skid of tires and the siren blaring. I didn't want to show my weakness in front of the DA, so I tried to look like a man who is used to living under pressure, hoping she wouldn't notice how ill I felt.

"What's the matter, Ranieri? Don't you feel well? You're the same color as the linoleum in my office."

Right, that worked.

"No . . . I just get carsick . . ."

"Hold on, Ranieri. It won't take more than fifteen minutes."

"I bet! At this speed, it's a miracle we don't take off," I blurted out.

"I'm sorry we had to summon you like this, but there is some news, unfortunately."

"Unfortunately?"

"This morning, I asked a police psychologist to go and inform Mrs. Salvioni about her husband's death. However, she didn't answer the intercom or her cell phone, so the psychologist asked the landlord to open the apartment door, and she found Mrs. Salvioni dead."

"Dead? No, Patty! What do you mean 'dead'? Patty was murdered, too?" I asked, bewildered.

"Yes. From what the psychologist described, we think she was hit over the head with a golf club."

I exclaimed, "Christ, what the fuck is going on? Poor Patty . . . I can't believe this . . . Patty, Massimo . . . They were such nice people!"

"We still don't know the motive for either of the murders, so I'm afraid I can't help you. Perhaps you can help us, though."

"How?"

"Before being murdered, Salvioni's wife tried calling you on your cell. By the way, have you found it yet?"

"Uh, no, I didn't even have time to look for it."

"Anyway, the police officers at the scene saw that Mrs. Salvioni had called you, so now we need to understand why she would do that."

"I haven't got the faintest idea! Probably Patty wanted to ask me if I'd seen her husband."

"To tell the truth, in the space of a few minutes, Mrs. Salvioni called you, Mr. Ranni, and some other people at the club who were among the last to see her husband."

I had only just noted the disappointment on her face when I was overcome with an unstoppable need to be sick. I rolled down the car window, but, damn, it only opened halfway, so I had to stick my head out as far as I could and just surrender to my stomach. Thank God it had been a long time since I'd eaten so I didn't make too much of a mess on the car, but I had the impression that in the eyes of the DA and the townspeople, my reputation had just gone down the drain. While I was cleaning my face with a tissue, I could sense her gaze and the ironic smirks of the two officers sitting in front.

"I'm really sorry about that; I couldn't hold it in any longer . . ." I mumbled, feeling totally mortified.

"Don't worry, Ranieri. Think nothing of it. I'm sorry we're in such a hurry, but in cases like this, time is of the essence."

"Yeah, I understand. It's just that, since this morning, it's like I've fallen into some kind of vortex, and to learn that both Massimo and Patty were murdered so violently is a terrible shock."

"Tell me about your relationship with them," Dal Nero asked me.

"There's not much to say. We meet most Saturdays and Sundays to play golf at Frassanelle, but we've never spent time together anywhere else."

Our conversation was interrupted by Schumacher, the officer driving, telling us we'd arrived.

We piled out of the car and entered the elegant apartment build-ing where the Salvioni family had lived. When we reached the second floor landing, I slowed down to catch my breath and steady myself before seeing yet another horrifying scene. Not understanding why the DA needed me there, I really didn't want to go in. I suddenly realized that, like it or not, I was up to my neck in this mess, even if just for the simple fact that I'd found Massimo's body. There was something else, though, something I felt like I was forgetting . . . I thought back to the day before. We'd played golf, and we'd talked about all sorts of things on the course, but I couldn't remember anything in particular. Even our arguments with Arcadio didn't give me any useful hints, despite being so unpleasant. After the match, Massimo and I had moaned a bit to Alessandro, who'd agreed with us about Arcadio being insufferable, and then . . . That was it! Then Massimo had said he would go and talk to Arcadio's father. That's what I'd forgotten to tell Corporal Cipolla!

I went to the door of Massimo and Patty's flat, where the sight of her feet confirmed that Patty was lying dead on the floor. The officer who had driven our car held me back and told me to wait until the DA called me. While I'd lingered on the landing, the DA had already gone inside. She had her back to me now, and I could see that her shoes were covered with cellophane. She was wearing latex gloves and a shower cap while talking to someone I couldn't see, either a forensics person or a ghost. As if she could feel me looking at her, the DA turned around, slightly embarrassed in her rather unflattering getup. I wanted to tell her about Massimo's planned visit to the Count of Nogaredo, but she turned back to the work and swiftly moved out of my line of sight, making me even more convinced that she didn't want to be seen dressed like that. All things considered, though, she was still ahead on points; I might have just seen her with a shower cap on her head, but she'd seen me barf out the window of a squad car. I turned to the officer and told him I'd wait downstairs where I could get some fresh air. He used his walkie-talkie to tell the officer outside I was on my way down. So much for trust!

On the stairs, I wondered why they hadn't let me in and worried that the police had found something that might somehow make them suspect I was involved in the murder. A shiver ran down my spine. The forensics team would know better, I told myself. I'd recently watched a National Geographic documentary where, with just a fragment of excrement, technicians had been able to determine what sort of animal had killed a brontosaurus 150 million years ago, so surely the forensics techs would be able to figure out that I'd had nothing to do with these murders?

The police officer outside asked me if I still felt sick.

"I just need some fresh air."

I sat down on the pavement and lit a Toscano; they always help me think and relax.

The officer looked at me with reproachful disgust, saying, "You call cigars 'fresh air'?"

Just what I needed: a know-it-all.

I wanted to tell him to mind his own business, but he was a police officer, after all.

"Cigars are less harmful than cigarettes and much more pleasant," I replied.

I hoped my trite answer would convince him to let it go, but he said, "All smoking is harmful, and it's the leading cause of death in Italy."

I didn't want to get dragged into a discussion about how stupid I was, so I let loose. "Do you know something? Neither of the Salvionis smoked, and they also liked to remind me how many people die from smoking! Strange coincidence, no?"

The officer snorted disdainfully at my hostility and dropped it.

I got back to thinking, wondering whether Massimo had managed to talk to the Count of Nogaredo yesterday evening, or whether he'd been killed before he got the chance. I could have called the golf club and asked for the count's number to ask him myself, but I felt I should tell Dal Nero first and let her decide what to do. All I could do right now was wait.

I'm a financial reporter for the *Mattino di Padova*, the most popular newspaper in Padua. I wondered whether it'd be unethical to call Gibbo Piovesan—his real name is Giovanni Alberto, but I don't think even his mother has ever called him that—the editor of the current affairs section. I abandoned the idea, partly as it didn't seem right to capitalize on the death of people I knew, but mainly because, with my cell phone still at large, I didn't have anyone's number.

I wasn't even halfway through my cigar when the officer, who'd never taken his eyes off me, said DA Dal Nero had called and wanted me back upstairs. I found her in front of the Salvionis' door, now without all the accessories she'd been wearing to prevent contaminating the crime scene. She was very attractive in a simple pair of jeans and a light-blue, close-fitting sweater that outlined her figure and set off her blonde hair.

She addressed me in her usual professional tone. "Ranieri, there are a couple of things I need to talk to you about."

"OK. First though, I remembered something about Dr. Salvioni."

"What's that?"

"Yesterday, after the golf match, we were having a beer together with Alessandro, and Massimo said he wanted to talk to Conte Alvise di Nogaredo, Arcadio's father, about his son's awful attitude with everybody. Arcadio had been getting on our nerves all day, and Massimo was really fed up. I don't know if they spoke or not, but the count could tell you."

"Of course. I'll get someone to call him right away. Do you mind if we go back to the office? I've asked Mr. Galli to come there, as well, seeing as the doctor's body was found in his club."

We went downstairs while Dal Nero was ordering someone on the phone to call the count. When she'd finished, before we got into the squad car, I proposed taking a taxi.

She laughed, and I couldn't help noticing how lovely it was, sunny and spontaneous.

"Don't worry, Ranieri. We're not in a hurry now. We can drive slower."

"Just promise me that Schumacher here can keep his Formula 1 syndrome in check."

Once in the car, we resumed our conversation.

"Did they find anything about Patty's murder? I noticed that the door to the apartment didn't seem damaged."

"No, it wasn't. Mrs. Salvioni must have opened it. We can't assume anything, but she probably knew the murderer. Ranieri, let's clear something up straight away. I hope you're not planning on screwing up my investigation with headlines in the *Mattino* tomorrow morning?"

"Don't worry. I write about finance, not current events. I mean, the thought crossed my mind, but I wouldn't feel right about speculating on the deaths of people I knew and liked."

I thought it better not to tell her I couldn't remember Piovesan's phone number.

"The less media coverage, the better we can work. Tell me, Ranieri. How did Mr. and Mrs. Salvioni get along with the other club members?"

"I didn't spend as much time with Massimo as some other people did. I'd pretty much just play golf, take a shower, and then head home. But as far as I know, Massimo and Patty got along with everyone—except for Arcadio maybe, but nobody really gets along with him."

The DA gave me a knowing smile.

Galli was waiting for us outside the DA's office. He looked surprised to see me get out of the police car with Dal Nero, and I wondered if the president was torn between envy at the attention I was getting and suspicion that I could be the guilty party.

We went upstairs, but instead of going into Dal Nero's office, Galli and I were led to a small waiting room and left there alone.

Galli looked at me searchingly, and I knew he was dying to bombard me with questions. One, two, three . . . and he was off! "Ranieri, what were you doing in the police car?"

Feeling slightly sadistic, I decided to let him brew in his curiosity and also to play up my own importance. "Well, I shouldn't say anything that could compromise the investigation. I'm sure you understand. Did you know Patty's been killed too? I can't believe it, one after the other . . ."

"Yes, I heard. It's crazy! But what do you have to do with it? Are you a suspect?"

"You really are reassuring, Galli. I sure hope not."

We were interrupted by an officer who asked Galli to come with him to answer some routine questions.

I stood up and began pacing to try and relax a bit. Then, glancing into the corridor, I saw Alvise Casati Vitali, Count of Nogaredo, enter the office of DA Dal Nero.

CHAPTER THREE

Three hours later, I was still waiting in the same room.

It was eight o'clock, I was tired, and my dogs needed feeding. I went into the corridor and knocked on the door of Dal Nero's office but got no reply. I knocked on the next door—still nothing.

After three doors, somebody finally answered. "Yes?"

I slowly opened the door to find a man sitting at a desk poring over some papers.

"Excuse me, but do you know where DA Dal Nero is?"

"No. Who are you?" he asked me, looking carefully at my face.

"My name's Riccardo Ranieri, and I'm a witness in the Salvioni case."

"Witness? Do you mean you saw who killed the Salvionis?"

Just what I needed, a semantic argument about the word *witness*.

"No, no . . . It's just, I'm . . . Look, I was their friend and . . ." I was too tired to try to explain. "Listen, let's leave it there. They asked me to wait until somebody came to get me, but it's been three hours, and I've got to get home to feed my dogs."

"If they told you to wait, then wait."

"Ah, great idea! Why didn't I think of that? Thanks a lot."

I shut the door in a way I hoped would make all those supposed public servants understand how I felt. They think they have the right to make everyone else feel rotten, just because they're carriers of red-tape viruses for infecting people like me, whose immune systems can't fight them off.

Trying to look casual, I listened at the other doors to see if I recognized anyone's voice. Total silence. I began to suspect that they had actually forgotten about me. What a blow to my ego: from leading player to outcast in less than three hours.

I decided to go downstairs to see if someone there knew where to find Dal Nero.

A female officer was on duty.

"Excuse me, Officer, I'm looking for DA Dal Nero. Do you know where she is?"

"I saw her leave over an hour ago. Why are you looking for her?"

"The DA wanted to talk to me about the Salvioni murders. She told me to wait in a room upstairs, but she never came back."

"I'm sorry, but I can't help you. I just know she left with a police patrol, and it must have been urgent because the sirens were going."

"Again?" I blurted out, amazed.

"What do you mean, again?"

"She's been running around in a police car all day."

"There must have been another emergency."

"Look, could you call her and ask her what I should do? I really need to go home because my dogs are there with nobody to feed them," I repeated.

"Wait a minute, I'll try."

At least she was helpful. Quite short, she probably just met the minimum height requirement to get onto the force, and she had a strong Roman accent. We kept looking at each other while she was waiting for Dal Nero to answer, and after about ten seconds I began to lose hope, but then she started talking. Thank the Lord, finally a bit of good luck . . .

"District Attorney Dal Nero, good evening. This is Officer Silvia Buoni at your office. I was looking for you because—"

I motioned to Officer Buoni to pass me her phone, but she covered it with her hand and whispered that she was just leaving a voice mail.

So I sat in the lobby with Officer Buoni, waiting for DA Dal Nero to call back, and as it was dinnertime, I suggested that we order pizza. I'd been too stressed out all day to realize I was hungry, despite not having eaten anything since the night before, and now I was starting to feel a bit dizzy. In less than ten minutes, the delivery boy arrived on his scooter with a cheese pizza for me and a pepperoni pizza for Officer Buoni. As soon as I caught a whiff of the aroma from the closed boxes, my appetite came right back. I paid the delivery boy quickly and bit into my first piece.

At that moment, Officer Buoni's phone rang, and after answering, she handed it to me.

"I'm sorry, Ranieri, I should have informed you. Unfortunately, there was another emergency I had to attend to, and it's late now, so you are free to go home if you wish. We can talk tomorrow morning," Dal Nero explained.

"OK, but I don't know if I'll be able to find a taxi willing to take me to Bastia this late."

"Don't worry about it. Put Officer Buoni back on."

I handed the officer her phone back and began devouring my pizza. I heard the officer replying in the affirmative to the DA's requests, nodding her head as if Dal Nero could see her. Hanging up, she told me she would take me home in about twenty minutes, as soon as she had finished her shift and, of course, her pizza.

Officer Buoni drove an old VW Polo with windows so fogged up it was like climbing into a glass of milk. There was an unpleasant smell inside, but I was careful not to react. Officer Buoni drove slowly and smoothly, and after being in the flying squad car, it was like relaxing on the sofa at home. We chatted a little, and she told me about a few cases she'd been involved in, mainly small brawls outside the football stadium or during public events. I've always imagined that women in uniform feel obliged to show they're better than the men to prove themselves, at the risk of becoming Rambos in skirts. But Officer Buoni didn't hide the fact that she was afraid and uncertain sometimes. After a while, I looked at the speedometer and saw that, despite the fact that there was no traffic, we were scarcely doing the speed limit. The dogs were going to have to wait a little longer, but at least I wouldn't get sick again.

"Forgive my directness, but seeing as, technically speaking, I could have killed the Salvionis, how come you trust me enough to be in the car with me?"

"First of all, there is no way you could have killed the wife. And anyway, who said I trusted you?"

"Why couldn't I have killed her?"

"Because the homicide occurred less than an hour before she was found, so between nine and ten this morning while you were at the golf club. Furthermore, District Attorney Dal Nero says you wouldn't hurt a fly, and I trust her judgment."

I was beginning to suspect that I needed to work on my air of seductive mystery.

"I mean, I wouldn't, but doesn't it bother you to be in the car alone with someone who's even potentially a murderer?"

"Ah! Well. You just think about touching me, and you'll find Onofrio's canines in your jugular."

"Who's Onofrio?"

"The Rottweiler sitting behind you."

I turned around, and, even before I saw him, I could feel him watching me. I love dogs, but being less than twelve inches from an animal that could have sent me to my creator with just one bite made me feel very exposed and very, very nervous. They say that dogs can tell when someone is frightened: when I looked into his yellow eyes, I was sure even a rabbit would have noticed my terror.

"Holy Christ, you should have told me!" I protested.

"I didn't think you could have missed him! Didn't you notice the smell in here? What, did you think I smelled like that?"

"It's just . . . Should I be worried? Onofrio doesn't seem like he likes me very much."

She laughed. "But Mr. Ranieri, I thought I was the one who was supposed to be afraid?"

"Go ahead and laugh, but you haven't got a Rottweiler staring a hole through your back. When we get to my house, I just want to see how he stands up to my German shepherds."

Christ, what a day! When so much happens at once, sometimes you lose control of yourself a little. I felt as though I had been catapulted into somebody else's life. I would have thought I could deal with stuff like this, but here I was feeling very vulnerable and totally unprepared to handle such an intensely emotional experience. If I felt this vulnerable with somebody who was here to protect me, just imagine how I would react to someone who was out to get me! DA Dal Nero was right: I was definitely not killer material.

"Is DA Dal Nero married?" I asked the young officer out of the blue.

"Oh! You like her, then?"

"She is an attractive woman, and, yes, maybe I like her, but I don't know her. So, is she married?"

"Don't you think that question is a bit inappropriate?"

Why do some women always have to make things difficult? I knew I'd have to lay it on thicker.

"Fine, Officer Buoni, I'm desperately in love and want to marry her, but before my dramatic, public proposal, I want to be sure I'm not going to hurt the feelings of any hidden husbands. Now will you tell me?"

"OK, don't get worked up. No, she isn't married, or rather she isn't anymore; she got divorced about a year ago. Don't tell her I told you, though, because the DA is very reserved and wouldn't be very happy if she knew I was talking about her—especially with someone involved in an investigation."

I decided to make the most of my advantage. "So why did you tell me, then?"

"I might have been imagining things, but when DA Dal Nero was telling me about you earlier, she sounded more like a woman than a district attorney. Do you get what I mean?"

"No."

"Come on, Ranieri! Are you messing with me, or are you really that stupid?"

"Whatever, maybe I am, I don't know, but yeah, I get it. In your opinion, DA Dal Nero can hardly wait to marry me!"

"Right, those were totally my exact words, and don't forget to tell her I said so!"

I turned back toward Onofrio and stretched out my hand to stroke his head and try to win him over. His head was huge, and he didn't seem interested in my attempt at bonding, but I know a dog's weak points, so I started scratching him under his ear, and, just as I predicted he would, Onofrio tilted his head to the side in pleasure. Onofrio was putty in my hands; maybe DA Dal Nero would be next.

"It appears that your bodyguard has been conquered by a scratch behind the ear," I said jokingly.

"You're good with dogs. How about with women?"

"To use a phrase you've heard before, when it comes to women I'm a serial killer. Meaning I kill any chance I have with every one of them!"

Officer Buoni burst out laughing again with her throaty, infectious laugh.

I laughed, too, maybe in an attempt to release some of the tension that had built up over the last day, and suggested we were good enough friends now to be on a first-name basis.

"We're almost there, Silvia. In two hundred yards, make a right at the gate."

I opened Giuseppe's gate with my remote while Silvia slowed down to a crawl.

During the short trip along the lane, I could see Giuseppe and his family looking out of the window. I could just imagine their disappointment in seeing I hadn't been locked up! Still, the fact that there was a woman with me would pique their interest and give them something new to gossip about. As far as the neighbors were concerned, I had already been crucified for my guilt in who knows what terrible crimes. The evidence against me was crushing: I was a stranger—from Milan, to boot—useless at gardening, never in church on Sundays, and, last but not least, never seen in the local bar.

Mila and Newton bounded toward the car, barking frantically, which set off Onofrio. Newton jumped up on the car door, showing his teeth through the window, which Onofrio was simultaneously trying to destroy by butting his head against it.

I couldn't hear a word Silvia was saying in that infernal chaos. I waved at her and got out of the car, trying to hold back Newton, who wanted to get in and fight it out with his new rival. Mila continued to bark menacingly at Onofrio while greeting me at the same time, her muddy front paws placed firmly on my leather jacket. I was trying to close the car door but lost my balance, thanks to Mila, and that's when the car window exploded. I felt a pain in my hand and heard Silvia shouting something, all three dogs still barking like crazy. I was on the ground when Silvia got out of the car and shot her gun one, two, three times in the air. Everything was so confused I couldn't make sense of what was happening. Onofrio jumped out of the car and started a terrifying fight with Newton. My adrenaline spiked, I heard sharp, shouted orders leave my mouth, and for a moment, the world seemed to stand still. Then, a few inches from my foot, the organic waste bin I keep just outside my gate suddenly exploded. The dogs fell silent and looked toward the irrigation canal, about thirty yards away, where I could just make out the silhouette of a person.

Silvia was asking if I was injured.

"No . . . I don't know . . . It hurts . . ."

"So get behind the car, you idiot! Or do you want to stay there and get shot at?"

"Oh God, someone's shooting at us?"

"Get over here, for fuck's sake!"

Silvia sounded hysterical, and justifiably so, but as I still hadn't gotten my head around what was happening, I felt foolishly calm. My survival instinct, I learned, was buried deep under the illusion of immortality that a boring daily routine gives us, especially us trade reporters.

The dogs had run over to the irrigation canal and stopped there, so I figured that whoever had shot at us was on the opposite side and must be fleeing. We were behind the car now, and our attacker probably hadn't expected Silvia to return fire.

I called Mila and Newton, and for once they obeyed me, coming straight away.

I heard Silvia calling police headquarters to tell them what had happened and to ask them to send an ambulance.

"Who's the ambulance for? Me?"

"No, for my granddad. Of course it's for you! Can't you see your hand's bleeding?"

In fact, it did seem to be bleeding heavily, and it hurt so much that I suspected something was broken. It was too dark for me to examine it.

Suddenly, Silvia pointed her gun toward me and shouted at someone behind me to stop and put up their hands. I was confused: the shooter had been all the way over on the other side of the irrigation canal, so this had to be someone else entirely! A man with a broad, local dialect demanded to know who we were, and I immediately recognized his voice. Despite the shadows, I could see he was pointing a gun at us.

"I am Police Officer Buoni. One more step and I'll shoot!"

I jumped up between the two cocked guns, yelling, "Officer, calm down! It's just Giuseppe, my neighbor. Giuseppe, lower your weapon. She's a police officer."

"But what's going on? We heard shots!" said Giuseppe.

"Nothing, it was just the dogs, don't worry. I'm sorry for all the noise; I hope your family wasn't frightened."

"Of course we were frightened! What the hell is going on? This morning: the police car with the siren going. This evening: gunshots. What the devil have you gotten yourself into, Ranieri?"

"Giuseppe, this isn't a good time now, but I'll explain everything as soon as I can. Don't worry—"

I'd hardly gotten the words out when Onofrio jumped onto Giuseppe and knocked him over. I could hear his wife and daughter screaming from where they stood a ways behind him, and then I heard Silvia ordering her Rottweiler to halt. Being so well trained, Onofrio obeyed instantly, but Mila and Newton were barking menacingly at the two women behind Giuseppe. I tried to call my dogs off, but I hadn't trained them like Onofrio. The two women raced back to the house like they were trying to win the hundred-yard dash!

While Silvia was helping Giuseppe up and the three dogs were cautiously getting to know each other, I pulled myself together. I had to get into the house to take care of my hand and finally feed the dogs. Silvia tried to dissuade me on both counts, but I was even more determined than she was, and I made it inside without further ado.

There was nothing much in the house to bandage my injury with, but I found the dogs' wound disinfectant in the laundry room and deemed it good enough. When I poured it onto the deep cut, a searing pain coursed through my body and I understood why Mila and Newton had always been so reluctant to have their injuries treated with the infernal stuff. I wrapped my hand in a napkin and filled the dog bowls, trying to spill less kibble than usual, and then carried the bowls out to the garden where the dogs had their kennels. Then I heard sirens coming toward the house. I still hadn't fully processed the fact that someone had just tried to kill me, right after the Salvionis, and the whole thing seemed unreal. It seemed more like a nightmare, or an insane crime that only happened on TV and not in the real world.

I left Mila and Newton's bowls in front of their kennels and went back to the gate, where Silvia was still talking to Giuseppe. It seemed like he was interrogating her, rather than the other way around. The police car came through Giuseppe's gate followed by the ambulance and pulled up in front of us.

I let Silvia explain to her colleagues what had happened and went to the first aid team that was getting out of the ambulance.

"Good evening, gentlemen. I'm sorry you've had to rush here, but it really isn't an emergency, just a cut," I said as convincingly as possible.

The older of the two, a tall, gray-haired man the size of a refrigerator, asked me to get into the ambulance so he could look at my injury. When I climbed in, I was met with the unmistakable smell of hospitals, and I took off the blood-soaked napkin. The paramedic took my hand and turned it toward the light and asked, "Were you shot?"

"To tell the truth, I'm not sure, but I think I got shot at. Rather, I'm sure I got shot at, but I don't know if it was a bullet that hit me or a piece of glass from the car window when it exploded," I tried to explain in a rather confused manner.

"OK. Now, Mr. . . . ?"

"Ranieri."

"Now, Mr. Ranieri, we're going to take you straight to the hospital to get an X-ray," he said, bandaging my hand.

As he said "X-ray," the ambulance door closed in the face of Silvia, who'd just come over to see what was happening. I didn't get the chance to say good-bye, but I felt pretty certain that she'd be there to greet me at the ER. Through the ambulance window, I could see Mila and Newton happily chowing down on their kibble with total disregard for their beloved owner.

I heard the ambulance siren start up, and this time I'd had enough. I shouted at the driver to turn it off; there was no emergency and no reason whatsoever to wake up the entire village on account of a tiny cut. While I was shouting, I had the strangest feeling that the siren was getting farther away. I realized my mistake too late; the driver, a man of about thirty, turned and looked at me with resigned pity. It was the police car siren I'd heard as it had screeched off again over Giuseppe's plants, chasing after the swine that had tried to kill me. The ambulance hadn't moved.

I muttered an apology while fridge man asked me to lie down so he could strap me to a gurney with the safety belts.

"Don't worry, Mr. Ranieri. Is there anyone we should contact to tell them we're taking you to the hospital?"

"My parents are dead, I'm an only child, and I'm not married or engaged. To be honest, I think the only person who could be even mildly interested in my fate is the tobacconist in Bastia, but I bought a pack of Toscanos from him last week, so he probably won't miss me for a while."

"Come on, don't play the martyr. If you knew my wife, you'd be glad you don't have any relatives. Anyway, it's not true that nobody cares about you! There's somebody out there who cares enough to shoot you, right?"

"Yeah, and I don't even know why."

CHAPTER FOUR

On the way to Abano Hospital, I realized that this was the second time in one day somebody was taking me away from my home against my will.

The stomach trauma of a police car going full speed had been dramatic enough, and I confess that lying in a moving ambulance while trying to digest a whole pizza was no less so.

"Sorry, but I get carsick. Could I please stand up?" I dared ask.

"Sorry, but we have to follow procedure. Anyway, you've lost blood, and, if you stand up, you could collapse and make everything worse."

"I know, but it's just a cut . . . ," I said, trying to convince him.

"It is not just a cut! It's actually quite an injury, and anyway, you have to lie down. Hold on a few more minutes. Be brave."

"What do you mean, 'quite an injury'?"

It's one thing to say something like that yourself, but another to hear it from a paramedic, seeing how they tend to minimize things so as not to upset patients.

"Well, Mr. Ranieri, as far as I can tell, a bullet passed through your hand. Don't worry, though—they'll know more at the hospital."

Fridge guy began busying himself with a very daunting syringe.

"Excuse me, but what's that syringe for?" I asked in alarm.

"We have to take a small blood sample to check your type; it's normal practice to save time when you get to the hospital."

I must admit that being trussed up like a turkey on a gurney while a gigantic paramedic was prepping a massive syringe, with the ambulance bouncing along like a horse-drawn buggy pursued by Indians, really didn't help my already-frayed nerves.

To make matters worse, the paramedic made three painful attempts before he located the vein in my arm.

"All done, Mr. Ranieri! Calm down now—we're almost there."

A few minutes later, the ambulance stopped and, as the doors opened, I was overcome by the desperate need to throw up. While a nurse helped the giant pull the gurney out of the ambulance, I barfed my pizza all over the hospital entrance. The small consolation that DA Dal Nero might not have seen me throw up for the second time in a few hours soon vanished when she appeared close by. That's when I decided to seriously reconsider my idea of trying to seduce her. I figured I'd better attempt some less demanding challenges, like running a marathon barefoot or swimming across a couple of oceans.

As I was being wheeled into the hospital, I saw DA Dal Nero talking to the paramedic, and then I was taken into a room filled with so many machines it would have impressed even a NASA engineer.

The nurse who had wheeled me in began removing the bandage the paramedic had just put on.

"What happened?" she asked.

"I got shot," I calmly replied.

"Oh! Why?"

"I've been wondering that myself."

"Do you at least know who it was?" the nurse pressed, seemingly interested in my case.

"Would you believe that I don't know that either?"

"Yes, but don't worry. In cases like this, we have to inform the police, but I see they're already here asking about you. I'll leave the questions to them. I'm going to disinfect your injury, and then we'll go for an X-ray, but I can already tell you the bullet has damaged some of the flexor tendons in your hand."

"Some of the what?" I exclaimed.

"The flexor tendons, the ones that enable you to move your fingers."

"Oh . . . Does that mean I'm going to die?"

"No, but you'll need surgery and we'll have to check for any other injuries."

"Meaning?"

"Meaning bones or nerves."

"I really must compliment you."

"Why?"

"To tell the truth, until now I always thought that nurses just pushed the gurneys and looked after the patients, but you act like a doctor."

"I am a doctor. My name's Dr. Sonia Migliorini."

It seemed like the only thing in my life that hadn't changed was my unwavering ability to make a jerk of myself.

"Oh, well . . ."

Just then, DA Dal Nero and Silvia came into the room.

"So, Mr. Ranieri, how are you feeling?"

Before I could answer, the doctor turned to the two women saying, "I'm sorry, but no visitors are allowed in here. I'm going to need you to wait outside."

"Excuse us, Doctor, but I'm the DA in charge of investigating a double homicide and what now looks like a third attempted homicide. This is Silvia Buoni, the police officer who defended Mr. Ranieri during the shooting. I just want to ask the patient a couple of questions and then we'll get out of your way."

"I understand, but Mr. Ranieri's injury is serious and I don't know how much blood he's lost. Give me a few minutes of silence to finish this, and then you can walk down to radiology with us. You're welcome to talk as much as you want on the way there."

At that, the doctor inserted an IV into my arm with such force I feared it might come out the other side.

After three or four colored tubes were attached, the doctor turned to DA Dal Nero and told her it was time to go to radiology on the floor below. A nurse came to fetch me and take me down on the gurney. DA Dal Nero approached, staring daggers at the doctor, who calmly returned her gaze. Finally, they both decided to follow me at marching pace. For a moment there, I'd been afraid their natural female competitiveness before a desirable male of my stature might lead to a race, at the risk of overturning the gurney and its precious cargo!

As we approached the elevator at a speed similar to that of a pace car on a racetrack, DA Dal Nero leaned over and said, "So, Ranieri, tell me what happened."

Keeping my eyes down, I replied, "There's nothing much to say. Officer Buoni drove me home and then, when I got out of the car, I heard the window explode, and then the waste bin near my feet blew up."

"So you heard two shots?"

"To be honest, I didn't have any idea what was happening, because a crazy scuffle had broken out between my dogs and Onofrio."

"Who's Onofrio?"

"Officer Buoni's lion."

Officer Buoni, following a few steps behind, interjected, "He's a Rottweiler."

"Right, as I was saying, the dogs were going crazy, and in all that confusion, it wasn't clear what was happening. In fact, I would have remained in the line of fire like an idiot if Officer Buoni hadn't shouted at me to get behind her car."

DA Dal Nero nodded, then continued. "Did you manage to see who shot you?"

"I saw somebody standing on the far side of the irrigation canal about thirty yards away, but it was dark, so I can't tell you much except that they were probably around average height."

"So about five eight?"

"I'd say so, but I can't swear to it since I only caught a glimpse. Right after that, Onofrio jumped on Giuseppe, and . . ."

"Is Giuseppe one of your dogs?" DA Dal Nero asked me seriously.

"No, Giuseppe is my neighbor. He heard all the commotion and rushed over with his shotgun. That's when Onofrio jumped on him."

"Hold on, Ranieri. Are you saying Giuseppe rushed over to shoot Officer Buoni and maybe you, as well?" Dal Nero asked, perplexed.

"No, absolutely not! Giuseppe was just frightened by the shots, so he came out to see what was going on. He only brought his gun as a precaution."

Dal Nero turned to Silvia. "Officer Buoni, send Ricciardi to this Giuseppe's house to see if he saw anything that you two didn't. And check whether he has a license for that firearm."

"Excuse me, DA Dal Nero, but do you really have to bother Giuseppe this late at night? I'm just asking because he's not what you could call the ideal neighbor. And after all this, I don't think he or his family will ever talk to me again."

"Ranieri, perhaps you don't fully realize the seriousness of these events. Two people have been murdered, and a third has a target on his back—and if you still haven't figured it out, that third person is you!"

Dal Nero nodded to Silvia, who headed off to follow her orders as the nurse wheeled me into radiology.

Once I was in the room, Dr. Migliorini put a small tube in my right hand that was connected to a sort of small mechanical crane and said, "Now, DA Dal Nero, I must ask you to leave the room with me. I'm going into the next room to take the X-ray, and you, Mr. Ranieri, must not move until we've both returned."

To be truthful, I was grateful for the break, as I hadn't been alone for a moment since I was shot, and I had the chance to realize that the injury didn't hurt too much. I had always wondered what sort of pain you felt when you got hit by a bullet, and I must confess that I felt a touch of male pride at how muffled the burning sensation was. Unfortunately, the feeling only lasted a few seconds, until I looked up at the bags hanging above my gurney: if one was blood, then the other two must certainly have contained anesthetic.

Resigned to the fact that I was not Bruce Willis, I was finally overwhelmed by the burden of this crazy day, and I crashed hard. I heard DA Dal Nero and the doctor come back in, but I could no longer fight the exhaustion that was washing over me like an incoming tide.

The next morning, they operated on my hand, and I spent the day under the effect of the anesthetic and the accumulated fatigue. In a brief moment of consciousness, when a very bright light was coming through a curtainless window, I realized that my right arm was immobilized, but I couldn't understand why. It took another day for me to fully come to. From that time, all I can remember are various sensations: an artificial metallic flavor in my mouth, then, in rapid succession, a burning thirst, as if I were lost in the desert, and the desperate need to pee.

The next day, I felt able to go to the bathroom by myself, so I looked around for a bell or a button to call a nurse. Finding nothing, I tried to call for help. The raspy sound that came out was nothing like the confident "Anyone there?" I was trying for, but it was enough to attract the attention of the policeman on guard outside my door. Within minutes, the room was invaded by people throwing questions at me and talking among themselves. Luckily, a nurse arrived and herded them all out. I asked her why I couldn't move my arm.

"Your arm has a rigid dressing and is strapped in place so that you couldn't hurt yourself while you were asleep."

I tried to lift my head to look, but there was so much pain in my neck that I decided to believe her.

I just said, "I need to go to the bathroom. Can I get up now?"

"Yes, if you feel ready, but I'd better help because you could get really dizzy."

She undid the straps around my arm and slowly helped me to sit up. It wasn't easy to move, but after a few moments, I could feel some strength coming back, and my mind was clearer; the dizziness and shooting pains stopped.

Then Dr. Migliorini came in. She looked at me and asked, "How are you feeling, Mr. Ranieri?"

"I think I'm starting to feel better. I'd like to get up now because I need to go to the bathroom."

"Of course, but you'll need to be extremely careful and take your time. The nurse can help you if you need her."

My right arm was in a cast up to the elbow to prevent me moving it, so I wouldn't be able to use my right hand. The nurse and doctor helped me to get out of bed, and once standing, I decided I could manage by myself. With as sure a step as I could muster, I headed toward the en suite bathroom and closed the door behind me.

I was wearing a white hospital gown that opened on the sides and I was completely naked beneath. Unfortunately, I'm not left handed, and anyway, I needed one hand to hold the gown open, so the entire operation was a bit "imprecise," and the result was one of those things that women complain most about in men! I tried to clean up the mess or, as DA Dal Nero might have said, to cover my tracks. Then I washed my left hand and went back into my room.

The doctor was the only one there; her assertiveness and medical priorities had won out again. She'd closed the door to ensure the others remained outside.

"Could I have something to eat or drink?" I asked.

"Today, it's better if you just drink fruit juice and eat something very light and easy to digest, like cooked fruit. Tomorrow, you can start eating normally again. So tell me, Mr. Ranieri, how do you feel?"

"Not too bad. It's a bit awkward not being able to use my right hand, and I suppose it means I'll have to move my bike bell to the left side of the handlebars."

"So, do you ride your bike often?" she asked, smiling at my stupid joke.

"No, I was kidding. Sometimes my mouth gets ahead of my brain. Sorry."

"Not at all. I wanted to explain what my colleagues and I did during your surgery."

"Go ahead, Doctor."

"We operated on your hand to reconstruct the flexor tendon in your forefinger that had been damaged by the bullet. As we didn't find any other damage, we closed the injury with five stitches on both sides. It was a simple operation, but you'll need to keep the dressing on for ten days and then begin physical rehabilitation to recover movement in your hand. Do you understand?"

I nodded and asked, "When can I go home?"

"We're preparing your discharge papers now. However, DA Dal Nero is waiting in the hall to talk to you. Do you feel up to it?"

"Sure."

"OK, I'll send her in. I'll see you back here in ten days to take the stitches out and check on your progress."

"Agreed. Thanks for everything you've done, Doctor."

I shook her right hand with my left. She smiled at me with a look of intense compassion that said I was in trouble up to my neck. Then she turned around, opened the door, and told the district attorney I was ready. I got a glance at the other people waiting in the hall, who appeared to be reporters.

I noticed that DA Dal Nero wasn't wearing the jeans she'd had on the day before, but a smart, straight skirt that really enhanced her walk.

"Good morning, Mr. Ranieri, how are you?"

"Fine, thanks. I think the worst is behind me."

"Medically speaking, I'm sure you're right, but as far as the investigation is concerned, far from it."

"Meaning?"

"As you were the first person to discover Dr. Salvioni's body, and as there is someone out there trying to kill you, I would say that 'the worst is behind you' is rather optimistic. What do you think?"

"You really know how to reassure a person."

"It's not my job to reassure you, just to tell you where things stand. From now on, you will be accompanied by an officer to protect you at all times."

"No way—I'd rather get shot!"

"Sorry, Mr. Ranieri, you have no choice. Can't you comprehend that someone is actually trying to kill you? Don't be crazy. Why the hell wouldn't you want protection?"

"For one thing, because I have nothing to do with all this mess!"

"Uh-huh. Go and explain that to the shooter."

"And for another, a bodyguard would get on my nerves. I'm used to being on my own, having my freedom. I wouldn't let a supermodel cramp my style, much less a policeman!"

"Listen, Mr. Ranieri, I can't force you to think rationally about your situation, but if you insist on behaving like an idiot, the officer will be obliged to simply follow you everywhere without your consent. It'll be that much more difficult for us to protect you."

"Look, thanks for your concern, but—"

"My concern? You're way off, Mr. Ranieri. The only thing I'm concerned about is avoiding another dead body, especially if that body could have given me some useful information."

"What information do you think I can possibly give you? I don't know why Massimo was murdered, I don't know why his wife was murdered, and I certainly don't know why anyone would try to murder me."

DA Dal Nero stopped a moment and looked me in the eyes, as if she were considering whether or not to tell me something. The pause gave us both the chance to take a breath and calm down. After all, we were on the same side, and arguing wouldn't help anyone.

In a much quieter tone, DA Dal Nero said, "We found Dr. Salvioni's cell phone. He'd sent you a text message just before he was killed."

"Oh . . . What did it say?"

"Wrong blood."

CHAPTER FIVE

"Wrong blood. What does that mean?"

"That's what I want to ask you. If Dr. Salvioni sent you that message, he thought you could understand it."

"But it means nothing to me. Wrong blood . . . It's nonsense. It sounds more like a message he'd send one of his colleagues. It could mean something to another doctor, right? But I don't have a clue."

"Did Dr. Salvioni talk to you recently about any problems he'd had at the hospital? Perhaps with a patient?"

"Massimo really kept to himself, and we never talked about work."

"Mr. Ranieri, I think this message has something to do with why they're trying to kill you. So take your time and think about it, and try to find some sort of meaning for these two words."

"Of course I'll think it over, but to be honest, you shouldn't get your hopes up."

"There are some reporters in the hall, so please remember you're not authorized to tell them anything. Any information that gets out could be fatal for our investigation—and for you, if you get my drift."

"Great, thanks for reassuring me again! Don't worry, DA Dal Nero. If you want, you can even be present when I talk to the reporters," I suggested naïvely.

"Oh, I most certainly will be! Just stick to telling them how you are, got it?"

"Well, that shouldn't be too difficult; about the only thing I do know is how I am!"

"What I mean is I don't want them to know you can't find your phone, or that Dr. Salvioni sent you that message before he was killed, or that we don't know who the shooter is," DA Dal Nero replied with an exasperated look on her face, like a mother reprimanding her witless son.

"But what if the reporters ask me why I haven't returned their calls or something?" I objected.

"Mr. Ranieri." Her tone was quite sharp now. "Just tell them you had other things on your mind, OK?"

"OK, OK, don't get worked up. After all, this is the first time somebody's tried to kill me, so I don't have much experience with these things."

I managed to get only a half-ironic and half-understanding smile from her, but it was enough to transform her face beautifully.

While I was wondering how I could tell her so without it sounding trite, she turned around and went to open the door to the reporters. Among my various colleagues, there was Gianluca Grandi, the editor of the *Mattino,* Piovesan, another colleague from the finance section, and I don't know who all. The room got so full I seriously considered escaping out the window.

They immediately barraged me with questions, all talking at the same time, until DA Dal Nero took matters into her own hands.

"Please, gentlemen, we're in a hospital! You'll need to speak one at a time, and remember what I've already told you: you can only ask him questions about his health. Is that clear?"

Piovesan began. "So good to see you're OK, Ranieri. Can you tell me who shot you?"

I was about to start laughing, and DA Dal Nero spoke again. "Did you not hear me, sir? Am I speaking gibberish?"

"I'm sorry, DA Dal Nero, but Ranieri's shooter has something to do with his health, right?"

Before the district attorney could eat him alive, I broke in. "Gibbo, don't try to be cute. The district attorney has enough on her hands dealing with me, and you'll only make it worse. I'll tell you what I do know. In the last couple of days, two people have been killed, two people I used to spend time with at the Frassanelle Golf Club. On Sunday morning, I was the first one to find Dr. Salvioni's body, and then in the evening"—I exchanged glances with DA Dal Nero to check that I was on safe ground—"the police accompanied me home, but when I got there, someone shot at me from about thirty yards away. He hit my hand and then ran off, because the police responded to his fire straight away, and he probably wasn't expecting it."

I didn't even get the chance to tell them that was all I knew before I was besieged with questions again. I took a deep breath and turned to Grandi. "I don't know when I'll be back at work. I'll update you as soon as I can."

DA Dal Nero took the opportunity to tell them that I wouldn't be answering any more questions, and asked them to leave the room. After a few protests, I was alone with her again.

"Do you want to know something, District Attorney Dal Nero?" I asked her.

"What's that, Ranieri?"

"Just five minutes on the other side of the fence and I already hate reporters!"

She began laughing and threw her head back—a very natural and very feminine gesture, at last. "Come on, you did fine! Now, have you thought about the message Dr. Salvioni sent you?"

It was my turn to be exasperated. "I thought you told me to take my time and think it over?"

Her reply was interrupted by the return of Dr. Migliorini with my discharge papers.

"You can go now if you want, Mr. Ranieri. Your discharge form is ready for signing. Remember not to use your right hand, and don't get the bandages wet. Come back in ten days to get the stitches taken out and have us give you a checkup," she said as she handed over the papers.

"I don't think he'll need the checkup, Doctor," DA Dal Nero said. "If Mr. Ranieri here continues to refuse our escort, stitches will be the least of his problems."

I realized that the district attorney was trying to appeal to some kind of female solidarity in an attempt to get over my stubbornness. Or perhaps she was hoping to elicit the protective instinct we imagine is inborn in all doctors.

The doctor's sharp response surprised me. "That's no problem of mine. If Mr. Ranieri comes to the hospital alive, I'll take his stitches out. If he shows up dead, it'll save me the effort."

She bent over me so I could sign the documents that released me from my hospital prison, turned on her heel, and left, saying good-bye without even turning around.

"That woman really doesn't like me. Or you. Or probably either of us."

"I think you're right, but somehow, I'm not the slightest bit bothered by it."

She smiled again, this time looking me in the eye.

I plucked up my courage. "Do you think we could dispense with the formalities? I don't want to be presumptuous, but if I have to call you 'District Attorney Dal Nero' each time we talk, it takes me thirty minutes to get a sentence out."

Another smile. "OK, Mr. Ranieri. My name's Giulia."

"And mine is Riccardo."

A moment of embarrassed silence followed; then I decided to change the subject and get back to reality.

"Tell me, Giulia, were you able to reach Count Nogaredo?"

"Yes, but he couldn't tell me much. He just told me that on the evening Massimo disappeared, he had spoken to him, and he said that the doctor had been complaining about his son Arcadio's behavior. Massimo said that he was taking too many liberties and was always rude."

"Knowing Massimo, it seems strange that he'd call just to complain like that."

"I agree. And it's ludicrous to imagine that Dr. Salvioni was killed just for tattling to the count about his son."

"Yes, of course. I'd like to know what they really said to each other. Look, Giulia, I've signed the discharge papers, and I'd like to get out of here as soon as possible. Seeing as it's almost eight o'clock, what about continuing our talk over a pizza?"

She studied me uncertainly for a moment, then looked at her watch as if she wanted to verify my claim.

I pressed gently. "That way, you can escort me. You are armed, aren't you?"

"Definitely not. I would never dream of it. However, we'd certainly have an escort."

"That's it, then: argument over. Let's get some pizza!" Before she could reply, I added, "And look. I'm sorry, Giulia. I'm sure you're dying to see me naked, but I really would appreciate a few moments of privacy while I put some clothes on."

"I'm going, Riccardo, but you're going to make me regret being on a first-name basis."

"Don't worry; I promise to act like a complete gentleman."

Shortly thereafter, Giulia and I left the hospital accompanied by a plainclothes police officer named Paolo Battiston. She and I went in her car, a Mercedes Class C, while Battiston got into a Ford Fiesta. I must admit that, despite my bravado, I didn't feel quite as calm as I had in the hospital a few minutes earlier. Knowing there's somebody out there who wants to shoot you really gets under your skin.

We drove over to a pizzeria on the road between Abano and my house. The police officer joined us, and we found a table by the wall. I ordered my usual pizza margarita, promising myself I wouldn't throw it up this time.

While we were waiting for our food, I returned to the investigation. "No matter how much I think about that message, I can't make sense of it. If Massimo was killed for the 'wrong blood,' he must've thought that sharing the secret with me would make him safer, right? That if others knew about it, too, there wouldn't be any reason to murder him. But how something about wrong blood could ever upset someone to the point of killing him that way, I just can't imagine."

"We've looked in the hospital files for cases of erroneous blood transfusions, but there hasn't been anything like that in the last ten years. In fact, it was really hard to find any complaints at all about Dr. Salvioni, and certainly no serious claims against him. To be honest, I think we're better off keeping our focus on the club. I did get the feeling that Count Nogaredo was hiding something from me when I called, and I think it'd be useful if you and I went to talk to him together. If you really are connected to this in some way, he might react emotionally to seeing you. If somebody feels nervous and under pressure, it's often enough to make them slip up."

"Sure, everyone knows that!" Battiston declared in what I considered a rather condescending tone.

"OK, but remember I only know Count Alvise by sight, and I don't think I've ever been personally introduced to him. You rarely see him at the club, and when he's there, he only interacts with a few people."

"Including Dr. Salvioni?"

"Yes and no. I mean, Massimo knew everybody. He could jump into any group, and it was like he'd known them for years, when probably he'd never even seen them before."

"Yes, I know the type. Well, regardless, I'd like you to be there in case it helps the investigation, and I was thinking perhaps we should tell the count about the message."

"Let's just hope he doesn't pull out his gun and shoot me! It's one thing trying to hit someone in the dark from thirty yards and another in broad daylight at close range."

Battiston found it hard not to laugh.

"If he does, we'll have solved the case! What's more, we'll have saved Dr. Migliorini the effort of seeing you again," Giulia replied ironically.

I confess, she was growing on me more by the moment. Being able to smile under pressure, even if it was my life at stake, was a lovely thing about her. It made her even more fascinating, and I really wanted to know whether she found me as attractive as I did her.

When our pizzas arrived, I realized that not being able to use my right hand meant that I either had to swallow my male pride and ask somebody else to cut the slices for me, or follow Dr. Migliorini's advice and opt for a liquid diet. I was skeptical about whether my new bodyguard could really deter any assassins, so I decided to get him to at least cut my pizza for me. It was a small compensation for his intrusion into my life.

After dinner, Giulia and Battiston accompanied me, or rather escorted me, home. When we went through Giuseppe's gate, I showed Giulia the angle I had been shot from. Recalling the scene from just a couple of days before sent shivers down my spine. I was returning home once again at dark and, once again, I had an escort.

I got out of Giulia's car very tentatively, then opened my gate to let Mila and Newton out. The dogs immediately checked out the entire area, including the entirety of Giulia's and Battiston's legs, patrolling like well-trained soldiers. To be honest, Mila ended up doing most of the patrolling because Newton was too busy letting Giulia fuss over him. Months of training and discipline out the window for some ear scratches and praise!

After describing what had happened during the shooting, I invited them both into the house. I showed them into the kitchen and then went to fill the dogs' long-empty bowls with food and water. My kitchen has an open fireplace and Provence-style furnishings, which took me more than three years to save up for. To me, the kitchen is the most welcoming room in the house. I have a large living room with comfortable sofas and panoramic windows overlooking the nearby hills, but I prefer the warmth of the kitchen and hoped my visitors would, too.

"Riccardo, do you live alone here?" Giulia asked me in surprise.

"After twenty years in a two-room flat in the center of Milan, I felt the need for open spaces and lots of countryside around me. When I saw this farmhouse for the first time, I knew right away it was waiting just for me."

We sat down at the table, and I offered drinks to Giulia and my escort, who was obviously inseparable from me now. After eating a whole pizza, I was as thirsty as a camel, and we managed to run through my entire supply of Coke, beer, and bottled water. We talked about how we should approach our chat with Count Nogaredo, or rather, Giulia told me how we'd approach it.

"I'd like to avoid bringing the count down to headquarters. I'd prefer to bring you to his house."

"What am I supposed to say when we get there?"

"Don't say anything until I prompt you. But when I ask, you'll talk about the message you received, and let him believe you have a few ideas about it."

"Ideas?"

"You have to make him think you understood the message and that you've talked to me about it. Nothing more. If Count Alvise asks you for an explanation, you'll just tell him you're not authorized to give one, and then we'll see how he reacts. Unfortunately, all we can do is hope to provoke him in some way."

"Good thing I'm an expert at annoying people. What time are we going?"

"I don't know yet. Tomorrow morning, I'll phone the count to see if we can visit him around eleven. As soon as I know, I'll call you."

"How are you going to call me, though? I don't know where my cell phone is, and the battery must be dead."

"Well, look for it this evening, but it really makes no difference. I'll call Paolo and he'll tell you. He'll sleep here. Given the size of your house, there's no concern about him invading your privacy."

Paolo wasn't quite as tall as me, but with such a large gut on him I wondered how he managed to keep his balance. I didn't like the idea of having a stranger in the house, but given the circumstances, I realized I had to go along with it.

"If I agree, will you promise to go to dinner with me tomorrow evening?"

"Definitely not. What are you talking about? Why should I?"

From the corner of my eye, I could see Paolo looking embarrassed and fidgeting in his chair; maybe he wished he were somewhere else even more than I did at that moment.

I decided to lie. "So you can update me about your thoughts regarding the case."

"Riccardo, don't try to be smart. I don't know, we'll see. I'm not obliged to update anybody. It's time for me to go. I'll be in touch tomorrow morning."

We all stood up, and, together with Paolo, Mila, and Newton, I accompanied her to her car. Newton was forlorn, but at least Giulia gave him a loving pat, while all Paolo and I got was a curt good night.

We stood looking at each other while Giulia's car drove off. I'm not used to having guests over, especially not men who are staying the night.

Paolo understood. "I bet you'd have preferred for the district attorney to stay here instead of me, wouldn't you?"

"No! What are you talking about? Come on . . . I love spending the night with a strange, armed man!"

"Seeing as I'm here to prevent you from getting shot again, it's a good idea for me to be armed, don't you think?"

"Of course, Paolo, I was kidding. So how should we get organized for the night?"

"If you've got a spare mattress, I'll bunk down in front of your bedroom door and we'll be fine."

"Ah! Keeping really close, then?"

"Since I'm here, let's do things right."

"It's safer than Fort Knox here, you know. As soon as Mila hears a leaf drop she starts barking, and Newton would never let anyone in."

"Yeah, but what if the assassin shot the dogs?"

I'd totally overlooked that obvious possibility.

"At that point, I'd be so furious that not even a bazooka would stop me!"

"In my opinion, a lady's .35 caliber would stop you."

The Bruce Willis tough guy act clearly didn't suit me.

"Fine, Paolo. Whatever you say. Can you help me look for my cell phone, please?"

CHAPTER SIX

Hungry again in spite of the pizza, Paolo decided to concentrate his search in the kitchen while I covered the rest of the ground floor and utility room.

I was still firmly convinced that the best deterrent for any evildoers was my German shepherds, so I decided to let them in to help me look for my phone.

I may have had a touch of unfinished-move syndrome, and my utility room was so disorganized that it could have inflicted serious psychological damage on anyone not sufficiently prepared. Originally, I had intended to use it for laundry, but three-quarters of the room was occupied by boxes full of the remains of my previous life, stacked up so high they blocked two of the three windows overlooking the garden. The work surfaces were covered by a dozen or so bottles of detergents, cleansing products, and medicines. I tried to think where I could possibly have left my phone. While I was considering the matter, I had the clear sensation of a shadow passing by one of the windows. Mila and Newton began barking furiously in the direction of the window, and I was overcome with panic. During the shootout, I'd been so surprised I hadn't even had time to process what was happening, but now I was fully aware that some psycho was determined to take me out. I realized I had better act quickly if I wanted to live another day.

I called Paolo, but it was obvious he would never hear me above the barking dogs, whose rage at this violation of their territory confirmed my fear. I didn't want to open the door that led outside because if whoever was out there was armed, he might go after my dogs. So I chose the biggest bottle of fabric softener and held it tight in my left hand. In vain, I tried to hush Mila and Newton, then I hid behind the door, out of sight of the window. Bad decision! Hearing the dogs, Paolo ran downstairs and threw open the utility room door so hard I thought I would pass right through it. It hit my face and the injured hand I'd instinctively raised to try to protect myself, and the impact was so violent I felt as if I had been struck by lightning.

I ended up on the floor with Paolo standing over me asking what had happened. I noticed the dogs had stopped barking and were happily wagging their tails trying to get outside. It could only mean one thing—they'd realized they knew the intruder. I told Paolo there was someone in the garden, and, as he rushed to check it out, the doorbell rang. It was Giuseppe, full of innocence and wanting to know why I wasn't answering my phone. I would have liked to lay into him, but I held back.

"Who's been beating you up?" he asked, looking me carefully in the face.

"What are you talking about?"

"Your eye."

"I bumped into the door."

"Sure, and I'm Shirley Temple."

"No, it's the truth. Just now, Paolo rushed down when he heard the dogs barking . . . Look, never mind. Let's drop it."

I went to look at myself in the bathroom mirror, and, in fact, my right eye was turning a deep shade of purple. Between that and my bandaged hand, I definitely wasn't looking my best.

Behind me, Paolo was trying to apologize while I cursed him. "If that's what protecting me means, I'd probably be better off with the killer in the house. At least he's a rotten shot."

"What was I supposed to do? It wasn't my fault you had to go and hide behind the door."

Giuseppe broke in to ask me what the liquid was on the floor.

"What liquid?"

"This bluish stuff."

I went back downstairs and saw the thick liquid slowly spreading over the utility room floor.

"Shit. It's fabric softener!"

"Fabric softener? You were doing the laundry at this time of night?"

"No, I was holding it to defend myself."

"You thought you could defend yourself with fabric softener?"

"Yeah, well . . . It was the biggest bottle within reach."

We were quite a comic trio, and I began wondering who needed a killer, anyway. If things kept going this way, I would never survive the night.

It took more than half an hour to clean the utility room floor as best I could, and afterward, I was so tired I told them both to give up the hunt for my phone, because I was going to bed.

I was accompanying Giuseppe into the garden, escorted as ever by Mila, Newton, and Paolo, when I noticed something shiny in Newton's mouth. I ordered him to "drop it," but of course, Newton took no notice of my command and just lazily wagged his tail. I was pretty certain of what it was now, and all three of us set about getting it out of his jaws. It was almost as hard as cleaning the utility room floor, but finally my cell phone was back in my hand. It was slick with drool, covered in scratches and dents, and a few numbers were missing from the keypad, but at least it hadn't ended up in the stubborn dog's stomach.

When I was finally in my room, lying on the bed, I managed to plug my mangled phone into the charger and turn it on. I found Massimo's message, which I still couldn't decipher: *Wrong blood*. Actually, reading it for myself was quite disconcerting. There was also the missed call from Patty. And then there were a dozen or so other calls from relatives, friends, and colleagues, and about thirty messages from people who wanted to know what was going on. A message from an unfamiliar number caught my eye. It was the first message I'd ever received that was so formal—more suited to a wedding invitation than a text. *I apologize for the disturbance, but I feel it is rather urgent and essential that we meet. Alvise Casati Vitali, Count of Nogaredo.*

I figured that Giulia would need to know about this right away, so I decided to call her, despite the fact it was past one in the morning. I opened the door and found Paolo lying on his mattress outside.

"Paolo, I need to call Dal Nero. Could you give me her number?"

"Why on earth do you want to call her this late?"

"Something important for the investigation. I got a text message from Count Alvise asking me to meet him. Seeing as Giulia and I planned to go see him tomorrow morning, I should probably let her know now."

"Ok, here it is. 334—"

"No, damn it, I don't have a 3."

"What do you mean, you don't have a 3?"

"Newton probably ate it."

"Use my phone, then."

Paolo typed in the number and passed me his phone. After four rings, Giulia answered sleepily.

"Hi Giulia. It's Riccardo. Sorry it's so late."

"Ah, Riccardo, it's you. What's the matter?"

"I finally found my phone, and there's a message from the Count of Nogaredo asking me to meet him."

"Huh! Well, this throws a different light on things. Let me think . . . Now it's probably better if you go see him alone and hear what he has to say to you. If I came, I'm afraid the count would just repeat the pat speech he gave me before. Yes, that's the best plan. I already contacted him when I left your house. Never mind, though. Tomorrow morning I'll call him again, and we'll fit you with a concealed mic before the meeting."

That woman continued to amaze me with her quickness; I'd woken her in the middle of the night, but she'd immediately worked out how to conduct the meeting.

"OK, see you tomorrow, then."

"Good night, Riccardo."

"Good night, Giulia."

The next morning, I woke around seven o'clock and went into the bathroom, but the sight of my face made me shudder: my eye was dark purple and almost swollen shut. Furthermore, because of my sensitive skin, I've always used a safety razor, which I hold in my right hand. After I'd shaved left-handed, the result was, predictably, a disaster—my face ended up looking like a battlefield.

I went down to the kitchen to make some coffee. Paolo was there, trying to ward off Newton's attentions, while reserved Mila just kept her eye on them both from a safe distance. When Mila saw me, she ran between my legs to claim her daily affection, alerting Newton, who abandoned Paolo and came over to greet his master.

"Do you want some coffee, Paolo?"

"Yes, please. What on earth have you done to your face?" he asked, curious and concerned at the same time.

"Are you talking about the cuts?"

"Yeah."

"I tried to shave with my left hand."

"I think you should consider growing a beard until your right hand's better."

"I'd rather not, because, apart from itching, a beard doesn't suit me. Mine grows like Che Guevara's. I'm going to jump in the shower. If Giulia arrives before I'm done, please let her in."

"No problem. Just one thing though, Riccardo."

"What's that?"

"The coffee."

"Right . . . Sorry."

After showering, I stood in my room, wondering what to put on. I had to admit to myself that Giulia was already having a certain influence on me.

In the kitchen, I found Paolo, Giulia, and a short, thin man of about fifty, wearing a pair of glasses with lenses so thick I wondered how they managed to stay in the frames.

Giulia greeted me straight away, asking, "What happened to your face, Riccardo?"

I was starting to get used to the question.

"Hi Giulia. If you're referring to the cuts, they're my fault because it turns out I'm no good at shaving left-handed. The black eye is thanks to your brilliant idea to have Paolo here to protect me."

Paolo answered resentfully, "It's your fault! You hid behind the door."

"Why were you hiding behind a door, Riccardo?" Giulia asked.

"Paolo and I heard someone in the garden. We thought it was the killer, but it was just Giuseppe, the neighbor I told you about."

"And what did Giuseppe want this time?"

"I think he just wanted to chat. You know, I've become a sort of celebrity here in Bastia recently, and having firsthand information would boost his credit at the local bar."

"Well, you're a mess! Anyway, I called the count on my way over and told him our meeting had been put off due to other urgent factors. So now you can call him and make your own appointment."

"OK. Just one thing, though."

"What's that?"

"If he's the person who's trying to kill me, won't this just make things easier for him?"

"That is a risk, but it's one that we have to take, and it's another reason why you'll have a concealed mic on you. Don't forget we'll be nearby, and if we hear that things are taking a turn for the worst, we'll be on him in fifteen seconds."

"A bullet travels faster than that!" I objected.

"Riccardo, if that's what you're worried about, you could end up under a tram while crossing the street."

"Great! Now I really feel reassured!"

"Let me introduce Piero Giacomini, our expert who's going to conceal the mic on you."

I shook his hand and couldn't help thinking that, if he could hear as well as he could see, my number was definitely up!

"Good morning, Mr. Ranieri. To be honest, we won't have to do much. Can you see this button?"

Seeing as he was holding it right under my nose, it would have been hard not to. Still, I didn't want to offend the man, so I just nodded.

"This is the microphone, or 'bug' if you prefer. It is extremely sensitive, so all you have to do is keep it in your pocket. It is calibrated so that from your pants pocket it can perfectly hear your conversation with someone up to six feet away. Furthermore, it can transmit that conversation to this switchboard within a radius of three miles. However, as District Attorney Dal Nero has told you, we'll be much closer than that, ready to step in if needed."

Having grown up in the James Bond era, I couldn't resist the temptation to quip, "Does it shoot lasers too?"

With absolutely no sense of irony and seeming rather offended, Giacomini answered, "No, sorry, it's just a microphone."

"Sorry, I was just kidding."

Dal Nero graciously broke in, saying, "It's already ten o'clock, Riccardo. How about calling the count now?"

I found his message in my phone and tried to call the number, but no one picked up. I tried again fifteen minutes later with the same result.

To avoid raising the count's suspicions with numerous attempts, Giulia and I decided to wait for him to call me back. The first three hours' wait cost me my entire stock of canned tuna and no fewer than ten apples picked straight from the trees in the garden.

Every so often, I caught Giulia's eye; perhaps I was kidding myself, but I had the strong feeling that a certain complicity was developing between us, as if we were both sorry we weren't alone. A couple of times during those long hours, I went into the garden to play with Mila and Newton, and to see whether Giulia would follow me and stop reading the documents she had brought with her, obviously foreseeing a long wait. Despite the fact that I played a few aces by picking some ripe pomegranates and even some sweet and rare jujubes, I was disappointed—Giulia never stopped working.

Instead, I was rewarded with the constant and truly boring companionship of Giacomini, who showed an almost unhealthy interest in my entire harvest and ate more in a morning than I managed in an entire season.

Even though Giulia was a compelling distraction, I had the distinct impression that I was on the verge of uncontrollable events that could cost me my life. My anxiety felt like a tight belt around my chest and reminded me of the feeling I had on September 11, 2001, while watching the events in New York. Now, as then, I felt I was being carried along by negative energy that was overturning my safe, everyday life and dragging me into an unknown dimension full of peril.

It was like watching a hurricane coming toward me and knowing full well I didn't even have an umbrella, let alone somewhere safe to hide.

CHAPTER SEVEN

At about half past five that evening, I had run out of patience and jujubes.

I couldn't wait any longer, so I said to Giulia, "Look, it's hard to imagine the count would be the type to always have his cell phone in his hand. The fact that he sent me a weird, formal message—with punctuation and everything—makes me think he just turns it on once in a blue moon. So I was thinking, what if I go straight to his house and ring the bell?"

Giulia agreed. "It's strange, though, because when I called this morning to cancel our meeting, he answered at the first ring. Still, since he doesn't have a landline, going over there seems like the only real option. Worse comes to worst, we'll just come back."

The count lives in a castle on a hill above the hamlet of Montemerlo in the Colli Euganei Park, which isn't far from my house, and it dominates the village of Nogaredo, as if Count Alvise still wants to exercise his feudal power over the surrounding land. It is a very large castle, but as I later learned from some golfing buddies, it's not all that old. It dates back to the postwar period, when it was built following the instructions of the count's father, who wanted his family to leave an indelible mark on the land.

I got into my Volvo. Luckily, it's an automatic, so I could drive without my hand causing too many problems. We had agreed with Giulia that she'd follow in her own car with Paolo and the ravenous Giacomini, all ready to intervene if necessary. When I reached the castle, I parked in front of the gate at the border of the estate. Apart from the entrance for cars, there was a smaller pedestrian gate as well. I got out of the car and was surprised to see there was no intercom, but the small gate was open, or, rather, it had a handle to open it. I looked around for another entrance, but I didn't see one, so in I went.

My feet crunched on the gravel, which reminded me of my childhood, when my mother used to take me to her friend's house that also had a gravel path. The happy memory just brought home how different my current circumstances were now, and the closer I got to the house, the less courage I felt. I was full of doubts: What would Count Alvise think, seeing me enter his castle? What if he had a gun and shot me? If he really might do something like that, why was I worrying about the rest of the investigation?

I felt my body tensing up with fear. I slowed down and peered nervously around to see if there was anybody watching. With each step forward, the castle got bigger and bigger. It was really imposing, despite the white, Provence-style, wooden shutters that softened its fortress-like appearance. The enormous, arched entrance was about thirty feet high and at the sides there were two sliding doors; one looked partly open, but just then, I heard a noise in the distance that froze the blood in my veins.

If entering the home of a shadowy figure I didn't know made me nervous, the scene that now unraveled before me was like a nightmare. It was difficult to calculate distance due to my swollen eye, but no more than a hundred yards away, there were three enormous dogs charging toward me at terrifying speed. I considered retracing my steps, but it was impossible: I would never have reached the gate in time. My only chance was to reach the sliding door to the right of the entrance, so I sprinted as fast as the loose gravel would allow.

I was about thirty yards away and the three assassin dogs were gaining on me. Their barking grew louder, and I was really, deeply afraid; I could feel the adrenaline coursing through my bloodstream and carrying desperate energy to my legs as I tried to reach my only hope of salvation. I was still about twenty yards away, which could have meant the difference between life and death. To try and release some tension, I yelled at the top of my voice, "Of all the shitty ideas I've ever heard, this is the worst of all. Bastards! Bastards!"

I have no idea how many times I said "bastards" and even less idea who exactly I was talking about. The three dogs were about fifty feet away and I was about thirty feet from safety, but I had the advantage of a straight shot through the door, while they had to come around the corner of the building, which should slow them down, or so I hoped.

One dog had overtaken the others. It was all black and looked like a Doberman, but a Doberman as big as me. I could still hear myself shouting something, probably just nonsense, while with my good hand, I slid the door open and threw my body inside. I twisted around and slammed the door shut so hard that if the Doberman-beast's head had been in the way, it would have been crushed. The three dogs stopped short at the door, barking ferociously, climbing over each other in an attempt to find a way through the barrier that separated me from their rage. As they showed their fangs, they also managed to slobber all over the glass, covering it top to bottom with drool.

I tried to breathe. Bent double from the effort and the fright, I whispered to Giulia and the others, "I'm inside. I managed to escape being torn apart by the dogs by the skin of my teeth, but it's OK now."

I turned away from the door, where the dogs were still barking, and looked around to see if there were any other signs of life.

The entrance foyer was very large and poorly lit, just as I'd imagined. It had a light gray marble floor and an impossibly high ceiling. The wide staircase was covered in dark red carpet, and there were imposing portraits hung on the walls; everything seemed to tell guests that whoever lived there was still powerful, despite article one of the Constitution ostensibly ending the Italian monarchy.

I tried calling out to see if anyone was there, but the only answer was the music coming from the speakers. Classical music. Despite my relative ignorance of classical music and much more besides, I was pretty certain I was listening to a toccata and fugue by Bach. At least the music meant someone was home. I tried calling louder but got no reply, so I headed toward the staircase, where there was a large door I hadn't noticed before. As I placed my hand on the doorknob, a small voice in my head asked me what the hell I thought I was doing. I'd clearly broken into somebody's home, into a castle owned by some guy who could be trying to kill me, and I thought I could just go around opening doors?

Standing there, my hand on the doorknob, I tried to think. No way was I going back outside; the three lions waiting to tear me to pieces were deterrent enough. I would have liked to ask Giulia for advice, but the microphone couldn't receive and, as Giacomini had somberly informed me, it didn't shoot lasers, either. Right then, my self-esteem took yet another blow when my cell phone rang. Shit! I'd been so totally inside my 007-style mission I hadn't thought of something as simple as a phone call.

"Hello, who is it?" I hissed impatiently.

"It's Giulia. What happened? We heard the dogs barking in the distance and you swearing."

"Not that distant. Three more feet and a Doberman the size of a yeti would have been devouring your precious collaborator."

"Where are you now?"

"Inside the castle, but I can't find anyone. I couldn't even ring the doorbell because the dogs were on me, so I found an open door and just ran in. By the way, is this breaking and entering?"

"Riccardo, you're not there to steal anything!"

"I know, but what do I do now? I can't find anybody . . . Just a minute."

"Why?"

"Wait . . . It sounds like the music got louder."

"Music? What music?"

"I can hear classical music, so maybe there is somebody here? I'm going to look in the other rooms."

"If you have any more problems, call me."

Encouraged by Giulia's voice and determined to talk to the damn count, I finally opened the door.

Asking if I could come in, I entered a large lobby about two thousand square feet, with a rectangular table in the center at least sixty feet long and fifteen wide, with a fireplace in the left wall as big as my bedroom. It was like stepping into a film about King Arthur. There were speakers playing Bach here, as well. I closed the door behind me and could hear that the music had been turned up again. It's strange how volume can alter your perceptions; while the music was soft, it made the austere setting seem elegant and full of charm, but as the volume rose, the atmosphere became increasingly tense and unpleasant. It was so loud now that I knew it'd be pointless calling out unless I screamed at the top of my lungs.

There was a corridor to the left that looked as though it led to the kitchen. Being generally well-mannered, I continued to call out as I walked along the corridor, even though I knew it was useless. Even more than the lobby I had just left, the kitchen was impressively sized, with a massive brick-and-wood island in the center. There were all types of furnishings around the walls, sideboards, cupboards, and sinks. The saucepans hanging above the island were proportionate to the vast kitchen: as big as the ones I used to have to wash when I was doing military service. There were no signs of life in the kitchen, and seeing everything so tidy and clean that it seemed fake made me even more anxious.

Increasingly concerned, I turned back. The music got even louder, and anxiety gripped my chest like a vise. I tried to find some courage by rationalizing the situation, even though there was precious little rationality there. I kept repeating to myself that it was music, just music, and somewhere there was an idiot having fun playing with the volume and my nerves. I retraced my steps and, through the sliding glass door, saw that the three dogs were still waiting for me. As soon as they saw me, they began barking again—or that's what I assumed. In all honesty, the music was so loud now that I wouldn't have heard the barking even if they'd been inside.

By now, there was nothing to do but climb the sweeping staircase and check upstairs. As I climbed, the volume was increased even more, and I marveled that the speakers didn't explode. I could feel my heart racing, and I couldn't understand the reason for the music. I was no longer able to think clearly, or even think at all because I could no longer hear my thoughts. I tried to cover my ears with my hands, but the bandage on the right one prevented me. I felt totally defenseless.

I rushed up the stairs. It was like being underwater when you are starting to run out of air and trying to get back to the surface as fast as possible. At the top, I could see a room to the left that looked like a reading room, though given the size it was more like a library. A long corridor stretched out in front of me with about ten doors opening to the right and left; I took five steps forward and opened one without knocking; knocking would have been pointless because anyone inside wouldn't even hear a gong with all that noise.

It was a bedroom with a double bed, a wardrobe, two windows overlooking the garden, and speakers suspended in the four corners of the ceiling belting out that music at an inhuman level, and although I wouldn't have thought it possible, the volume went up even more.

The speakers began to distort the sound, producing an effect that was even more devastating to my nerves. I couldn't stand it any longer. I wanted to curl up in a corner and wait for someone to come and save me from this torture, but I got a grip on myself and leaned against the door. While closing it, I had the impression of seeing a shadow disappear at the end of the corridor. I instinctively shouted in that direction, but even my own ears couldn't hear my voice. I really couldn't stand this any longer; I didn't even know if I was holding my breath or not. I began running along the corridor, determined to follow the shadow I had just seen, until I saw that the last door on the left was open. I reached it and looked in.

The scene before me was so apparently normal that in that absurd situation it became surreal: an elderly woman was sitting in a chair with her hands in her lap, totally motionless, as if all that noise didn't bother her at all. Despite the totally crazy situation, I realized there was something off about the woman's pose. Her head was in an unnatural position with respect to her shoulders, her neck at a forty-five degree angle. The shock from the sight of the woman and the infernal noise from the crescendoing toccata and fugue didn't prevent me from sensing an evil presence behind me. I knew it was him; I could feel it. My heart sped up so much it just about burst, and I could feel the stark contrast of his calm, cold demeanor. He had finally reached his goal and was enjoying the inevitable finale. Perhaps due to the excess of adrenaline, I began thinking a thousand disconnected thoughts, one being that if I died it would at least end the torture of that hallucinatory music. Another thought was something an old girlfriend once said to me: "A loser isn't someone who loses, but someone who gives up without a fight."

At that moment, I felt the cold steel at the base of my neck and imagined it was a blade or gun. That cold touch triggered some kind of survival instinct: I felt myself rotate my hips while my right arm swung out to come down like a sledgehammer on my assassin. The action was so fast there was barely time for my hand to close into a fist. It wasn't fast enough, though, because in that infinite fraction of a second, I felt the steel hit my neck with amazing violence. I perceived the unstoppable force of that metal from hell rip deep into my flesh, until my senses began to recede as if washed over by a wave. As silence overcame me, I realized I could do nothing more.

Everything went black, and I became aware of my own death.

CHAPTER EIGHT

Every morning in Africa, a gazelle wakes up, and it knows it must out-run the fastest lion or it will be killed. Every morning in Africa, a lion wakes up, and it knows it must run faster than the slowest gazelle, or it will starve. It doesn't matter whether you're a lion or a gazelle—when the sun comes up, you'd better be running. OK, I know. I risk offending ancient African wisdom, but in my opinion, it does matter whether you're a lion or a gazelle, and right now, that goddamn gazelle had just kicked me in the back of my neck with what felt like an iron.

"Ouch!" It was really painful.

"Hold still, Ranieri. I'm trying to put this pillow under your head."

"Where am I?"

"Welcome back. You're in the ambulance."

"Again?"

"That's right. If you keep it up, we'll give you a season pass: take three trips, get one free."

I don't know what the odds are of being loaded into an ambulance twice in the space of a couple of days. I suppose it's not so strange for someone who's ill, but to find yourself tended to by the same gigantic paramedic twice in a row must be against the odds.

"My head is killing me . . . What happened?"

"The carabinieri told me you fainted and hit your head on the corner of a dresser when you went down."

"Carabinieri? The military police are here?"

"Yes, Ranieri, we intervened."

I hadn't even noticed the officer sitting in a small chair on my right. He exclaimed, "It looks like you're in serious trouble, Mr. Ranieri!"

"Nothing new there, then."

Clearly, Giulia hadn't told the officer that she'd sent me into the castle. Still, I was so confused by the ringing sound in my ears that I decided to keep quiet and not mention my assignment from the DA.

No matter what I did to try to regain control, these past few days made me feel like I was being swept along by events like a leaf in the wind, so I just closed my eyes and decided to let them take me where they wanted. Until a few minutes earlier, I'd been convinced I was dead, so all in all, things were improving.

I don't know whether I fell asleep or fainted again, but when I opened my eyes, I was in a hospital bed. It was like reliving the night of the shooting, but this time I immediately recognized the nurses, doctors, and officers. Experience counts for something . . .

My head hurt terribly, and as I regained consciousness, the awful ringing in my ears came back. The first person to realize I was waking up was one carabiniere I recognized straight away: Marshal Costanzo.

He said, "So, Ranieri! What have you been getting up to?"

"Good evening, Marshal Costanzo. I'm sorry, but I really don't feel well. Do you mind if we let the doctors rescue me first?"

"Look, Ranieri, I'm going to need you to explain what the hell you were doing."

I expected the doctors to make him keep quiet so they could look after me, but they didn't say a word. In fact, I had the distinct impression they came closer to try to listen in. I almost wished Dr. Migliorini was there.

Seeing no other choice, I decided to play my ace right away.

"Marshal, you need to talk to District Attorney Dal Nero. She sent me to the Count of Nogaredo's castle."

"Leave District Attorney Dal Nero out of this, and tell me what you were doing in the castle."

Despite feeling so woozy, I could hear the change in his tone and understood it was better not to provoke him, but I had to repeat the truth.

"I told you. District Attorney Dal Nero sent me there."

"Sure, sure. And did the district attorney tell you to kill the count's mother as well?"

"What are you talking about? You can't possibly think I killed that woman?"

"Why not? The first time I see you, you're next to Dr. Salvioni's body. Then the next time I see you, you're next to the body of that poor old woman. Yeah, what a crazy conclusion. I guess I'm just suspicious by nature. Come on, Ranieri! Tell me the truth and let's get this mess sorted out as fast as possible."

"Look, Marshal, please. Call the DA and I swear she'll clear this up. Look, I'm sorry, but I really feel terrible. I have a splitting headache and there's a horrible ringing in my ears."

Finally, the seemingly eldest doctor in the group decided to speak up. With his thick head of hair the same color as his shirt, and the confident expression of someone who is accustomed to dealing with much more serious matters, the man that I would later discover to be Dr. Angelo Banfi, head physician in traumatology, addressed me in a reassuring tone. "Don't worry, Mr. Ranieri. The ringing in your ears is just tinnitus, which is a normal reaction when you're exposed to a loud noise that damages the cochlear ciliate cells. It should be much better in a couple of hours and should resolve itself completely over time."

"What about the headache?"

"You've been under a lot of stress. You fainted, and when you fell, you banged your head on a dresser, causing a lacerated contusion to your temple. We did a CAT scan while you were unconscious and found nothing to worry about. The headache should improve soon, as well."

Dr. Banfi's cold, detached analysis of my case helped me gain a minimum of rationality. I realized how close I'd come to identifying the killer.

I turned back to the marshal.

"Listen, Marshal, if you give up this inquisition for a minute, there might still be time. Call the DA and tell her the assassin we're looking for is in Count Alvise's home. He's probably still hiding there waiting for things to calm down."

"Ranieri, let's get one thing clear: District Attorney Dal Nero is on her way here, and she's furious, because she says you should have informed her of all your movements inside the castle. But not only didn't you inform anyone about what was happening, you even decided to kill some old woman."

I really didn't feel like arguing with him; my head was about to explode, and each thought was stabbing at the base of my skull.

I turned to Dr. Banfi. "Doctor, could I have something for my headache? I can hardly take it anymore."

"You'll have to wait, Ranieri, because we have to see if the pain goes away by itself or not. Pain is a signal from our body to tell us something is wrong. I told you that the CAT scan was clear, but you never know. With this sort of trauma, we have to be certain that there are no other complications."

Maybe Banfi was right, not that I really understood. Still, it seemed best to close my eyes and not ask any more questions, both to minimize the pain and to avoid learning more about what kind of complications he was talking about.

I could sense the marshal was getting ready to question me again, but I decided to pretend I wasn't there, which wasn't too tough as I felt like I was on the verge of death.

He gave up, but my moment of calm didn't last long. I could hear shouting and swearing in the hall and realized it must be Arcadio. The officers tried to stop him from coming in, but he pushed them away, shouting something like, "You bastard, I'll kill you! I'll rip your heart out!" and other equally kind words. If the carabinieri hadn't been there, he would probably have torn me apart like his dogs had wanted to at the castle. It's true what they say about dogs taking after their owners.

In the midst of all that ruckus, I saw Giulia behind Arcadio, and from her expression, I thought it would be easier to face Arcadio. So, a quick tally: one hand with a hole in it, my face diced up by a razor, a black eye from the door Paolo banged into me, a lacerated temple and my head on fire, and, last but not least, that infernal ringing in my ears. The last thing I needed right then was a furious district attorney and a marshal accusing me of triple homicide. In short, the asshole who had tried to murder me was the least of my problems right now.

Unlike Arcadio, Giulia had no need to shout; the icy tone of her voice when she asked how I was fully expressed her contempt. Without waiting for my answer, she added, "I thought we agreed that you'd keep me informed of all your moves."

When I want, I can maintain a certain aplomb. "I thought we agreed that you would intervene if something went wrong."

"You never told us you were in danger."

My voice began to get louder as my headache got worse. "Didn't you suspect there was something wrong? In your opinion, Bach blaring at ten thousand decibels was normal? How on earth could I tell you to come in when I couldn't even hear my own voice?"

"At least tell me now what you did in the castle," Giulia said, cutting me off.

Arcadio, still held at the door, started shouting again. "He killed my grandmother! That's what he did, the bastard!"

The marshal made his first good call so far: he ordered the carabinieri to remove Arcadio, who continued shouting that he'd be waiting to kill me as soon as I got out.

I found it hard not to shout back that he'd have to wait his turn, but I turned instead to Giulia. I could see how irritated she was, probably because of the almighty mess this had turned into rather than because she really thought I'd done something wrong. I told her how I'd entered the castle to escape from the count's dogs, I told her about the awful music, about the shadow I'd seen at the end of the corridor, and finally, I told her about the woman sitting in the chair with a broken neck.

"Now, you explain why you didn't come in after me!"

"After I called you, the mic started screeching, so we thought you'd broken it. We tried to enter, but couldn't come in on foot without attracting the attention of the dogs. We were about to ram through the larger gate with the car when we saw the dogs chasing someone in the park. We tried to drive in that direction around the property, but by the time we got there, he was gone."

"Maybe that was the assassin! And maybe he didn't get away and he's still hiding somewhere on the grounds."

"I don't think so. We called other squads and they've been patrolling the estate and surrounding area for two hours now."

"I don't understand a couple of things. If he killed that woman—"

The marshal broke in. "She was the count's mother."

"OK, the count's mother. As I was saying, if he killed the count's mother, why was he hanging around listening to Bach, turning the volume up to an infernal level, instead of just running off before he got caught?"

"Come on, Ranieri, catch up," the marshal said. "That infernal music, as you call it, is a burglar alarm that is activated by the sensors inside the castle. When you pass in front of them, the music begins and increases in volume. It's like a siren, but much more sophisticated."

"A burglar alarm?"

I didn't know whether to feel more humiliated by the fact that I hadn't understood or by the fact that the marshal had lost his accusing tone and seemed now to consider me some sort of simpleton.

Giulia spoke again. "Yes, Riccardo. That's what put the mic out of commission."

"OK, I get it now, but that's no reason to be angry with me or accuse me of murder!"

"I haven't accused you of murder; I just said you should have contacted me."

I noticed that the marshal was no longer looking at Giulia or me.

"How the hell was I supposed to do that if the mic wasn't working?"

"Come on, Riccardo. With your cell phone!"

"In your opinion, I could phone you with all that chaos? Anyway, there's no number three on my phone anymore, and I don't exactly have your number on speed dial."

"All you had to do was press the call button and find my number among the incoming calls, seeing as I'd called you a minute before."

"OK, you're right, Giulia. Look, let's put it like this: this is not my job. I'm not used to going into other people's houses, and I'm definitely not used to finding myself in that sort of situation."

There was a lull, and I took the opportunity to think over something: I still didn't understand what had happened behind me when I found the body of the count's mother.

"When I entered the room where the dead woman was, I felt someone behind me shove a knife against my neck and then something really hard hit me."

The marshal interrupted to explain. "No, no knife. That was the barrel of my Winchester."

"The barrel of your Winchester?"

I was stunned. I couldn't believe it.

"Yes, Ranieri, you see, the castle alarm is linked to the Bastia police station, so we came to the scene. We didn't see the dogs you're talking about, though."

"Because the dogs were chasing the guy who was running away," Giulia pointed out.

"I guess, yeah. So, we entered the castle. When I reached Mrs. Roncadelle's room, I saw the back of the person I thought had killed her."

"It was just me!"

"But you could have been the assassin."

"Give me a break here!"

"I shouted, 'Carabinieri! Don't move!' But you moved, so I tapped you on the neck."

"A tap? You fucking tomahawked my neck!"

"Come on, don't exaggerate!"

"Exaggerate my ass! You hit me so hard I passed out!"

"You shouldn't have moved! I told you to stop!"

"Didn't you realize I couldn't hear you?"

"Well, I did suspect that—"

"Thank God you suspected it, otherwise what would you have done? Just shot me?"

"Yes."

"Marshal, the doctors told me I'd banged my head against the corner of a dresser."

"I told them that."

"There wasn't a dresser in the room."

"Come on, Ranieri, don't split hairs."

"Split hairs, nothing! You almost kill me with your gun, and then you lie to the doctors and accuse me of murder."

Dal Nero broke in to try to calm us down. "Look, let's not make a fuss over nothing. We'll leave you to rest now, Riccardo. Marshal, you'll need to help me find the count."

Right, the count. In all that chaos, I'd forgotten the reason why I was in a hospital bed again. If nothing else, it meant that the key to everything that had happened was the count and his family. In fact, if we found him, dead or alive, maybe the nightmare would be almost over.

As I was trying to think between one stabbing pain and the next, they all left the room, and I turned off the light. At first, it seemed pleasantly dark, but once my eyes adjusted, I realized there was still way too much neon light coming in from the windows to the hallway. Why did hospital rooms always have to be like that?

Despite my efforts to analyze the situation from the various viewpoints—the killer's, the victims', and mine—there was one thing I just couldn't understand: What could push a man, or more than one, to kill so many people? I was convinced that the assassin, or assassins, had lost control of the situation. The first murder, Massimo's, was obviously a message for someone, because they'd stitched his lips shut. That someone, perhaps me even, hadn't reacted as the assassin had expected, so he was forced to kill again. And if, as I thought, the count was the key to everything, what was Arcadio's role in it all? Much as I didn't like him, he didn't seem capable of murder. Anyway, his fury at me over his grandmother's murder was certainly convincing. What was the connection between the Salvionis and the count's mother? Finally, where was Count Alvise, who hadn't answered his phone and wasn't in the castle? I had no answers, and as another stabbing pain seared my skull, I decided it wasn't my job to find them, and so I just drifted off to sleep.

I woke up some time during the night. I firmly believe that a hospital is the ideal place to lose all sense of time. I looked at my watch. It was four o'clock. I'd been woken by a lively discussion in the hall between two doctors or nurses.

To my relief, my headache and the ringing in my ears were gone. To test my hearing, I tried to eavesdrop on what the people in the hall were saying. I couldn't make out all the words, but I understood they were discussing the best procedure for a blood transfusion in a very urgent case. One word in particular sent a shiver down my spine: *incompatibility.*

I thought back to the message Massimo had sent to my cell before he was killed: *Wrong blood.* What if the answer was an incompatible blood type! Some types are totally incompatible with each other, not only to save a life but also to create one.

Massimo was an obstetrician. He delivered babies.

CHAPTER NINE

At forty years of age, I can now read the signs to know if it's going to be a good or bad day.

A nurse as ugly as sin had woken me at five thirty for breakfast, which was a cooked pear, or a soggy mass that might have been a cooked pear, a cup of milk stained with some instant coffee, and two brightly colored pills.

My hearing was back completely, and my headache was still gone. As I started to feel better, my mood improved, as well, and as the hospital menu fully conformed to comic stereotypes, I couldn't help joking and asking the nurse if I could have some broth with tiny pasta stars it in. I expected a witty response, but instead, she looked at me with surprise. I guessed she wasn't Italian and I immediately felt sorry for making fun of someone who was just trying to do her job, and what's more, was looking after me.

As the nurse walked away looking confused, I got up and went into the bathroom. I would have liked to shave, but I didn't have my razor; I looked at the mournfully empty shelf that should have held a toothbrush and some toothpaste. Returning to my bed, I felt dirty, my mouth was furred up, and while dreaming of the first-class luxuries on Air Emirates, I worked up the nerve to taste the milky "coffee." Amazingly, it tasted even worse than it looked, but at least it woke me up like a slap in the face.

Paolo came to the door, so I figured he was still responsible for protecting me or, as Marshal Costanzo surely would have said, checking up on me.

"How are you today, Riccardo?"

"Recently, whenever I say I'm OK, something awful happens, so let's skip it. More importantly, can I get a decent cup of coffee?"

"First of all, I'm not a waiter. Second, who said you can drink coffee?"

"Why shouldn't I? I'm not suffering from insomnia—just the opposite. These past few days, between fainting and tranquilizers, I spend more time asleep than awake. Anyway, I never asked you to bring me coffee. If you tell me where the machine is I'll go and get it myself."

"How am I supposed to know?"

"Look, Paolo, on all the detective shows, the supercool American cops are always carrying a hot cup of coffee and superfattening doughnuts."

"Yeah, but I'm not American."

"Where are you from?"

"Adria. I mean, Papozze, really, so nearby, but not quite Adria."

"Yeah, you're right. It's not the same . . . Do you know what I'm going to do?"

"No, what?" Paolo asked.

"I'm going to get dressed and go home."

"You've got to wait for the doctors, and I've got to ask District Attorney Dal Nero if she has other plans."

"Doctors, district attorney, plans . . . Quite frankly, I'm fed up. I'm going home, and if that bloody idiot wants to kill me, let him get on with it. I don't care anymore. I've got to feed my dogs and get back to my job, if I've still got one."

"You bet you do! In fact, starting today you've got two jobs."

I looked past Paolo to see who was talking: Piovesan had suddenly appeared out of nowhere.

"Starting today, you're on the breaking news beat."

"Hello, Piovesan. Why two?"

My cold greeting was an attempt to show my contempt for his rude interruption and also my resistance to the professional implications of what he was saying.

"Two what?"

"You said two jobs."

"I told you: you've been assigned to breaking news."

"I get that, but that's just one job!"

"And the other is your old job on finance."

"Let me get this straight. I've got double the amount of work to do, so I suppose I'll get paid double, as well?"

"No. If you're good at breaking news, you can leave the financial page."

"What gave you the idea I want to move to breaking news? For one thing, I've got a damn degree in economics!"

I was really beginning to be over all this shit, and I could hear my voice getting louder. It was one thing for these terrible events to mess up my life for a few days, but to have someone just totally change my job responsibilities was taking it too far.

"Calm down, Riccardo. I'll explain. At the paper, we need someone to cover the events you're involved in, and who better than you?"

"Gibbo, I'm not stupid. I get why you want me on news. What I don't get is how you could decide without consulting me first."

"Obviously, if you don't want the gig, then that's that. But in my opinion, you'd be perfect. Anyway, news is always a career boost."

"Sure, and next I'll win the Pulitzer Prize. Come on, Gibbo, give me a break."

Piovesan's interruption had been so sudden and our conversation so heated that Paolo hadn't even had the time, or the wits, to ask who he was. If the damn assassin approached the way Piovesan had, I'd be dead on the spot if it were left to Paolo.

While I was trying to find my clothes, someone appeared behind Paolo and Gibbo and made me feel even more wretched; the poor nurse, presumably Moldavian, came in with a bowl of hot broth, stars and all, and left it on my bedside table.

I was finally getting dressed when a doctor with a rather important air entered, followed by a crowd of other white coats.

After looking at my broth with a mixture of curiosity and horror, the doctor introduced himself as the chief consultant and came over to shake my hand.

"I see you're hungry and in a hurry to go home, Mr. Ranieri."

"Let's just say I've already caused you enough trouble. I feel fine now, and there's no reason for me to stay any longer."

"I'm sure you're right, but still, just to prevent any surprises, let me have a look."

I'm like Onofrio: I'll try to act tough, but if someone scratches me behind the ear, I'm putty in their hands. I took off my jacket and, meek as a lamb, got ready for my checkup. The doctor confirmed my optimism, and he authorized my discharge.

It was only seven thirty in the morning, but when I got outside, there were about thirty reporters waiting for me. I turned to Paolo, who had been trying to get in touch with Dal Nero.

"What do you think, Paolo? Should I spill everything to the press and get the weight off my chest?" I joked.

"Don't even think about it, Riccardo. You'll be in serious trouble—"

Before he could recite the whole sermon, I looked him straight in the eye and said mockingly, "I was just joking. Calm down! You should worry more about the poor creep who's trying to do me in. I'll never be alone again; I feel almost sorry for him."

"I can imagine how sorry you'll feel for him if he puts a bullet in your brain."

"Thanks, Paolo, I'm so glad you're here to make me feel better."

Piovesan, who I'd asked to give a ten-euro tip to the nurse, hurried to join us, exclaiming, "Eh, Riccardo! Don't forget—not a word to any other papers, eh?"

Paolo felt obliged to point out, "I already told him."

"I dunno, Gibbo. Maybe I should promise the exclusive story to the *Corriere della Sera* in exchange for a job in breaking news."

I've never been the type to exploit situations for my professional benefit. In fact, I've always had the naïve conviction that you can only enjoy professional success if it's achieved through your own talent and hard work. Otherwise, all you get is a fleeting ego boost that evaporates as soon as you hit the first bump in the road. But I like provoking people, and I imagined that my below-the-belt blow would cause Gibbo some concern, but I was wrong.

He promptly answered in the same tone, "Nah, they wouldn't be interested. It's a decent story for the *Corriere,* but not that big a deal. We're in the Veneto here and it's the Veneto people who care about this."

Still, all the television channels were there—the RAI national channels, Mediaset. All that was missing was Al Jazeera. For a moment, I imagined I'd be on all the news channels in Italy, and maybe abroad as well, because let's face it: three homicides, almost four if we count me, is like manna from heaven for the media.

Even though I wasn't actually looking to be a local celebrity, I must admit that when I left the hospital I felt a slight exhilaration and, I confess, a touch of narcissistic vanity. Just like on TV, the reporters went wild, bombarding me with questions all at once, but Paolo took my arm and managed to maneuver me through the crowd like an offensive lineman. The reporters kept hitting me in the face with their microphones until I decided to stop before the whole thing got ridiculous. After all, it was the first time I'd appeared on TV, and I didn't want to look like a cartoon character.

With as much self-determination as the situation allowed, which is to say very little, I turned to the reporters and solemnly stated, "I'm very sorry, but I'm not authorized to answer any questions."

For a fleeting instant, a surreal silence fell over the frozen crowd. It was just an instant, though, because right after, they burst out again with their questions and incessant shoving. The situation became increasingly grotesque when, after what felt like ten minutes, Paolo and I, still surrounded by rabid reporters and cameramen, and unable to see where we were going, realized we were heading in the wrong direction.

Paolo had parked his ancient Fiesta about a hundred yards from the exit, obviously not anticipating this feeding frenzy. After far too long, we finally saw his car and moved toward it. While I was getting into the car, one of the most persistent reporters called out, "At least tell us how you are!"

I couldn't help but think how frustrating it must be to get up at five o'clock in the morning to go and interview someone, wait hours outside a hospital, and never get a single answer. I decided they deserved something, to hell with Piovesan, Paolo, and all the rest.

"I feel fine, and the doctors have just given me authorization to go home."

I got in the car, closed the door, and asked Paolo to drive carefully. The last thing we needed was an injured reporter.

Stupid me. Paolo turned toward the center of Padua to take me back to the DA's office.

"Seriously, Paolo! I told you I wanted to go home," I objected in dismay.

"Come on, Riccardo, don't make a fuss. We'll go to see District Attorney Dal Nero, see what she has to say, and then I'll take you wherever you want."

"Brilliant. From attempted homicide to kidnapping in one fell swoop. What a great life," I grumbled.

"What do you mean, 'kidnapping'? The DA isn't answering her cell phone, and if I take you home instead of to her office, do you know what'll happen?"

"No. What?"

"Have you ever seen Dal Nero when she's angry?"

That fleeting hint of Giulia's temperament reawakened my curiosity about her. The violent rushes of adrenaline caused by recent events had distracted me from my attraction to her, but this return to normality, if you could call it that, had rekindled my interest.

"She seemed pretty angry yesterday evening."

"Yesterday was nothing. When the DA really gets mad, it's best to keep your distance."

"Have you ever made her angry?"

"Not personally. But once my captain turned up an hour late for a meeting she'd called. When he entered her office, he couldn't find a chair to sit on because she'd had it removed, and he had to stand while she informed him he was off the investigation, because one unreliable person could compromise everyone else's hard work. I'm not kidding. And it wasn't even so much what she said as how she said it. Believe me, that woman knows how to hit the mark."

"OK, Paolo, I'm convinced. Let's go and talk to the big scary monster, and then you can take me home so I can get back to my life."

"Sure, as long as that guy who's trying to do you in doesn't take that life first."

"You said it, Paolo. 'Do me in.' The truth is this whole business is starting to do me in."

"I didn't mean—"

"I know, Paolo, I know," I said and stopped him with a smile.

As we entered Padua, I saw a newsstand and asked Paolo to stop. I hadn't read a paper for three days, a record for me. Paolo asked me to hold off because he'd noticed a motorbike behind us. I pointed out that it was rush hour in Padua, so the only strange thing was that there was only one motorbike instead of an entire platoon.

"Believe me, Riccardo. They're following us."

"Who?"

"I don't know, but there are two of them."

We stopped at a red light, and the motorbike stopped, too, even though there was plenty of space to pull around us. Peering into the rearview mirror, I spotted the video camera.

"Great, now I've got the paparazzi on my tail! When they set their minds to it, reporters can be real pains in the ass," I moaned.

"See? Now that you're on this side of the fence, maybe you'll see what a nuisance people like you are."

"Touché, Officer."

Ten minutes later, Paolo and I reached the DA's office and, still being filmed by one of the guys on the motorbike, entered the building.

"Hello, Riccardo. How are you?"

"Silvia, my dear! Not bad, thanks. Between one attempted murder and the next, I'm getting by. What about you?"

Silvia couldn't restrain that bubbly laugh, replying, "Great. Now I'm famous, thanks to you. Loads of people are calling. Even my parents remembered I'm alive."

"Why are you famous?"

"What do you mean? Haven't you read the papers?"

I scowled at Paolo.

"No, nobody's given me the chance."

"Read them! All they're talking about is you and your story."

Up until this week, I'd spent my days on Reuters, Bloomberg, and Ansa, scanning for stories worth looking into. I'd been better informed than *The Times* server. Now that I was the story, I hadn't so much as glanced at a paper in days.

Silvia turned to Paolo and asked if he was looking for Giulia.

"Yes. Do you know where she is?"

"She's not here yet, but she's on her way. I think she was going to the hospital, but I guess they'll send her back here. If you'd like, you can go up and wait."

I suggested to Paolo that we make the most of the break by having breakfast in the bar across the street, and for once he agreed without objecting about my safety. We crossed the street under the watchful eye of the motorcyclists' camera and went into the bar. As soon as we entered, we ordered two coffees: one decaf with a splash of milk, and the other a single shot of espresso in a mug.

The bartender obviously wasn't a morning guy and looked at us like we'd asked him to explain Bell's theory of quantum mechanics. I'd just managed to pick out a delicious-looking brioche when the biker-reporters appeared behind me, introducing themselves as a correspondent and a cameraman for *Repubblica*. The reporter wasted no time before asking me about the Frassanelle murders. I was ready to reply that I was obliged to keep the details of the investigation confidential, but I'd just bitten into my brioche and didn't get the chance to swallow before Paolo, with his usual eloquence, threatened to throw the reporter out on his ass if he didn't get lost in five seconds. The two reporters left, mumbling about police brutality.

"Paolo, what if you just let me talk to them politely?"

"I know what those people are like! If you don't treat them rough, they never give up."

"Have you considered that I also know what they're like, seeing as I'm one of them? Anyway, they're just trying to do their job."

"Exactly, and I'm trying to do mine. That OK with you?"

"Ok, Paolo, let's drop it."

We finished our breakfast without another word, and went to leave the bar, looking around for any more reporters or, worse, assassins, but we were halted by the bartender. He seemed rather skittish and offended.

"Excuse me, gentlemen. I heard you saying that you're doing your job, but I'm doing mine as well, aren't I?"

"Of course. What's the problem?"

"Maybe you'd like to pay for the coffee and brioches?"

CHAPTER TEN

When we entered Giulia's office, she seemed strangely distant. She was sitting behind her desk reading some files. Looking up, she gestured for Paolo and me to sit down, then went back to her work.

I can't say I expected a hug or anything, but I thought she might at least shake my hand . . .

We both waited in a rather embarrassed and tense silence until Giulia had finished reading. After another minute with the files, she set down the papers that had formed a physical barrier between us, apologized politely, and then gave us her undivided attention.

"I sent a patrol to fetch you from the hospital, but they said you'd already left."

"Yeah, I couldn't stand being there any longer," I explained.

"Did the doctors sign off?"

"Of course. The chief consultant himself came to look me over and said I'm as fit as a fiddle."

"Good. This morning I heard they want to transfer you to front page news at the *Mattino*."

"Word travels fast around here. I'm not even sure I want the job."

"No problem. The only thing I ask is that you keep the details of our investigation confidential, so that you don't risk compromising our work."

"Don't worry, Giulia, they won't get anything from me. By the way, have you found Count Alvise?"

"Yes. The count was off golfing at the Frassanelle Club during our adventure at the castle. There's no reception on the course, so he didn't have a clue we were looking for him."

"That's crazy! But it's so obvious. Why didn't we think of that?"

"Riccardo, *you* didn't think of it."

"Hey, it wasn't just me looking for him."

"I know, but we wouldn't have known there was no reception on the golf course, whereas you should have. Anyway, it doesn't matter now. I don't think his mother was murdered because you broke into the castle. To tell the truth, your visit allowed us to establish a few things."

Right then, Giulia was about as pleasant as famine in Africa, but I didn't want to give her the satisfaction of seeing that she was upsetting me. I refrained from swallowing, even though I needed to.

"Meaning?"

"Well, to start with, the count, or his family, is deeply involved in these events. What's more, Count Alvise's mother is not his mother. Or rather, wasn't."

I swallowed. "So who is she? Or was she?"

"The person everyone in the village called 'the countess' was, in fact, Stella Roncadelle, and it seems that she had always lived with Count Alvise because she was his nanny. Basically, she was the housekeeper and estate manager. And, according to the count, she's the only mother he ever knew. I take him at his word that he was really close with her because, when he learned of her death, or rather, murder, we had to rush him to the ER. The shock caused a heart attack that nearly sent him to his creator, as well."

Until then, Paolo had just listened, but at this point he seemed to think it was time to score some points with Giulia by means of some pointless commentary. Knowing how afraid of the DA he was, I found it hard not to laugh at his ineptitude.

"Well, District Attorney Dal Nero, we're certainly keeping the hospital busy these days, aren't we?"

Giulia's expression went from cold to freezing. Slowly and purposely, she turned to Paolo and replied in an accusatory tone, "Yes, Officer Battiston. So busy that I'm told a reporter from the *Mattino* managed to enter Ranieri's room without any interference from the officer assigned to protect him."

"Yes, but Ranieri knew him—"

He didn't get the chance to finish because Dal Nero continued. "I'm also told that you two pushed your way through a crowd of fifty or so reporters. Is that correct?"

"But, but—"

"Officer Battiston, do you have any idea how to protect someone?"

What really hurt was that Giulia's tone never changed. She never raised her voice, as if she couldn't be bothered to really get angry at someone who was so clearly a bumbling idiot.

Paolo understood that there was nothing he could say to help matters, so he just hung his head.

I felt obligated to try to say something in his defense. "Giulia, it's my fault we didn't wait at the hospital; I just couldn't take it anymore—"

But she interrupted me, too. "Riccardo, you still haven't gotten your head around the fact that there is an actual person out there, or maybe more than one person, who wants to kill you."

"What do you mean, more than one?" I asked in alarm.

"This morning I got the autopsy report on Patty Salvioni."

"And?"

"As we suspected from the start, whoever hit her wasn't very strong, maybe an elderly man or a small woman. Even though she was hit on the head at least fifteen times, only three of the blows caused actual skull fractures. That many blows suggests the same sort of ferocious rage that killed Dr. Salvioni, but he was definitely murdered by somebody else."

"So how did Massimo die? What killed him before he was butchered that way?"

"Somebody came up from behind and strangled him with fishing line. It takes a lot of strength to kill someone that way, especially considering the victim's size."

I steadied myself to ask the question that would determine whether I could ever go back to a normal life, not to mention keep my life at all. "Do you have any idea who it could have been?"

"If you mean names, no, but if you mean a psychological profile and motive, we're working on it."

"A profile?"

"The ferocious nature of the first two homicides leads us to suspect someone very close and familiar to the victims. In the case of Mrs. Salvioni, there was less force, but not less violence or malice. The fury on display in these attacks is far from rational. The only thing that's out of place, that could lead us to consider premeditation, is the perpetrators' apparent lack of cell phones. From the GPS data, we can verify that there were no unknown people present while the homicides were taking place."

"What about the motive?"

"It could have been a betrayal, or a question of money. In any event, both the detectives and I are convinced that the murders are directly linked to the Frassanelle Golf Club. It can't be a coincidence that first the Salvionis and then the count's surrogate mother were killed, but there could be more than one killer, because the homicides are too different, and the victims are as well." As if she'd read my mind, Giulia said, "Let's get this straight. That shouldn't reassure you in any way—just the opposite. While a serial killer works methodically and takes care not to betray himself because he wants to go on killing, the person or persons we're dealing with here have no established patterns. We don't even know if they want to remain in the shadows or are prepared to strike out in broad daylight. So," she continued, looking at Paolo, "you two have to take all possible precautions and avoid contact with *anyone* who tries to approach you. I want to be perfectly clear, Officer Battiston: If Ranieri dies, you are out on your ear. Have I made myself understood?"

I wanted to play down the idea that someone would still be trying to kill me at this point, but I knew Giulia would just feel obliged to insist that I was still in denial.

I decided to keep quiet, but Paolo began stuttering, "Yes, but, but—"

"Good, you can go now. Riccardo, one last thing . . ."

"What is it, Giulia?"

"Breaking news or no, remember our agreement. I've told you everything I know, not because I want to read it in the *Mattino* tomorrow morning, but to better equip you to defend yourself and perhaps even help us figure out who tried to kill you. So remember, if anything of what I've shared here leaks out, you'll find that I'm a much more formidable enemy than the person who tried to shoot you. Do we understand each other?"

"And here I wanted to invite you to dinner to celebrate my new job."

Despite my playful tone, Giulia's tone got colder still. "I already have plans, and anyway, I don't make a habit of socializing with people involved in my investigations."

If challenged, I'm prepared to lose, but I always have to play all my cards, so I retorted, "What a shame. I wanted to bring you up to date about some thoughts I had regarding the message Massimo sent me before he was killed."

"Meaning?"

"Oh, no, I mean, since you don't want to come to dinner . . ."

"Riccardo, don't waste my time."

I realized that she wasn't one for going along with a joke, or at least not right then.

"'Wrong blood' could mean a blood transfusion that leads to a death, or maybe incompatibility in generating a life. Massimo was an ob-gyn, and maybe he'd realized that a child's blood type meant its mother had stepped out on some husband who paid less attention to her than to his Tuesday evening football game."

Giulia studied her hands on the desktop, perhaps to help her concentrate better.

"Hm, yes, that's a distinct possibility. But if Dr. Salvioni sent the message to you, it must have been because he thought you'd understand it. Perhaps you're the father of this hypothetical illegitimate child. Have you ever had any affairs with married women or women who got married shortly after breaking things off with you?"

"Well, that could complicate the investigation considerably!"

"Excuse me?"

"Sorry, but I have more than my share of exes. Believe it or not, women find me quite irresistible."

At last Giulia smiled, albeit ironically. Looking like the cat that ate the canary, she replied, "Strange, because according to our information, over the last ten years you've been in three relationships—four at the most."

"Information? You've been digging around in my private life?" I was impressed, but annoyed, as well.

"Dear Riccardo, we have put your life under a microscope. Relatives, colleagues, friends, women, phone calls, even the websites you've visited over the last ten years. We know what you ate when you vacationed in Sicily last year."

"You know I went to Sicily!"

I was really unsettled. I'm not famous, so I always imagined I could enjoy a certain amount of privacy. But to hear that Giulia, or the people who worked for her, had so swiftly been able to unearth absolutely everything about me, even the most intimate details, was kind of horrifying.

"OK, so if you already know everything, it seems pointless to ask me if I ever got anyone pregnant. Maybe I should ask you!"

Despite my attempts at self-control, my voice betrayed panic and dismay.

"Riccardo, we didn't obtain this information out of nosiness or curiosity. It's de rigueur in any investigation these days. In fact, 90 percent of criminal cases are now solved through cell phone records."

"So what did you discover about me?"

"Well, what are you referring to?"

"Did you discover anything interesting? Come on, tell me."

Smiling again like someone who knew she had an ace up her sleeve, Giulia replied, "No, not much. You're a very ordinary person, not very computer literate and not on any social media networks. You don't even look at online porn and, apart from work, you only visit sites about golf, golf equipment, and golfing trips. Really, you're quite boring."

Here I was, proud of my lack of digital dependence, convinced that social networking was worse than drug addiction. The people I considered "boring" were the ones who spent all their time in a virtual world instead of the real one. I could accept that Giulia favored men who might be a little more with-it, but no way could I let her call me "boring" just because I didn't spend my time composing tweets.

"Look, if you ask those three—or 'four at the most'—exes about my flaws, not one would say that I'm boring, just the opposite—"

Giulia cut me off, laughing. "Wow, Riccardo! You're awfully good at joking and teasing, but even though you can dish it out, you clearly can't take it!"

I stuttered, "I, uh, look, I thought . . ."

Giulia had me pegged. I love joking around, and for me, irony is a sign of someone's intelligence, but I always have trouble realizing when someone is turning it back on me. Lots of times, I only figure out I was being played a few days later. It's probably related to my chronic inability to distinguish a lie from the truth. You can tell me anything. I mean, I'm still not entirely convinced that Santa and the reindeer don't come visit at Christmas. I mean, it wasn't just anyone who told me about them—it was my mom!

I didn't want Giulia to know she'd hit the bull's-eye. Trying to maintain a modicum of dignity, I said as aloofly as possible, "So if you know everything about me, why are you asking me all these questions?"

"Well, we know who you went out with and that they don't have criminal backgrounds. They aren't drug addicts and they weren't married when they were with you. But we haven't investigated their lives after you split up."

"Whatever. As far as I know, none of them got married or had children right away."

"We'll check it out; it won't take long. But until we're certain, I prefer not to dismiss any possibilities. I'd like you to be thinking about any possible links between you and the count's family. I suspect the key to everything is in the relationships between the various victims."

"I don't want to argue with you, but technically speaking, I'm not a victim."

"Apart from the fact that the assassin or assassins could try to kill you again at any moment, as far as our investigations are concerned, you are already a victim."

I didn't want to seem vulgar, so as casually and discreetly as possible, with my left hand I gestured toward my private parts to ward off bad luck. I'm not superstitious, but given the circumstances, I needed all the help I could get.

"But there's no link. I only know Count Alvise by sight, and I always lose to his son at golf—which is the only thing that matters to that jerkoff. As for the count's mother, or nanny, or whatever, I saw her for the first time yesterday, when it was too late. To be honest, the members of the noble family I'm most closely acquainted with are the guard dogs."

"Clearly, but think it over anyway. You can both go now, but don't forget, always be available. If I try to call and don't get you, then you're both in trouble. Have I made myself clear?"

"I've got some doubts here regarding my civil rights, privacy, freedom, and the like."

"Riccardo, get out. Otherwise, I'll place you under house arrest, and then you won't have any of those things for several months at the very least."

"OK, say no more. I'm going."

CHAPTER ELEVEN

As I left the DA's office trailed by a chastened Paolo, I took Giulia's advice and tried to review my connection to the murders. Try as I might, I couldn't find any link between me and the victims, couldn't pinpoint anything that involved us all, apart from that damn message Massimo sent before he was killed.

Everything about my meeting with Giulia had put me in a bad mood: her cold demeanor, which I thought unjustified; the fact that my life had been turned inside out like an old sock by people I didn't know; my bandaged hand which hurt; the speculation about my career; and last but not least, Paolo was still there like a button sewn on my shirt, robbing me of my last vestige of presumed privacy, a constant reminder that someone wanted to kill me. In short, I felt like an unarmed man sent into enemy territory. My typically carefree nature was taken over by anxiety. As I was thinking it all through, I realized that maybe the murders weren't linked by one single motive. If that were true, which one was linked to the attempt to kill me? Logically, Patty's murder should be linked to Massimo's, given that they were husband and wife. However, the idea that someone who wasn't very strong had killed Patty made the whole scenario much more complex. Massimo had been strangled by someone powerful, and then his mouth was stitched shut as a message to intimidate someone else. Whoever had done that had to be a bloodthirsty monster. Patty had been killed ferociously, Dal Nero had said, but with much less force and probably by someone she knew. I had been shot by a small-caliber bullet from pretty far away. Finally, Stella's neck had been broken, but she'd been left sitting in her chair, in a gentle, almost respectful way, as if the murderer had had to kill her, but there was no malice in it. In that intricate weave of facts and conjecture, something must be escaping me. What if something emerged from the investigation into my past that could somehow lead the detectives to suspect me?

As I climbed into Paolo's Fiesta, I wondered whether I should talk to a lawyer. I asked Paolo, not so much because I wanted his opinion, but mostly just to think out loud.

"Why would you?"

"Mm . . . I'm realizing that perhaps I've been a bit naïve. Not once did I imagine the investigators might dig into my life like that. What if they found something I can't even remember and decide it's incriminating? It wouldn't be the first time an innocent person ended up on the rack. I mean, if you think about it, apart from Patty, technically speaking, I could have killed Massimo and Stella."

"Are you stupid?"

"What do you mean?"

"Do you really imagine Dal Nero would let you go free if she thought you were the killer?"

"Why not? It could be a tactic to see if I betray myself!"

"Yeah, right, Dal Nero using a dumb tactic like that. Believe me, she's a bloodhound, and if she thought you were guilty, first she'd lock you up and then work you over until you sang like a bird."

"Mm . . . Put like that, it almost sounds fun."

"Yeah, fun like a sledgehammer to your knees."

"But really, she hasn't let me go free, seeing how she's got one of her assistant bloodhounds on me. Of course, judging from what she said earlier, you may not be her favorite one!"

"Riccardo, my job is protection, not surveillance. The assassin tried to kill you, too. So unless she's decided you paid someone to shoot you in the hand, it's highly unlikely that Dal Nero thinks you're guilty. I mean, do what you want, but if you show up at her office with a lawyer, I think the DA's feelings toward you would take a definite turn for the worse. Trust me, Riccardo, it's better to go along and have her on your side."

"Oh, Paolo! From the way you talk about her, it sounds as if you'd prefer to spend time with the psycho who killed Massimo."

"No doubt about it. You saw that back there. When Dal Nero gets angry she's worse than the Hunchback of Notre Dame."

"He wasn't a bad guy!"

"I know, but he was still revolting."

Rest in peace, Victor Hugo.

"OK, Paolo, no lawyer. Let's go to my house and then over to the *Mattino*."

Paolo was spending more time looking in the rearview mirror than at the road, and he informed me with great annoyance that two motorbikes were following us. He'd spotted them waiting outside the DA's office.

"If I were the killer, I'd dress up as a reporter. That way I could get close to the victim without causing alarm," I teased.

"No way! If someone got too close, I'd shoot them down before saying 'halt.'"

"Uh-huh, sure. Like Dal Nero said, if Piovesan had been the killer, I'd already be with the Creator, negotiating a shorter penalty for my sins."

"Hey, don't think I didn't consider that. But Dal Nero wouldn't let me explain. I realized right away you knew that guy. That's why I didn't do anything."

"Paolo, what if the killer and I know each other?"

"Oh, shit, you're right . . . I didn't think . . . But even if it was him, he would have had to pull out a weapon and I'd have gotten him first. I might be a bit on the heavy side, but I'm as quick as a lion."

"You might be underestimating just a little, there."

"What do you mean? I weigh less than 220 pounds."

"Which is an awful lot at your height! Look, Paolo, we'll both be more careful. If someone is coming for me, let's at least try to make his job as difficult as possible."

As if they were aware of our newly heightened vigilance, the two motorbikes hung back about fifty yards behind us, but strangely enough, when we reached Bastia, they disappeared. Paolo and I couldn't explain it. They'd been waiting all morning outside the DA's office, they'd escorted us as far as Bastia, and then they left us at the last minute? Seriously weird.

I took the opportunity to convince Paolo to stop in town so I could buy newspapers and a few essentials, like kibble for Mila and Newton and some cigars, as I'd forgotten my stock at the hospital.

The advantage of a small town is that all the main shops are within a hundred yards of each other. A tobacconist, a newsstand, and a small market that in two hundred square feet stocks everything you'd ever hope to find in a sprawling supermarket. A pharmacy where the owner asks for a prescription even if you buy toothpaste stands next to the office of a veterinarian who, understandably, competes with the pharmacist by selling under-the-counter medicine without a prescription. Within spitting distance, there's even a clothing shop, its window display staggeringly out-of-date, plus the bakery, a stationery shop, a café-bar, and the obligatory hunting and fishing supply store. Of course, there's also Town Hall, with the mayor who's also the vet, and the church with its adjacent oratory and rundown basketball court, which they've turned into a small soccer field in a desperate attempt to attract community members—but to no avail. In Bastia, the young, like the old, prefer sitting around a table drinking or playing cards to wearing shorts and chasing a ball.

Before I even got out of the car, I saw the poster with the headlines of the day. They all centered on the same theme: "Killer Strikes Again: Countess Nogaredo Murdered." Below were the photos of the victims, including me, which I found in really bad taste. I entered the newsstand and realized from the owner's bright expression that, for the first time in seven years, I would no longer be considered an outsider. I bought two local and two national newspapers, further reason for the owner to look at me with new respect.

I motioned to Paolo to wait while I crossed the road to go and buy some cigars. Every Friday for seven years, religiously, I've bought a carton of Antico Toscano, but the tobacconist has asked what I wanted every single time, as if he's never seen me before. But things change, and, before I even reached the counter, there he was, holding a carton of cigars like a trophy and welcoming me like an old friend. After seven years of the cold shoulder, though, I wasn't about to give him the privilege of knowing me just because I was famous now. I looked at him as if I'd never seen him before, and, making out like he'd mistaken me for someone else, I asked for a carton of Toscano Originale. I knew I'd be sorry: Originale has a completely different aroma from Antico, and it's much spicier, but the tobacconist's surprised look was worth the sacrifice. Then, without giving him time to comment or strike up a conversation, I took the carton, paid, and left him standing there like he'd turned to stone.

Not fifteen steps away, with Paolo watching like a hawk from the car, I entered the market. Cramming everything people need into such a small space is great, but it does mean that, between the boxes of biscuits, the stacks of bath mats, and the rack of cell phones, there's very little space to move around. The manager is a woman over seventy, one of those Veneto women whose skin is as tough as a rhinoceros's hide. I don't think she's ever missed a day at the shop, not even when she gave birth, which, as far as I know, happened at least four or five times. Like all women of her generation, she only speaks the local dialect, which I still struggle with. More than once, I'd brought my shopping home to find an alarm clock instead of a lemon, or a plum-and-walnut tart instead of nutmeg. Nevertheless, going into the cramped market was always a bit like entering a magic cave.

Unlike the other shopkeepers, she welcomed me with her usual smile and no sign of caring about my newfound celebrity. I wondered if she read the news. She greeted me as ever with a few words of welcome, totally incomprehensible to me, and asked what I wanted. I asked for some dog food and she replied with a question I didn't understand. Not wanting to waste too much time, I nodded quickly, hoping that she hadn't asked if I wanted another tart. I was lucky that time and left the magic cave with food for Mila and Newton and a lovely box of crayons, to boot.

When I got back in the car, Paolo asked me why in the world I'd bought crayons.

"Would you have preferred the plum-and-walnut tart?"

"What?"

"Forget it; it's a game between me and the shop owner."

We turned down the road to my house.

When we were still a mile or so away, we both spotted the reason why the reporters on the motorbikes had stopped following us. They'd determined where we were going and took another route to beat us there, parking in front of Giuseppe's gate, though there was such a crowd we couldn't even see it.

No way could we get through in the car, so I suggested that Paolo hang back and park behind the TV vans. The reporters were so focused on interviewing Giuseppe and his family that we managed to blend into the crowd and sneak through, like in some silly cartoon. Despite the temptation to stop and listen to what Giuseppe's wife and daughter were saying about me, I decided not to press my luck and scuttled through the gate and up the lane. The reporters noticed us then, but it was too late, and to discourage any further attempt to approach, Paolo pulled out his gun. It deterred my colleagues enough that we were able to reach my own gate unmolested.

I opened it out of habit, not stopping to consider how Mila and Newton must feel about the reporters' invasion of their territory. They set off like rockets toward the reporters, growling and baring their teeth. The reporters' sprint for safety was as fast as it was chaotic; Giuseppe's family was nearly trampled in the panic, and it took all the authority I could muster to get my dogs to stop short of them. They settled for barking their disapproval from about halfway down the lane.

The stampede had left some expensive cameras, two hats, a scarf, and probably my reputation lying on the ground. Clearly satisfied with her work, Mila decided to turn her back on the escapees to trot back up and greet me, followed by Newton. Instead of pats, the dogs were met with my reprimands, shouted loud for the benefit of the reporters, and with Paolo's compliments for their police-like methods and results.

Once peace had been restored, I could hear the reporters shouting their resentment. I apologized and invited them to come closer; in short order, the group reformed in front of my gate. I repeated my apologies for the dog attack and, in exchange for their forgiveness, granted a short interview from the far side of the protective gate. All the questions focused on my relationship with the dead victims. However, I remembered Giulia's instructions and did not mention Massimo's message and did not answer any questions about my visit to Count Alvise's house. After a dozen or so "ums," "hms," "I don't knows," and various other stammerings, I decided it was enough. It was late, and I wanted to make it to the *Mattino* before dark.

It might seem silly, but reading the papers and seeing the news on TV gave me a much better idea of what was going on than being in the middle of this business. The events involving me were headlines in all the papers and lead stories on all the TV news shows. Seeing myself occupying more space than Merkel, Hollande, and President Monti combined gave me a real sense of the mess I was in. That said, the articles all contradicted each other: some said I was potentially actively involved, while others just presented me as a passive victim who'd escaped by the skin of his teeth. I wondered if the killer had also read or heard the news and what he was thinking.

I felt a bit better after a shower and decided that, active or passive as I may have been up to this point, it was time to make some decisions. I got dressed and asked Paolo to take me to the *Mattino* office, determined to handle things my way.

I made two phone calls on the way: one to Grandi, telling him I wanted to talk, the second to Piovesan telling him that I wanted him to be present when I met Grandi.

The *Mattino* occupies a two-story building in the center of Padua. The entrance is manned by a security guard and our receptionist, Giannino, who has been sitting at that desk ever since he was hired back in 1975. He is a good and patient man, perhaps too patient because, even though he'd gained the right to retire some time ago, he still lived in the hope of being promoted and joining the editorial staff. From the way he welcomed me, I realized that things weren't going to be the same from now on in the office either.

"Good evening, Director Ranieri. At last! We were afraid you wouldn't be coming back, you know?"

Clearly, Giannino, eager to flatter my new status, had promoted me to some kind of director in his mind.

"Don't worry, Giannino. Weeds never die," I reassured him with a laugh.

"It's a real pleasure to see you, Mr. Ranieri. With all the bums working here, we could never bear to lose a great reporter like you."

Even though it was hard to admit, being welcomed back with so much adulation was somewhat gratifying. On my way to Grandi's office, I initially greeted some of my colleagues, but as it was six in the evening and the office was very busy, I realized I'd need to get a move on. I hurried down the hall faster than a waiter during the dinner rush, avoiding everyone else. I knocked and opened the door without waiting for his answer.

"Ah, good evening, Ranieri! Come in and sit down. We were waiting for you."

Grandi is an intelligent and very somber person. Nobody has ever heard him raise his voice, and even though he has to make difficult decisions at times, he never gives the impression of struggling with them. He seems like a person who always knows the right answer.

Piovesan was sitting in front of Grandi's desk and tapped twice on the chair next to him to invite me to sit down.

Grandi spoke first and asked how I was.

"I admit, I've had a few rather lively days."

With much less aplomb and more pragmatism, Piovesan said, "They messed you up good, huh?"

"Sure, but I'm feeling better now. And I must confess that being the center of attention has its moments."

"Such as?"

"Well, to start with, I didn't have to drive and park today. The police double-parked my ride downstairs."

"What about your hand?" Grandi asked.

"It doesn't hurt too bad. Unfortunately, I'm right-handed, so it's hard to shave."

Grandi decided that was enough small talk and got down to business. "I know that Piovesan mentioned our idea to transfer you to news."

"To be truthful, Gibbo presented the whole thing as a fait accompli."

Piovesan felt obliged to defend himself, responding, "No, Riccardo. I told you that if you didn't want to, then that was it."

"But that meant it was decided, so all I could do was accept or refuse. If you don't mind, I'd like to suggest a different approach."

"Really, nothing has been decided," said Grandi. "It's obvious that your involvement in the Frassanelle Golf Club murders gives us a unique advantage over the other papers, so we decided to offer you the chance to go to news."

"So my promotion is all thanks to that psycho who's trying to kill everyone?"

While Piovesan snorted impatiently, Grandi showed the grace that made him so good at his job.

"Partly yes, Ranieri, but don't take it amiss. You're far from the only one to be in the right place at the right time. Careers are often, if not always, tied to unforeseeable events and strokes of good luck. In your case, luck was an essential condition, but not the only factor in my decision to offer you a posting on breaking news."

"What else, then?"

"You, Ranieri."

A pause to increase my attention.

"Do you really think I'd move you to the nerve center of the paper if I didn't think you were right for the job?"

Another short pause, then the grand finale.

"As you can see, Ranieri, all the parts of the puzzle are there: the right place, the right time, and, above all, the right person."

Inside, I was happy as a clam, but after all the fuss I'd threatened to make, I couldn't give in so easily.

"So is it a promotion, then?"

Grandi, calm but not naïve, took my meaning right away, so while Gibbo blurted out "Of course!" Grandi conceded, "No, not a promotion in terms of salary. Given the crisis, we can't consider that right away. But obviously, if you accept our proposal, you'll be much more in the limelight, and, if circulation remains at the current level until the end of the year, we can talk again. For now, let's say we're pointing you in the right direction, and then it's up to you to decide whether to get there quickly or not."

"What about the finance section?"

"I've spoken to Grossi, and it's OK with him."

I didn't doubt that Fausto Grossi, who'd become the editor of our finance section based on seniority alone, would be happy to get rid of a colleague who was constantly reminding him of his lack of qualifications. I smiled to myself, thinking of the jokes my colleagues made about the man and his unflattering name.

"When should I move?"

Piovesan answered, "You decide. Now, if you want. There's a free desk next to mine."

"OK. So if we're all agreed, then I'll move straight away. I'm anxious to do some research into this case."

"Speaking of the case," Grandi resumed, "together with Piovesan, we must decide how to proceed. I expect that the DA has forbidden you from disclosing any confidential information?"

"Exactly. She ordered me not to give any interviews, and not to write any articles about it."

"So, you are sworn to secrecy."

"Let's say we can work to deny certain false leads I read about today in the *Repubblica* and *Corriere*. In exchange, the police will keep me constantly updated about the developments. Then when the DA authorizes it, I'll be able to write everything in detail."

"Great. I won't waste any more of your time, Ranieri. Get on with your work, don't disappoint me, and I'll make sure you're very satisfied."

On the way out of Grandi's office, Piovesan put his hand on my shoulder and began grilling me about the case. I cut him off, reminding him of my promise to the DA.

Deaf to all reason, Piovesan continued, "Sure, buddy, sure, but at least tell me who the assassin is."

CHAPTER TWELVE

My office at the *Mattino di Padova* is a large room with five or six work-stations separated by partitions.

There are giant screens on the walls tuned to Tg24, CNN, Bloomberg, Al Jazeera, and others besides. Between the bustling copy-writers, colleagues' phone calls, and the droning of the TVs, the noise pollution is on par with a construction site. However, that background racket helps concentration and the spirit of initiative, or at least gives the impression that we're all very busy. Before Grandi came on board as chief, the screens were only in the office of his predecessor, a person I never had the pleasure to meet. I was hired after he left, but I'd heard plenty about the vain man's penchant for perks and frills that high-lighted his position at the top of the pecking order. Now, though, the screens were out in the open, giving life to a place that, as Grandi put it, had to be on its toes around the clock.

After collecting my personal belongings from my old desk—a toothbrush, a plaque commemorating my first article when I was still freelance, a photo of Mila and Newton, and an ashtray with built-in cigar cutter, a gift from an old girlfriend—I began to settle in at my new desk. The hardest part was shaking off Piovesan, who was determined to pry some sort of secret information out of me. First, he threatened to refuse me a swivel chair. Next he appealed to my duty to help a colleague who was fighting, single-handedly as he saw it, to ward off the inevitable decline of print in the digital age. This was also the reason Piovesan had wanted me in the news section: we had the right story to increase sales, at least for the moment.

Even though it was almost eight in the evening, the office was still very busy, and I wanted to try to fill some of the gaps in my understanding of the case. But, deluged with kind welcomes and requests for inside info from virtually all my colleagues, I decided to give up until the next day.

Before leaving, I called Enrico, head chef and manager of the Frassanelle's restaurant, to see if it was still open. The restaurant was definitely one of the highlights of the club; the chef was known to serve unusual, sophisticated dishes instead of relying on local staples, which lacked imagination and used mainly chicken and game. Add to that the really good prices, and you can understand why members and outsiders alike hung around the place long after they'd finished their eighteen holes.

Furthermore, unlike many such clubs, Frassanelle has a very warm atmosphere. The waiters are mainly students paying their way through college, and they need to be friendly and skilled, as well as possess exceptional patience for assholes. One of the most frequent and serious illnesses that afflicts a golf club member is pathological superego syndrome, which deprives him of the mental capacity to recognize that other human beings have the same rights as he does. The worst aspect of this treacherous illness is that it is easily transmitted to his wife. Despite the great progress made by medical science, it is still unclear if this is a genetic or viral illness, but the fact is, whenever a group of golf club members assembles at a bar, the syndrome's hideous symptoms are likely to be on display. The waiters are adept at seeing to those suffering from the syndrome and preventing the disease from spreading further.

I get along really well with Enrico; often, on cold winter evenings when playing golf is the exclusive prerogative of a few diehard head cases, I join him and five or six other members in front of the fireplace to watch a football match, talk about politics, or gossip about the other members. The main ingredient of these evenings is the lively debate. No matter whether the topic is politics or football, what counts is the discussion. To help spark this conversational fire, Enrico taps into his reserve of vintage grappa, chilled to the perfect temperature. After midnight, it's not unusual to see the parking lot's lampposts bent and flattened by drivers convinced they can win a fight against Bacchus.

Outside the office, I found Paolo looking black as thunder and asked him what was up.

"They took my car," was his lapidary response.

"What? Who?"

"The traffic police. People in the bar over there saw the tow truck."

"Where were you?"

"At the front desk, talking to Giannino."

"Great! Now what are we going to do? I just made dinner reservations at the club."

"Let's call a cab."

"It'll cost a fortune."

"Do you have a better idea?"

"Can't you call the towing company and tell them you're a police officer?"

"I did, but they're closed for the night. I'll have to call again tomorrow."

"What bullshit! Here I am boasting to my colleagues that the only advantage of having an escort is that I don't have to find a parking space! I'm going to look an idiot when they find out!"

I'd totally lost my patience.

"Piovesan already knows. I almost punched him."

"Why?"

"Because he wouldn't stop laughing."

In the end, we took a taxi to Bastia and picked up my car. At least my Volvo was more comfortable than Paolo's Fiesta.

It was nine thirty by the time we reached the club, and there weren't many cars left in the parking lot. Late October's gloomy fog and early sunsets had reduced the number of evening visitors.

When I entered the restaurant, Enrico seemed undecided whether to be angry I was so late or happy because one of his best customers was still alive. In the end, his business interests prevailed, and he opened his arms in a brotherly hug. Before everything got too sentimental, I broke away and asked if Arcadio was around. I didn't want to risk him coming at me again. With Officer "Quick Draw" Paolo on the job, something unfortunate could happen.

"No, Arcadio isn't here, don't worry. But how did you get that black eye?"

"Let me tell you, Enrico, when you've got a highly trained law enforcement officer to protect you, rest assured that nothing's left to chance."

Paolo gave me a shove that was only partially good-natured and pushed me into the dining room.

There were only eight people in the entire restaurant, but Paolo and I were soon surrounded by them and subjected to all the obvious questions. My secrecy agreement stood me in good stead—if I'd even started trying to answer them, I would have had to eat a cold dinner.

By ten thirty, it was just me, Paolo, Enrico, Francesca behind the bar, and Iury, a Serbian waiter who was studying engineering at Padua. Of all the Frassanelle staff, Francesca is the touchiest; quiet and reserved, she never smiles or jokes. Neither beautiful nor ugly, she seems to do everything possible to pass unobserved, and all in all, she does a pretty good job. The gravity of the recent events at Frassanelle was even more evident when even she decided to overcome her natural reserve and come to our table to listen in.

My tongue loosened by a glass of pear grappa, and as there were just us five in front of the homey fireplace, I relaxed a little and told Enrico that I didn't really understand anything about the murders.

"Yes, Riccardo, but you're a golfer."

"So?"

"Of course you don't understand anything."

"Aw, fuck off!"

Francesca was the first to head home, probably because she wasn't interested in the comradely, alcoholic ramblings of four men. Shortly after, we ended up reminiscing about the Salvionis, and, unable to shake off the melancholy mood, we decided to call it a night and go home.

By seven the next morning I was already up.

As usual when I'm under the shower, I ran over the things I had to do that day. My number one priority was to sit down and figure out the identity of the killer or killers—at least that way I could stop admitting I didn't have a clue what was going on. Next, I had to replace my broken cell phone, and then buy some pasta sauce to try and overcome the risk of famine I'd been facing since the ravenous Paolo had started living with me. Plans firmly established, I strode brightly out of my room to make my first cup of coffee for a day that, all in all, seemed promising. In October, it's still pretty dark at seven, but I figured I didn't need to turn the hallway light on. Maybe it was my good mood or maybe the grappa from the night before, but I forgot my guest was sleeping on the floor between my room and the stairs. My foot made violent contact with something, resulting in a thud and an unrepeatable series of curses. I lost my balance and threw my hands out to try to stop my fall, which, luckily, was softened by landing on Paolo, hitting him smack in the face with my elbow. Amid groans and swearing, we managed to untangle ourselves and I flipped on the light. Paolo was sitting on the mattress with his hand over his right eye. I apologized profusely and bent over to look at his eye: it was swelling up a bit, but didn't look too serious.

"I'm so sorry, Paolo! I totally forgot you were there. You know, I just had a feeling this was going to be a good day."

"Sure, awesome. What a great start!"

"Look on the positive side: I fell on something even softer than the mattress!"

I headed down to the kitchen, trailed by a soundtrack of curses that would have made an exorcist cringe.

Once the verbal storm had passed, we left home and got to Padua just after eight. The traffic was heavy but still moving. Claiming a serious allergy to the red tape needed to recover his car, I convinced Paolo to overlook Giulia's strict instructions, and we separated for the morning. I took him to the impound lot, and we arranged to meet at lunchtime outside the *Mattino*. Of course, I had to swear I'd go straight to the office without stopping and getting shot on the way.

As I drew near to the office, I began the hateful search for a parking spot. It would have been worth clawing my way up to editor-in-chief just to get the only reserved parking space at the *Mattino*. I finally found a spot in a paid lot a half mile away. I only had enough coins to pay until one o'clock. At lunchtime, I'd have to go and renew my street permit. It started raining and my good mood began to fade. As I was walking toward the office without Paolo beside me for the first time, I felt a shudder of fear. Still, I enjoyed having the momentary freedom to decide where to go and what to do, even though I knew it wouldn't last long. The rain got heavier and heavier. With no umbrella, squinting in the downpour, I tried making eye contact with the people I passed. I must confess, I did it not only to see if they intended to shoot me, but also to see if they recognized me. At last, I reached the office building and went past it to the coffee bar next door, where, for the first time, I didn't have to fight for the bartender's attention, because the bar was full of my colleagues, who all began asking questions. While I mumbled some vague answers, I was offered a shot of espresso in a mug with the sachet of raw sugar and a fantastic brioche. The day was looking up again.

As I was leaving, a woman entered whom I often saw there and who I presumed worked in the nearby notary's office. She was very attractive, about thirty-five years old, and looked a lot like Michelle Pfeiffer, though certainly shorter. Until then, I had repeatedly tried to catch her attention but had always failed miserably. I'm of the firm conviction that if a woman looks you straight in the eye for a few moments, it means she's probably interested, so if you're bold enough to ask her out, there's a good chance she'll accept. For the first time, the blonde looked me straight in the eye and held my gaze.

In spite of all my flirting with women I know a bit, I'm far from bold with beautiful strangers, and I let the moment pass. Still, though, I'd regained the bouncy optimism I'd found in the shower that morning. Wound tight as a spring, I entered my office and sat down. Luckily, Piovesan hadn't arrived yet, so I was able to begin my hunt for murderous demons undisturbed.

I decided to begin with some research into Count Alvise's family, and, as I was typing his name into the search engine, Piovesan materialized behind me and, looking as innocent as a baby, asked me what I was working on.

"Gibbo, at ten we've got a meeting to discuss how we're going to manage the articles on the murders, right?"

"Right."

"Good. So, how's about you let me gather my ideas and actually do some work until ten o'clock. Sound reasonable?"

"OK, OK, there's no need to get angry. I just wanted to chat."

"Gibbo, I'm not angry. It's just that I never have a minute to myself."

"That's what my wife's always saying."

"I'm sure she has her reasons."

"I don't think so. She doesn't go to work and our children are grown. How in the world doesn't she have time to herself?"

I was beginning to regret accepting the position in news.

"Gibbo, I don't know. What I do know is that the meeting starts in about an hour, so if I spend much more time talking to you, there's no way I'll manage to find the information I need."

"Fine, I'm going. Don't forget, the meeting's at ten."

Poor woman, I thought as Gibbo left me.

Finally left to my work, I turned up a lot of interesting information about Alvise Casati Vitali, Count of Nogaredo.

The first thing concerned his birth, on September 20, 1947, when his mother, Arduina, died of unclear causes while delivering him. Immediately thereafter, his father, Umberto, appointed Stella Roncadelle to raise infant Alvise. Umberto himself died in 1952, probably due to his dissolute life, seeing as he was found naked in a hotel bed in Venice. Tabloids from the era seemed to insinuate that there'd been more than a simple employer-employee relationship between the count and Stella, because when he died, Stella took over the management of the noble family's entire estate.

The more I read about the family and that woman, the more my curiosity grew. From nanny to empress in the space of a few years—an impressive climb, indeed. I decided to focus my attention on her and learned that Stella Roncadelle was born in Mogliano, Veneto, on April 5, 1928. And that was it; that was all I could find. There was virtually nothing about her background. She probably came from a poor peasant family. There wasn't much in between at that time in the Veneto: either you were a very poor peasant or a very rich noble.

There was no information about her before her employment with the Vitalis, but from that point, Stella began turning up at charity events. After a few months of attending them sporadically and alone, she and Count Umberto were a fixture at all such events from 1950 to 1952.

I was starting to have a clearer picture of Count Alvise's family, and I was quite intrigued. Unfortunately, Graziella the editorial assistant interrupted to tell me my colleagues were waiting in the conference room.

The meeting, or as Piovesan preferred to call it, spit-balling session, aimed at determining how our articles on the murders would be presented. I strongly opposed the suggestion that they should appear under my byline, fearing reprisal from Giulia. After fifty minutes, we decided that Fabrizio Pilotti, a colleague I respected and trusted, would write them under my supervision, and then Piovesan would sign them.

Fabrizio got to work straight away on profiles of the victims, including me, and analyzing all possible connections between them. For coverage, we would also publish an article about the count being rushed to the hospital when he heard about Mrs. Roncadelle's death. I'd just be responsible for reading and tweaking the finished work.

In the meantime, I was free to return to my research into Stella. I unearthed articles revealing that, after the death of the old Count Umberto, she had been formally named as Alvise's guardian. He was only five years old when he inherited the estate, so that left Stella in charge of everything. I may be suspicious by nature, but even I found it hard to believe that she'd taken advantage of the situation for the simple reason that, if she had, it wouldn't make sense for Alvise to still love her the way he clearly did.

For now, I decided to trust in Stella's moral virtue, and began researching Alvise, thus fulfilling my need for more information with Fabrizio's need for profile fodder. As soon as I began searching, I discovered an appalling coincidence: I already knew that Alvise was a widower, but what I didn't know was that his wife, Maria Teresa, had died while giving birth to Arcadio, just like Alvise's own mother. While bad luck sometimes seems to run in families, the symmetry seemed too perfect. The matter was further complicated by the fact that she'd given birth in a hospital in Santo Domingo.

The more I thought about it, the more convinced I was that these ill-fated births were the key to everything. However, I couldn't figure out Salvioni's connection to them. At Santo Domingo Hospital, the countess had been assisted by a Dr. Pedro Majoi. The articles claimed the complications were due to an internal hemorrhage a few hours after giving birth, and although I knew the joke was in terrible taste, I couldn't help thinking it seemed inevitable she would hemorrhage after giving birth to a prickly pear like Arcadio.

I discussed my findings with Fabrizio, and we decided to tuck this information into the end of the article, with no suspicions or conjectures expressed, leaving the readers free to experience the thrill of the hunt for the motive by digging into the family's muddy past. Piovesan was fearful of a libel suit from that powerful family, but he acquiesced to our including the facts without any interpretation. As Gibbo was the boss, though, he felt it his duty to quibble with something, so he took issue with the article's title. Fabrizio and I wanted something romantic like "The Past Returns," while Piovesan insisted on "The Vitali Casati: Just Like the Kennedys," claiming that if we printed that name on the front page, we'd sell more than three thousand copies to the American military on the base in Vicenza alone.

It was pointless to try reasoning with the silly man, who didn't want to hear that Americans, including those on the Dal Molin military base, spoke English, not Italian.

CHAPTER THIRTEEN

At about one o'clock, Fabrizio and I decided to work through lunch and ordered something up from the bar.

If I've got to break my rules regarding healthy eating, then I'm going to do it in style, so to celebrate my return to work, I ordered an enormous panino with mayonnaise and salami, followed by a chocolate muffin, washed down with an Irish stout. I confess that if it hadn't been for the adrenaline high I was getting from my research, I would probably have been comatose for the rest of the afternoon.

To overcome the first symptoms of drowsiness, I decided to see what dirt I could dig up on Arcadio. To my great disappointment, and with a touch of envy, I discovered that nearly all the articles were about his victories on the golf course. When he was thirteen, he had joined a special training team managed by the Italian Golf Federation. Arcadio had done well in several official competitions, but he was later expelled from the group due to his character. Another article revealed that, at sixteen, Arcadio had refused to accept a referee's call and, according to some witnesses, purposely hit a golf ball at a group of refs standing on the side of the course. In another competition, the boy was disqualified for mooning a competitor, whose crime had been disagreeing with him that a ball, which had landed a foot and a half off the course, should be considered in. If I hadn't experienced his shitty attitude firsthand so many times, I might have found all this bad behavior almost charming.

Apart from the article about his mother's death and a few about his golfing misdeeds, I didn't find anything useful for Fabrizio's profile or my research. However, when I unplugged from the database around five o'clock, I was finally beginning to have a clearer picture about everything that had happened. It was then I realized I'd never gone back to the parking lot. Regarding the case, I was even more certain that the mysterious circumstances of Alvise's and Arcadio's births were the key. The link with Stella was clear, but what Massimo had to do with it was still a mystery. And why did Arcadio's mother go to Santo Domingo to give birth? Finally, how big a parking fine would I have to pay?

I decided to call Giulia and tell her what I'd found.

She answered on the first ring and asked me to tell her immediately if something had happened.

"I'm sorry, Giulia, is it a bad time?"

"Not at all, why do you ask?"

"You seem a bit curt."

"Not in the least, but I'm working. What do you want to tell me?" Definitely curt.

"My colleague and I have done some research into Count Alvise's family."

While I was calculating the pause to kindle her curiosity, already savoring the foreseeable compliments, Giulia brought me right back to earth. "And you've discovered that both Alvise's and Arcadio's mothers died in childbirth."

I could feel a lump forming in my throat: How was she so good at making me feel like an idiot?

"You knew?"

"Riccardo, do you think that my detectives are just sitting here twiddling their thumbs?"

127

"Of course not, but you could have told me."

"So now I'm supposed to keep you up to date on my investigation?"

"I thought we had an agreement," I spat.

"Agreement? What on earth are you talking about?"

I was losing my patience and, like the burglar alarm in the count's castle, started to raise my voice.

"If you remember, we agreed that I wouldn't write anything about the investigation, and you would keep me informed about the developments."

"Sorry, you understood wrong. You won't write anything about the investigation, and I won't keep you informed about any developments unless I'm so inclined or I decide you need to know something for your own safety."

With the patient tone a dad might take with his daughter, I responded, "Giulia, that's not an agreement, that's a rip-off."

With the tone of a parent putting her disrespectful child in his place, Giulia replied, "Riccardo, this is not an agreement, it's the law. In this case, investigation secrecy. Ever heard of it?"

Pause. The lump in my throat was turning to frustration. Perhaps Piovesan was right: I should just go rogue, exploit my position to get record sales for the *Mattino*, and let the lawyers sort out the rest.

In a less argumentative tone, I said, "This changes things. I've been extremely careful not to reveal anything to my colleagues, so the paper couldn't write anything that might give the killer an advantage. But this way there's no reason why I shouldn't publish at least some basic details that the competition doesn't know."

Giulia changed her tone as well.

"Riccardo, seeing as you're the one the killer's after, you know even better than I do why you shouldn't publish anything about the case, even if it seems innocent."

Checkmate. I decided to be a bit more conciliatory.

"Can I ask you one thing?"

"Maybe."

"Why did the count's family go to Santo Domingo to have their baby?"

"Count Alvise is a major landowner in the Dominican Republic, and even before the child was born, they went there often. In fact, they once lived there for more than three months."

"So what's Salvioni got to do with it?"

A moment's pause, then her tone was as warm and friendly as before. I could sense a complicit smile in her voice. "I can't tell you that over the phone."

I might not be that great with women, but with an opening like that . . .

"So, perhaps tonight over dinner?"

"No, Riccardo. If you want to know more, I'll see you in my office at eight tomorrow morning."

"Damn! Missed!"

"What?"

"Nothing . . . OK, see you tomorrow."

Fabrizio noticed my disappointed look, which wasn't hard to do—I practically had tears in my eyes.

"What's wrong, Riccardo?"

"Nothing, Fabrizio, thanks."

"You should see your face. You look so crushed."

"No, it's just that . . . You know, ninetieth minute, goal kick, and it's offside."

The next morning, Paolo and I arrived at the DA's office a few minutes early.

I went to the entrance to see if Silvia was there, but she wasn't. Instead there were two rather bored-looking officers reading the *Gazzetta dello Sport*. Paolo introduced himself and asked if Giulia had arrived yet.

"Yeah, the DA's been in her office for a couple of hours already," one of the officers said. "Is she expecting you?"

"We've got an appointment."

"Go on up. I'll let her know," the other officer said.

Paolo hadn't shown any sort of emotion until then, but as soon as we got in the elevator, he let out a sigh worthy of the last scene of *Titanic*.

"Are you still afraid of Dal Nero?"

"No, I'm not afraid. She just makes me really anxious."

"Don't think about the pain. Just close your eyes, and it'll all be over in a minute."

Giulia's office door was ajar, so we knocked, and she told us to enter.

This time, Giulia paid attention to us right away and suggested we all walk across the street for coffee at the bar where I'd gone with Paolo.

Paolo looked mutely surprised, having expected her usual reserve. While Giulia was putting her raincoat on, I got a glimpse of her neckline and its promise of paradise. Despite my efforts to think of something else, I couldn't help imagining her naked in my arms. I immediately felt ashamed of my ogling and did my best not to let on.

"Riccardo, you're looking thoughtful. What's the matter?"

"Nothing. I was just thinking how your coat makes you look like the cops on TV."

"Sure, just like Columbo. Get a move on, Riccardo."

In a lot of countries, people drink their coffee hot and watery. In Italy, we treat coffee like positions in the Kama Sutra, using our imaginations to order all manner of creative variations on the theme. Still, not wanting to test the bartender's nerves, we three ordered a shot of espresso in a mug, a cold shot of decaf, and a hot espresso with a dash of milk. To that we added a plain brioche, a brioche filled with cream, and a whole-wheat brioche with honey. In order to ward off the bartender's suspicions about whether we might try to skip out on the bill, I decided to go to the register and prepay for everything. I overcame my companions' protests and opened my wallet, only to find that all I had was a hundred-euro bill. Trying to look as innocent as Bambi, I tried appealing to the barman's compassion, but that was obviously something he didn't have. His eyes burned through me like lasers, and he examined my banknote as carefully as if he worked for the Central European Bank. At last, puffing like a freight train, he counted my change out under my nose, exaggeratedly placing down one coin at a time. Then, with the expression of someone who'd just been swindled out of his life savings, he gave me my receipt and slammed the register.

As we were leaving, I suggested to Giulia that we find somewhere else to have breakfast next time, perhaps somewhere with a friendlier bartender. She laughed and confessed she had enjoyed seeing me so embarrassed over my hundred-euro bill.

When we got back to the DA's office, Giulia told Paolo to wait downstairs. I found myself alone with her in the elevator and, to disguise my anxiety, lapsed into teasing.

"If you wanted to be alone with me, you just had to say so. I'd have planned something more romantic."

Her expression was about as friendly as the bartender's had been. Was it me?

When we reached her office, Giulia sat down behind her desk and invited me to sit, as well.

"I read the *Mattino* today. Thank you for not publishing anything that wasn't already public domain. I liked the article with the story about the Casati Vitali dynasty. Did you write it?"

"Let's say I helped out the person who wrote it."

"Piovesan?"

"Investigation secret."

"Touché. I do have to say, the reference to the Kennedys is a serious stretch."

"Drop it, it's a delicate subject."

"I wanted to apologize for yesterday evening. I was short with you, and I didn't mean to be."

"Water under the bridge, and anyway, in the competition for who treats me worst, the bartender wins hands down."

Giulia's smile got even wider as she looked me straight in the eye. The more I got to know her, the less I understood her. The day before, I'd felt like an annoying problem she had to solve, but now she seemed to be looking for some kind of complicity. If that was her way of attracting my attention, it was a waste of time because I was already totally fascinated by her.

"Yesterday you asked me what Salvioni had to do with the death of Arcadio Casati Vitali's mother. Now, please remember that what I'm about to tell you is protected by investigation secrecy and privacy laws. You can't breathe a word of this to anyone. Is that clear?"

"Clear."

"In Dr. Salvioni's study, we checked all the case histories of his patients."

"And?"

"And we found the files of Count Alvise and his dead wife"—a melodramatic pause before the thrilling twist—"empty."

"What do you mean, empty?"

"Whoever killed Mrs. Salvioni tried to remove the folders from his files, but they just managed to pull out the documents, because the folders are made from tough plastic, and were tied to a safe by nylon wire, like fishing line."

It took a moment for me to absorb this new information.

"OK, so I was right that the key to everything is the count's family. But why exactly would they steal the medical records?"

Giulia was watching me like a schoolteacher waiting for a flash of genius from her student, and, when I caught her gaze, I finally understood: wrong blood.

"The message Massimo sent, 'Wrong blood.' That was the secret in the file. Massimo was a gynecologist, which means procreation, families, Count Nogaredo and his wife who wanted a child. Nobles always want a male heir, and Count Alvise probably did, too . . ."

"Well done, Riccardo, you're catching up. What Dr. Salvioni was trying to tell you is that Count Alvise's blood type is not compatible with his son Arcadio's. In other words, Alvise cannot be Arcadio's biological father."

I didn't speak, but I looked into her eyes. Her expression was profound and full of energy. I studied her face, hoping she'd speak again, that she would tell me it was finally all over, that she and her colleagues had figured out who the assassin was. She guessed what I was thinking, and a shadow crossed her face.

"Unfortunately, we don't have anything else. Whoever killed them did not leave any clues: no fingerprints, DNA, phone traces."

"You must have some idea, though! Who could be interested in keeping a secret like that?"

"Arcadio, for one."

"Arcadio, of course. Being the son of a count means being rich. And, I mean, that guy is a real shithead, but I can't see him killing Massimo and definitely not his adoptive grandmother."

"No, we know he didn't kill Dr. Salvioni."

"How come you're so certain?"

"Because Dr. Salvioni was killed on Saturday evening between nine and eleven o'clock. After playing golf with you, Arcadio went to the Venice airport and, at nine thirty, he boarded a plane to Rome for another golf competition."

"Does Count Alvise know you know that?"

"No, I haven't said anything to him yet because first I want to understand how involved he is in all this. Plus, I'm still waiting for the files from Santo Domingo about his wife's death. If Count Alvise isn't

Arcadio's father, but his wife was pregnant, then was it adultery or is someone else the real heir? And if so, where is he?"

"Wow, I've got it! So the killer is the count's real son?"

"No, Riccardo, this is all just conjecture and I don't want to make any missteps. There is the definite possibility that the count could be charged with various crimes ranging from murder to corruption, plus illegal immigration, as well, if it turns out Arcadio is actually Dominican."

Giulia stopped to ask why I was laughing.

"Just imagining Count Alvise as an accomplice to an illegal immigration. I'm sorry, but it's too funny. I can just imagine him in a vest with a cigarette in his mouth as he rows his dinghy ashore . . ."

She laughed as well, which restored a certain air of serenity for a while. Paolo was right: she was like a lioness on the prowl. She had caught the scent of her prey and was gearing up for the chase. I couldn't let myself get totally distracted by Giulia's charms, though. Thinking over the implications of what she'd said, I asked, "Does this mean the golf club isn't the center of the investigation anymore?"

"No, it means we just have more leads to check out, like missing puzzle pieces. Our current information does suggest that we should concentrate the investigation on the Casati Vitali family, but that doesn't mean we're abandoning other possibilities."

"What's the most logical hypothesis, in your opinion?"

"In my opinion, the family had a number of skeletons in their closet. Perhaps Dr. Salvioni, accidentally or otherwise, opened that closet and paid the price. In this case, though, simply identifying the most logical motive won't be sufficient."

"But if we figured out who wanted to keep the skeletons hidden, we'd probably find the killer, wouldn't we?"

"First, having a motive is not enough to make someone guilty. Furthermore, until all the pieces are in place, we can't be certain that the motive we imagine is correct. It could be a financial motive involving the inheritance. Or a crime of passion that has nothing to do with the Casati Vitali family's history."

"What do you mean?"

"I don't really think this, but for the sake of argument, what if Dr. Salvioni's wife had a lover who decided to kill off his rival? After which, the presumed lover could have been threatened with exposure or rejected by Mrs. Salvioni, so he was forced to kill her, as well. It's classic."

"But what's any of that got to do with me?"

"You could be the lover."

"Ah!"

That deadly look of a hunting lioness again.

"Still, that wouldn't explain why Mrs. Roncadelle was killed," I replied.

"We can't exclude the possibility that the crimes aren't related at all. Anyway, Riccardo, it's pointless to draw conclusions too early. We have too many findings still to wait for, including the forensics reports. If we just focus on one detail and overlook the rest, we risk giving the murderer or murderers the upper hand."

I had the impression that Giulia was parroting the party line rather than saying what those killer instincts really told her. Still, I decided to go along with it.

"Perhaps I'll go to the club today to see what's happening there."

"OK, but don't play detective. You think the assassin is like a normal person, but you really don't know what you're dealing with. At no point can you forget that there's someone somewhere who's trying to kill you."

"Thanks, Giulia! It's a good thing you keep reminding me. I wouldn't want to be confused if someone took another shot."

"Don't joke, Riccardo. Don't put yourself in the way of trouble. If I have any other news, I'll let you know. For now, I can't do much more."

"OK. As far as I'm concerned, I have no intention of leaving you without your favorite reporter. In fact, if you ever have a few minutes free to get a drink, just whistle."

I was expecting her usual suggestion that I get the hell out, but once again, Giulia surprised me.

"I'd like that. We'll see. Don't do anything stupid, and who knows."

"Really? Are you serious?"

"Well, just a drink, let's be clear."

"Sure, sure. I finally have a good reason to put up with your watch-dog day and night."

That deadly smile again.

"Ah, come on, Paolo's great. Of course, now we'll have to replace him."

"What do you mean, replace him? You can't give me somebody else. I've only just gotten used to him, and we've even seen each other in our underpants. You can't throw away such a profound relationship . . ."

That smile again.

"Bye, Riccardo. We'll see, we'll see."

CHAPTER FOURTEEN

I left Giulia's office, walked down the hall to the elevator, and pressed the button to go downstairs.

While the automatic door closed as slowly as could be, I saw the awkward guy who hadn't been of any help to me the week before when I was alone in the police station and asked where Giulia was. He sped up in the hope that I would hold the elevator. I looked at him and pretended to press the buttons, first with an expression of total understanding, then one of concern, until through the last tiny gap in the door, one of total resignation. What a great day! First, Giulia said she'd go out with me, and then I'd gotten revenge against that good-for-nothing pencil pusher. If the day continued the way it had started, I figured I'd find the killer by dinnertime!

I bumped into Silvia as I was leaving the elevator. She greeted me warmly as usual and offered to buy me coffee at everyone's favorite bar across the street.

"Thanks, Silvia, but if the owner sees me come in again, he'll probably throw a fit. Anyway, I've had my daily dose of caffeine so I'd better not. Can I take a rain check?"

I headed outside and asked Paolo to take me to the *Mattino*. It wasn't even ten o'clock, which meant I still had time to go through my mail and work with Fabrizio to prepare the next article before going to the club in the afternoon.

There's no chance of finding a parking spot in central Padua at that time of the morning, so I got out in front of the office and left Paolo to handle that mission impossible, promising myself that if the police ever offered me a driver in the future, I'd accept willingly. As a deterrent to homicide, Paolo was pretty useless, but getting picked up outside one office and dropped off at another in less than ten minutes was as precious as a free ticket to the Ryder Cup.

When I entered my office, I found Fabrizio sitting at his desk. "Hi! How goes it?"

Fabrizio looked up from his computer and crossed his hands behind his neck to stretch, responding, "Hi, Riccardo, fine. What about you?"

"Awesome. All I need now is to win the lottery."

"Have you seen DA Dal Nero?"

"Yes, and it's good news all around."

"Are they about to capture the killer?"

"No, not yet, but the circle's getting tighter."

"Is it someone in the Casati Vitali family?"

"Dal Nero says anything is possible, and the opposite is also possible. But in my opinion, only one thing matters at the moment, which is that all hell's broken loose in that family. There's some stuff I can't tell you, but I'd bet a year's salary that the beast is hidden in the nobles' garden. What are you working on?"

"At four o'clock this afternoon, Dal Nero will give a brief press conference, to update us on the progress of the investigation. So we have to have the article ready to go before then."

"Great. Then this afternoon I want to go to the club to look around, under the pretext of getting in a little golf practice."

"Practice? With your hand like that?"

"Just with my putter. Anyway, I really need to get some time in because lately I've been playing like crap."

I quickly worked through the various tasks I'd left hanging for a few days: I paid my car insurance, checked whether the hole in my bank account was an acceptable size, and then transferred two hundred euros to the woman who came to my house to clean three times a week. How on earth she managed, in just six hours a week, to iron my shirts, tidy up, clean the house, and look after my one-and-a-half-acre garden was a scientific mystery as confounding as the Higgs boson.

I said good-bye to Fabrizio and went downstairs to meet Paolo, who, as usual, was chatting with the security guard.

"Paolo, we're going to Frassanelle," I told him, interrupting his conversation.

"Seriously? It took me two hours to find a parking space—I've only been here ten minutes!"

"If you prefer, we can hang around for a bit. That way it will seem more justified. What do you think?"

"Great, we could go in about an hour."

"For God's sake, Paolo, I was kidding!"

We reached Frassanelle at lunchtime. It was Wednesday, and although it was overcast, there seemed no real threat of rain. Like on all weekdays, the majority of people at the club were getting on a bit in years—pensioners or former entrepreneurs who'd managed to sell their businesses and now lived off their earnings. They were people who found golf a great hobby and a good way to keep fit. With a few exceptions, they were all sitting in the restaurant for the prix fixe lunch that Enrico served for ten euros, including wine and coffee. I went in and greeted some folks I knew, just stopping for a few seconds because I didn't want to seem rude and because I didn't want to get caught up in the usual web of questions. Finally, I called one of the waiters to show us to a table, where we each sat down and ordered a first course and a beer.

While I was waiting for lunch to be served, I fiddled with the new company Blackberry that Piovesan had given me. I was attempting in vain to download a file attached to an email from Fabrizio when to my right I noticed somebody standing next to me. I looked up, and, when I'd focused on who it was, I realized that the happy part of my day had ended when I'd entered the elevator at the DA's office. Towering over me, Arcadio was holding a golf club in one hand and tossing a golf ball in the other, glaring into my eyes. I never took my eyes off him, but I also noticed Paolo's movements on the other side of the table, as he slowly and purposely pulled out his big gun, quite fitting for his size and placed it on the table.

I decided to break the silence, "Arcadio, I hope you're not going to make a scene here in the middle of the restaurant."

"Let's go for a walk on the course, then."

"No. First, because we're waiting for our spaghetti, and second, because punching each other is not the solution. If you want to talk to me, why don't you sit down with us?"

From his expression, I could see that he was willing to talk, at least for now.

With the rudest tone possible, he pointed at Paolo with his club and spat out, "Who the hell is this?"

I let Paolo answer for himself because when it came to manners, there was no doubt those two were a match made in heaven.

"I'm the guy who'll put this bullet in your ass if you make a wrong move."

"Listen, you bastard! If you make a wrong move, I'll split your head open with this iron. Got it?"

I decided to break them up before they ran out of compliments to pay each other and decided to move on from threats to action.

"OK, Arcadio, now that you've introduced yourselves, please sit down and leave Paolo alone. He's a police officer assigned to protect me from the killer. Just like you, I want to understand what's going on.

And to clear things up once and for all, I most certainly didn't kill your grandmother, who I didn't even know."

"So what the hell were you doing at my house?"

"Your father sent me a text asking me to meet him. I tried a dozen times to call him back, but he never replied, so I decided to go to the castle and see if he was home. Given the last few days, I figured his message might be urgent."

"So you just walk into someone's house?"

"I had no intention of entering your damn house, but as soon as I stepped into the garden, those insane dogs started chasing me, and I had no choice but to run inside. The carabinieri must have explained all that?"

"Sure, I spoke to a marshal, who said he can't understand why you're always next to someone who's been killed. He also said that if it were up to him, you'd already be behind bars."

"Was it Marshal Costanzo, by any chance?"

"I think so."

"Yeah, he doesn't think much of me, but luckily, he's not in charge of the investigation. Seriously, though, think about it: Do you think the investigators would protect me and let me go free if they thought I was guilty?"

As usual, Paolo felt obliged to interrupt so he could get his due credit.

"That's what I said—"

"Yeah, yeah," I cut him off.

I suddenly realized that, as things stood now, Arcadio was probably more frightened than me.

So far, I hadn't looked at the situation from his point of view. He was just a twenty-year-old kid whose family was involved in a series of murders. He might even be a target, too, and have some idea of the reason why—unless he was the killer, of course.

"How's your father?"

As I said the word *father*, I wondered whether Arcadio knew he wasn't Count Alvise's biological son. But knowing how cautious Giulia was, I decided it was more likely that Arcadio still didn't know anything.

"Not great. He's still at the hospital, but if the tests are OK, he'll come home tomorrow. He's really messed up, though, because he loved Stella. We all did."

I didn't mention that I knew she wasn't his real grandmother, even though I was dying to know what he knew about her relationship with Count Alvise. So I tried to come at it from another angle. "What do you make of all this mess?"

"I don't know. I can't understand who could have killed my grandmother. Who did she bother? She was the nicest person in the whole damn village. Maybe too nice. I swear, if I find out who it was, I'll kill him with my bare hands and reduce him to such a pulp they won't even be able to identify his shirt buttons," he said vehemently.

Right then, I felt more sorry for him than frightened. Still, I needed to know how much he knew about his family affairs.

So, as casually as possible, I asked, "Arcadio, do you have any brothers or sisters?"

"No, I'm an only child."

I smiled at him and said in my most fatherly tone, "Listen, let's stop playing Rambo for a minute. In my opinion, if we don't focus, the monster that killed your grandmother could get away with it."

Arcadio probably wasn't expecting me to level with him like that. He needed someone to show him the right way to deal with the whole drama.

"I just spoke to the district attorney in charge of the investigation, and they still don't know what the motive was, but they cannot exclude the possibility your grandmother was killed for a reason, and not just because she was in the wrong place at the wrong time. Do you get my meaning?"

"No, I don't. What are you trying to say? That my grandmother hurt somebody?"

"No, absolutely not. I mean that perhaps she was killed because she knew something, maybe even the identity of the assassin."

"Huh?"

"What I'm trying to say is that we cannot exclude the possibility that the assassin is going to come looking for you, as well, or that you, without even knowing why, could pose a threat to him."

"Hey, like I said, if I get my hands on him . . ."

Incorrigible.

"Arcadio, stop with that stuff for just a second. Right now, you should look into the past. Try asking your father if he has any idea what's going on. I mean, don't assume this hell has exploded into your life by chance or that it's all some tragic error."

Arcadio looked at the floor, thinking over what I'd said to him. If nothing else, he'd stopped flexing his muscles and had calmed down a bit. Maybe he was finally beginning to understand that whatever was happening was much bigger than him and his thirst for vengeance.

Unfortunately, I couldn't tell him much more.

That was Giulia's job, and I really didn't envy her.

CHAPTER FIFTEEN

The putter is the club a player uses to hit the ball a short distance on the green and try to get it in the hole.

No matter what they show on TV, putting is not easy. Unlike other shots, a putt doesn't require major physical exertion, but it does take great precision to read the line the ball has to follow to reach the hole. Above all, it requires you to carefully calibrate the strength needed for the distance. Of all golfing shots, the putt is the most important. It often happens that a golfer hits two perfect shots and covers four hundred yards to place the ball just a short distance from the hole, but then needs three or four more shots to actually get it in. I'm neither a professional nor an instructor, and I don't know what is needed for a perfect putt, but with all my experience, I'm an expert in everything needed to screw things up royally. The most frequent mistake is closing the shot with your wrists; as your arms move like a pendulum, you have to prevent your hands and wrists from interacting with the line of your arms. That in itself isn't so difficult, but the problem is that you also have to get some force behind the shot. Your arms alone aren't sufficiently sensitive to measure the impact—your brain needs information from your hands, and if your brain acts on it, then your ball ends up several yards away from the hole. For this and many other reasons, I'm convinced that, despite what others say, the less you use your brain in golf, the better you play. So if that theory is correct, my bandaged right hand and its inability to communicate with my brain should have been an advantage.

There are two putting greens at the Frassanelle Golf Club: one in front of the restaurant bar, where the other members can watch from their seats at outside tables, and one farther away, next to the practice green. For a small fee, members can store their sets of clubs in a room that goes by the imaginative name of the "bag room." In order to prevent expensive sets becoming a temptation to any light-fingered players, only the caddies are allowed access to the bag room.

I didn't feel like chatting, so I decided to go to the more distant putting green, with Paolo in tow, of course. There, I found the caddy master, Carlo, sitting outside the bag room, adjusting the weight of another member's driver head. Carlo is one of those naturally gifted men who can do everything, from woodcutting to engineering. He's got the trim physique of someone used to manual labor: unlike a body built up in a gym, his emanates natural strength. On top of that, his long blond hair and blue eyes make him a threat to all the club husbands. I tapped him on the shoulder to say hello, and as he turned around, he jumped like he'd seen a ghost. Like Marshal Costanzo, he probably imagined I must be guilty of at least one of the murders.

"Hey, calm down, Carlo! I didn't mean to scare you."

"Mr. Ranieri! I wasn't expecting to see you here."

I'd asked him many times to use my first name, but no way; Carlo thanks me, but he can't bring himself to do it.

"I've come to practice my putting a bit."

"With that hand?"

"As my instructor always says, I move my wrist too much. This time I want to go straight as an arrow."

Perhaps Carlo thought I was trying to make a joke, so he forced out a small laugh and then just looked at me in silence.

"Carlo."

"Yes?"

"I need my putter."

"Oh, yes, of course, I'll get it right away."

The only thing that makes boring putter practice bearable is that I can smoke a cigar while I'm doing it. Let's face it, trying to hit a ball into a four-and-a-quarter-inch hole from a distance of three or four yards is about as much fun as trying to thread a sausage through a needle.

It had been about a week since I'd held a golf club, and I was so ready to play that I would have ripped my bandage off if I could. Carlo gave me four balls, and Paolo and I went to the center of the putting green.

The grassy surface of the practice green is exactly like the one on the course, so that players are able to evaluate the smoothness. That's why players are only allowed on the greens wearing totally flat shoes. The surface of the greens must be perfectly smooth, with no unevenness that could divert the path of the ball.

In horror, I realized Paolo was wearing shoes with a heel and, given his size, he had left a track of scars in the grass visible even from a distance. I didn't get the chance to tell him to get off before a woman began squealing like a plucked turkey that his shoeprints were ruining the precious green. Paolo couldn't understand why she was so hysterical, so he just pulled out his gun and pointed it at the sky as if considering whether or not to shoot her. Trying not to start laughing at the ridiculous reaction, I explained to him why she was shouting and why she was now running like a maniac to the safety of the clubhouse.

A few minutes later, Galli rushed over, having being told by the hysterical woman that the assassin who killed the Savionis was back, and in my opinion, also because he was concerned about the cost of fixing the green. It took about ten minutes to explain why Paolo was with me, and, after we had cleared up the misunderstanding, there was no way I could prevent Galli from bombarding me with questions about everything that had happened.

After suggesting that he and the other members, who had inevitably gathered around us, should read the articles in the next edition of the *Mattino*, I was finally able to start practicing my putt. However, after the first four hits, my bandaged hand theory was blown to bits by the harsh truth of totally wrong lines: I hit two wide to the right and two to the left. I picked up the balls and noticed that Carlo had discreetly come over to the green next to Paolo, presumably with the excuse of chatting with him, but really because he wanted to talk me out of my stupid theory. After another series of disastrous shots, Carlo sauntered over with the air of an expert, despite the fact that he's never hit a golf ball in his life, and gave me a lecture. It took him almost twenty minutes to explain that, in his opinion, the theory could only work if both wrists were bandaged. I apologized that I hadn't managed to get shot in my other hand yet.

Carlo's response surprised me. "If the killer hasn't killed you yet, it shows that you've behaved yourself as far as he's concerned."

I didn't want to discuss it any further, so I went back to my putting. I couldn't help thinking about what he'd said, though. The fact that I hadn't been the target of another murder attempt might mean that I was no longer a threat. In other words, the fact that I still hadn't figured things out had probably saved my life.

I spent another hour on the green under the watchful eye of Carlo and the bored eye of Paolo. Then I put my putter in my bag and walked over to a spot where I could get cell reception. There were a number of missed calls, including one from Fabrizio and five from Piovesan. Even though my curiosity urged me to call them back immediately to see what they wanted, I thought it only fair to reward Paolo's patience and Carlo's professional aspirations, and so I offered to buy them each a drink.

Francesca was behind the bar, and she almost freaked out, too, when she saw me.

"Hi, Francesca. I'd like three beers and a box of .22-caliber bullets."

"Good afternoon, Ranieri. I'm sorry, I didn't expect to see you with . . . ," she replied, trying to get hold of herself.

I let it drop; I didn't know if she was referring to my company or what. Still, I decided not to ask, because with her sad sack attitude, Francesca could depress a lottery winner. She's one of those people who, if you've broken an arm, she's broken two; if you've got a flat tire, her engine just blew up, and so on. Given the current situation, the last thing I wanted was to be regaled with stories about inconceivably bad luck, so without paying any further attention to her, my guests and I toasted the killer's imminent capture.

Later, when Paolo and I were back in the car and far enough from the golf club's Bermuda Triangle of cell reception, both our phones began ringing furiously with notices of missed calls. As if taking after their owners, my tone was a singing bird while Paolo's was a mooing cow. I had three more missed calls from Piovesan, and Giulia had tried to reach Paolo. Seeing the eight attempts from Gibbo and one from Fabrizio, I decided to call the latter. Before calling a boss who's desperately trying to get hold of you, I think it's good practice to call a reliable colleague first to get the scoop on what's going on.

Fabrizio understood this and answered at the first ring.

"Hi, Riccardo. We've been looking for you."

"Yes, I know. I got a ton of calls from Gibbo. What's up?"

"I think you've won a grand prize trip to the Caribbean."

"I won what?"

"At the press conference today, Dal Nero announced that the detectives have uncovered some potential leads connecting the case to the Dominican Republic, and it seems the Dominican authorities are refusing to send the documents the investigators have requested."

"What's that got to do with me?"

"Grandi and Piovesan have decided to send you there to follow the developments firsthand."

"To Santo Domingo?"

"Exactly."

"Awesome."

"Hold on, Riccardo, don't think you're getting a week's holiday in a resort. You might only be there for one day."

"Mm, not so cool, then. Still, being in the Caribbean with Dal Nero doesn't sound half bad . . ."

"We don't know if Dal Nero is going or not. Do you speak Spanish?"

"*¡Sí, señor!*"

I called Piovesan back next. "Hi, Gibbo, I just saw your calls. Sorry, I was at the golf club, and there's no reception."

"I was calling you because there are some developments in the case, and it seems there are problems in Santo Domingo."

"Yeah, I just talked to Fabrizio, and he explained everything."

"Did he tell you we've decided to send you there?"

"He told me you've booked me a room with an ocean view at a resort for a week."

"Well, probably not for a week, and probably not an ocean view, either. But don't you dare complain about the assignment, otherwise I'll have to sock you in the nose."

"Don't worry, Gibbo. I'll play nice this time."

Paolo was listening as he drove. As soon as I hung up, he asked eagerly, "They're sending you to Santo Domingo?"

"Looks like it."

"Lucky bastard! Maybe Dal Nero will send me, too! I've never been to the Caribbean."

Paolo pulled over so he could call Giulia, but then sat there staring blankly at his phone, terrified at just the thought of talking to her.

Clearly, the poor man needed a pep talk. "I bet Dal Nero is absolutely furious with you."

Looking at me desperately, he asked, "Why?"

"Come on, I was kidding! You're really gullible. Look at you, 220 pounds of gibbering fear because you have to call the district attorney."

"I told you: it's not fear. It's anxiety. That woman makes me anxious."

After some more sighing like a steam engine, at last he dialed and said, "Hello? Good evening, DA Dal Nero. I saw that . . . Yes . . . No . . . Yes . . . I heard . . . Yes, I think so . . . OK, yes, sure . . . But . . . Yes, OK . . . Certainly, DA Dal Nero, have a good evening."

I was laughing so hard I was in tears.

"Paolo, you really have to be assertive with some women, or they'll wipe the floor with you. What did she say?"

"She wanted to know what Arcadio said to you."

"How did she already know about Arcadio?"

"Galli called her to check that I was really assigned to your protection."

"Paolo, you didn't get a single word in! What did Dal Nero say to you?"

Paolo answered as my phone started ringing again.

"That if I pull my gun out without a valid reason again, she'll make me eat it. Then she said she'd call you."

With a sense of foreboding, I answered my phone. "Hello? Oh, Giulia—"

In a cutting tone, she said, "Riccardo, I heard about the fuss at the club."

"Yes, but look—"

"Listen, get it through your thick head that you can't attract any more attention than you already have."

"Well, if you're talking about—"

"I'm talking about the fact that if you go around looking for trouble, you're going to find it. Do we understand one another?"

"Well, to be honest—"

"The next phone call I get complaining about your behavior, you'll be placed under house arrest, and Paolo will be directing traffic in Porto Tolle. Clear?"

Click.

"Hello? . . . Hello?"

I looked at Paolo in confusion.

"Listen to me, Riccardo."

"What?"

"You really have to be assertive with some women, or they'll wipe the floor with you."

"Oh, fuck off!"

CHAPTER SIXTEEN

After leaving the club it started to rain—an insistent and annoying drizzle, whose only purpose seemed to be in reminding me that summer was over and autumn had set in. This, on top of Giulia's call, had put me in a bad mood.

As we were driving along the enchanted road through the woods, my eyes were captured by the illumination of the headlights on the surrounding landscape, and while I was trying to come to grips with Giulia's irrational anger, I was fascinated by the effects of the lights as they hit the rain-moistened leaves and exploded into silver sparks all around. I felt like the light was dancing for me, magically trying to console me after Giulia's reprimand. As we pulled out of the woods, Paolo was looking even more crestfallen than me, if that was possible, so I suggested we stop off and get something to eat on the way. The thought of going home to microwave some colorless and tasteless frozen food was about as enticing as going to a funeral.

I proposed Trattoria da Aldo. The woman and her husband who run the restaurant are always smiling, and they welcome their guests warmly, in stark contrast to the traditional cold shoulder you get most places in the region. I've frequently eaten there alone, and quite often the owner has sat down with me to keep me company. This time, she greeted me with a warm hug and was delighted by the prospect of my companion's appetite—obvious from his girth—as she led us to our table.

"At last, you've brought a friend who enjoys good food! No offense, but you're so thin, and you eat like a little bird!"

Paolo was uncertain whether to feel insulted about his weight or flattered about his appreciation of all things gastronomic, so he just smiled at her inquiringly as if reserving judgment until after he'd eaten.

"Lucia, I'm sorry it's been so long. You know I come by as often as possible, but at the moment, between people trying to kill me and people trying to save me, I haven't had much free time."

"Well, I hope this handsome young man is one of the ones trying to save you, then?"

"Theoretically speaking, yes, but sometimes he's more dangerous than the folks trying to kill me!"

Paolo cut the small talk short with a shove that launched me ten feet across the restaurant, nearly knocking over several tables.

Dinner and Lucia's company restored some of my good mood. Naturally, Lucia wanted to know everything that had happened in return for filling me in on the various rumors around the village. After stopping by the Frassanelle bar, I had gone from being everyone's vague acquaintance to their best friend, and half the club members were now claiming that just before I was shot in my hand—they were unclear about whether it was the left or the right—I was with them, either in the bar, having dinner at their house, or walking through the village. Apart from the local gossip, Lucia told me something about Francesca the bartender, who Lucia had known since she was a child. Apparently, the morning after I was shot, Francesca had turned up in the village to hear how I was doing. Lucia and Paolo teased me, saying Francesca must have a crush, confirmed bachelor and Latin heartbreaker that I was. I thought it was strange that she'd come to town to ask about me rather than just keeping tabs on the news at the golf club—especially considering her shyness. I made a mental note to talk to Giulia about it.

The next morning, we were already on the road to Padua at seven—to Paolo's great disappointment as he, like Newton, would have preferred to sleep longer. I had tons to do and no way could I risk waiting until rush hour and losing time sitting in traffic. At seven thirty, we were already in the café next to the *Mattino* for breakfast. When I got into the office, Fabrizio was already deep in it.

"Fabrizio, didn't you go home last night?"

"Don't you start—you sound like my wife."

"How is Sandra, by the way?"

"Fine. But since all this started we hardly ever see each other. When I get home, I'm so exhausted I just have a bite to eat and then go to bed."

"Don't worry. In a situation like this, there's bound to be collateral damage."

"Are you talking about my marriage or my career?"

"Honestly, marriage, but if you say anything to Sandra, you're fired!"

As it wasn't even eight o'clock, we felt quite pleased with our philosophical musings regarding marriage and decided to move onto more mundane topics.

"What are you working on?"

"We're preparing for an interview with Count Alvise."

"Great. Have we got an exclusive?"

"Afraid not. But Piovesan is sticking to him like glue. What about you? Have you packed?"

"No, not yet. I don't even know when I'm leaving."

"I don't want to scare you, but I think you're leaving today."

"What? I don't even know if my passport's up to date. Has Grandi arrived?"

"No, nobody's in yet. But I think Graziella has made all the arrangements. You should talk to her."

"OK, I will. In the meantime, I want to look into Francesca Visentin who works at the golf club bar."

"Why? Is she pretty?"

"Pretty, no, but strange, yes. I just found out that she was asking about me in the village the day after the shooting."

"So what?"

"I don't know. It's usually impossible to get a word out of Francesca unless she's complaining about her life, and I just can't imagine her going around asking about me, so if she did there must have been a good reason."

"Maybe she's in love with you."

"Maybe she shot at me and wanted to know if she'd hit me or not!"

"Looking at you, I'd say that's more likely."

"Thanks, man."

I began my Internet search right away, but all I could find about Francesca was a forlorn Facebook page and a few appearances at a golf club gala. I was getting ready to access the newspaper database when I saw Graziella. I got up to go over to her and she, like everyone else seemed prone to doing, stared at me in horror.

"Ranieri? What on earth are you doing here?"

"What do you mean? I work here!"

"Didn't you read my emails?"

"When was I supposed to read your emails? I just got here ten minutes ago."

"So where's your Blackberry?"

"Shit, the Blackberry! I completely forgot about it!"

"Your plane leaves in less than three hours!"

"Damn it! I hate cell phones! OK . . . I can rush home, pick up my passport, and then go. OK, Graziella? I'll leave now, and then I'll call you for the details on the way to the airport."

"Fine, don't worry."

As I was rushing to the elevator, Graziella came over with a furtive expression and whispered, "Riccardo, the envelope with the plane ticket is on your desk."

Now I felt like a total idiot, but thanked her for her discretion; maybe my chronic disorganization could remain our secret.

I went back to my desk, passing Fabrizio's on the way, and put the envelope in my pocket. Fabrizio didn't even look up as he opined, "It's strange, isn't it?"

"What?"

"That you still need tickets to get on a plane."

"When I get back, you're fired!"

I bumped into Paolo on his way into the building.

"Oh, Riccardo, what's the matter?"

"We have to rush home and then go to the airport. My plane leaves in less than three hours."

"God, this sucks! I just managed to park!"

"While you're cursing, get a move on. There's no time to lose."

We rushed to the car and headed off for Bastia. Luckily, the traffic was mainly going in the opposite direction at that time of day, so there were no holdups. Due to the speed, though, my carsickness was kicking in again. Paolo begged me to call Giulia so that we didn't get another scolding. I'd finally put her number on speed dial in my damn Blackberry, and I called her and she answered right away. "Hi, Riccardo, what's up?"

"Hi, Giulia, how are things?"

"Fine, thanks. Look, I'm busy, so let's cut to the chase."

I was getting like Paolo and felt anxious every time she spoke to me so brusquely.

"I just wanted to tell you that after yesterday's press conference, my bosses decided to send me to Santo Domingo for a few days to find out what's happening down there."

"You're going to Santo Domingo?"

"Yes, aren't you?"

"Me? Why on earth would I go to Santo Domingo?"

Apart from the car sickness and anxiety, I now had a lump in my throat to deal with. "They told me the investigation was being moved to Santo Domingo."

"You reporters always jump to conclusions. I never said the investigation would be moved anywhere. What I said is that we're waiting for documents from the Italian embassy in Santo Domingo. You've got to be kidding if you think I've got the time to travel all that way just to talk to a few bureaucrats."

Despite my disappointment, I had to keep up my role as the determined Romeo.

"And here I was hoping to have a honeymoon with you in the Caribbean."

"Riccardo, I already told you, I don't have time for your antics right now. Have a good trip, rest up, and let me know when you get back. Bye."

Click.

I turned to Paolo. "If she's as aggressive in bed as she is at work, I'd rather share my bed with a pit bull!"

"What did she say?"

"In short, she's got no time for silliness."

"No, I mean about me?"

"We didn't talk about you."

"Damn it—I mean, do I have to come, too, or not?"

"Shit, I didn't ask!"

"Great. Now I've got to call her, and she'll tell me again I don't know how to do my job. This sucks!"

Paolo's snorts, alternated with deep sighs and unintelligible murmurings, lasted until Cervarese, about three quarters of the way home, when he finally decided to face his demons and call Giulia.

"Hello? Good morning, DA Dal Nero. I'm sorry to bother you, but I just wanted to know—No, of course . . . Yes, that's true . . . Oh, right . . . OK. Yes, have a nice day."

The call must have lasted between three and four seconds total—Telecom certainly wasn't making much money off those two!

"What did she say?"

"That if I haven't bought a ticket, what am I calling her for?"

"If nothing else, she's practical, eh?"

"I had a different adjective in mind."

When we got home, it took me about ten minutes to get ready: one minute to pack a case and nine to look for my passport, which I finally found in the kitchen on top of an old Milan telephone book, which I kept for nostalgic reasons. Then I had to swing by Giuseppe's house to ask him to fill my dogs' bowls every day until I came back. Altogether, our whole stop took less than fifteen minutes. Paolo and I jumped back into the car and onto the highway, breaking all kinds of driving laws on the way. We left the car in a no-parking zone and rushed into the airport, only to find that there were still two hours till departure. We peered up at the information screens and finally began to relax a little.

"I don't see it. What time should it leave?"

"On the note they gave me at the paper, it says 11:10."

"At 11:10, there's a flight to Moscow and another to Rome."

"Maybe it's the Rome flight, and it continues to Santo Domingo?"

Anxiety began to overtake my residual carsickness.

"Wait, let me read it again."

I took out the envelope Graziella had given me to double-check the time. Relieved, I saw that the flight time definitely was 11:10. I called her, and, in her usual efficient manner, she answered right away.

"What's the matter, Ranieri?"

"Hi, Graziella, I'm at the airport, but I can't find any information about my flight. Do I have a connection in Rome, by any chance?"

"Strange, no, there's no connection. The agency told me it's a direct flight from Verona–La Romana."

My blood turned to ice.

"Graziella, did you say Verona?"

"Yes, Verona–La Romana."

I read the note again, which clearly stated "VER–LRM." I thought I was going to faint. Knowing me, Graziella realized what had happened.

"Don't tell me you went to the airport in Venice!"

"Holy fuck! Of course I did! I'm from Milan, and there's no need to check which airport I'm leaving from. It's always Malpensa, and that's it!"

Graziella may have felt a little bit guilty. She knows I'm useless at organization and she should probably have told me twice. She tried to be encouraging.

"Look, Ranieri, it's 9:25; if you hurry, maybe you can still make it in time."

"I doubt it, but I'll try. In the meantime, call the Verona airport and ask them to hold the plane. Tell them there's a bomb or an Ebola outbreak or something."

"It won't be easy, but I'll try. I'll call you later."

We ran back out to the car and set off for Verona. When I was finally getting over my self-pity, in spite of Paolo's constant complaints, Fabrizio called to add to my stress.

"Don't worry. Piovesan said that if you miss the flight, he'll kill you himself. That way the case will be closed and we can all take a vacation."

Terrific. Just what I needed right now. It's good to know your colleagues all trust you and have your back. If nothing else, I was making things tough for the killer. Just try to anticipate my next move if you dare! Even the most sophisticated NASA computer would struggle—too many unforeseeable variables.

Graziella called me back a short while later.

"I just talked to the airline. They'll try and wait for you, but you have to be at check-in at least an hour before departure. Do you think you'll make it?"

"We're going . . ."—I leaned toward Paolo to read the speedometer—"Shit! One hundred five miles per hour!"

She calmly replied, "Great, then you should make it."

"Do you know what kind of car we're in?"

"No, what kind?"

"A Fiesta of indiscernible age."

"Good heavens. Take care, then."

"Going this fast in a car like this, I think luck's more important than caution. Never mind . . . If I get there alive, I'll let you know. If not, then you can have my ashtray with the cigar cutter—there's no way Fabrizio's going to get it. OK?"

Graziella laughed and hung up, so I turned to Paolo.

"Don't you think it's better to get there late, but in one piece?"

"Come on! My trusty Fiesta has never let me down."

"What's that got to do with it? I'm talking about the speed!"

"Don't worry. I took a speed-driving course to get into the emergency response unit."

"Oh, so you were in emergency response?"

"No."

"Why not?"

"Because I failed the speed-driving course."

After risking our lives repeatedly, we finally arrived at Verona Valerio Catullo Airport around ten twenty. I ran inside, weaving my way through groups of Japanese tourists. My check-in desk was easy to spot: an airline representative was frantically waving a piece of paper to catch my attention. I ran over, and, trying to catch my breath, handed her my documents and dumped my bag on the conveyor.

"I'm Riccardo Ranieri from the *Mattino di Padova*. Thanks for waiting for me."

"A bit disorganized, huh?"

"Look, until a couple of hours ago I didn't even know I had to leave. You're right, though. I am a bit disorganized."

Clearly pleased with my self-criticism, the rep said no more and pointed me toward the gate. I went through security and emerged holding my trousers up with my good hand because, when I took my belt off, I realized I'd lost the top button. I was hot, sweaty, and breathless, but I'd made it. The gate agent tore off my boarding pass stub and ushered me onto the plane.

Before turning my phone off, I sent Fabrizio a message. "I'm on the plane. It was a piece of cake!"

CHAPTER SEVENTEEN

The eleven-hour flight was hell.

Naïvely assuming I'd be traveling business class, I found myself in coach between a woman who could have been Paolo's twin sister, judging by the size of her, and a young male gaming fanatic who never took a break from his virtual world, not even to go to the toilet. When I tried to close my eyes, not so much because I was tired but because I wanted to shorten the trip, all I could see was plane crashes to compound all of my recent good luck. I decided to remain vigilant throughout the flight.

I arrived at Santo Domingo airport at four o'clock local time. It was cloudy and around eighty-five degrees, which felt tropical due to a humidity level even higher than the Po Plain in Italy. After an agonizingly slow trip through passport control and customs, I immediately spotted the person who had come to meet me. No more than five feet tall, he was shorter than the sign he was holding, which bore the Spanish version of my name: "Señor Ricardo Raneri." My escort introduced himself as Julio and immediately showed his generous nature and strength by carrying my superlight carry-on to the car, while I had the honor of wrestling the heavy suitcase.

Julio was about forty years old and had typical creole looks: short, curly hair and a chubby frame. He climbed behind the wheel of a red Peugeot 205 with windows for air conditioning and a trunk that didn't close. Still, after the close quarters of the plane, it felt luxurious. Julio said he had instructions to drop me at my hotel and then to be available anytime to assist in my attempts to make contact with the Italian embassy and the hospital where, many years before, the mysterious events had occurred.

I had no idea what to expect from the next few days, but I imagined I would have precious little time to actually enjoy the paradise I'd landed in. The ride in the car from the La Romana airport to the hotel in the city center was, therefore, a precious opportunity to admire the beautiful island. Alas, after a mere half mile, I was overcome by exhaustion, and, lulled by the constant buzz of the tiny engine, I passed out cold. I was woken by a car horn, which seems to be the most common sound in the streets of Santo Domingo. Julio and I were in the center of the city, which, based on certain preconceptions of tropical paradises, I'd imagined as significantly less modern and chaotic than it turned out to be. Nor were there any women dressed in flowers dancing in the streets with languid expressions full of promises of love. Despite myself, I had to replace that image with a reality of dirty streets full of indolent-and dangerous-looking individuals who seemed like they might commit crimes out of sheer boredom.

Julio and I reached my hotel near the Italian embassy about ten minutes after I woke up. It was a colonial-style building, and, from the outside, it had a reasonably dignified air. I said good-bye to Julio, and we arranged to meet at eight the next morning. After giving a generous ten-euro tip to a young boy who not only carried my luggage to my room but also proudly showed me all the luxury accommodations—a light switch and air conditioning—I finally got into the shower, something I'd been dying to do since the chase had begun the day before.

It was about ten to eight, so I decided to lie down for few minutes before going down to the restaurant for dinner. A fatal mistake: I woke up more than three hours later. At eleven thirty at night, the hotel restaurant was bound to be closed, but I was hungry, so I decided to go out and look for something. Outside, it had cooled down a bit, and, luckily, the symphony of car horns had died down considerably. As soon as I left the hotel, I was pursued by children asking for money or candy, as well as taxi drivers, real or pretend, who kept offering trips to the sketchiest-sounding clubs in the city. I gave a few coins to the children, thinking it would get rid of them, but that just made even more of them trail me with even more insistent demands. So I decided to accept the offer of a taxi driver who looked less menacing than the others, and climbed into his cab to the sneers of the other drivers and shouts from the children. With my stunted Spanish, which mostly involved adding an *s* to the ends of Italian words, I tried to explain that I was hungry and not interested in being taken to any women.

Convinced I was a homosexual, he took me to a bar full of men dressed in a way that left no doubt that they were. The second bar seemed more geared toward bisexuals, as far as I could tell from the folks loitering around the door. I surrendered to the third attempt, which seemed more hetero and where, apart from the compulsory presence of a couple of hookers, it looked as if I'd at least be able to get something to eat. I have no memory of what I ordered or what the food tasted like, but it filled my stomach. I had to eat my meal with one knowing hand on my groin and the constant friction of a breast against my left arm. When it was time to leave, the girls sulked until I pulled out two twenty-euro notes. Somehow, I managed to escape among kisses, caresses, and promises of future meetings and got into the cab that was still waiting outside the bar to take me back to the hotel.

The next morning, I found Julio at the reception desk, chatting away with the two hotel clerks. He broke off to accompany me to the breakfast room. Like all hotels worthy of the name, the breakfast buffet was a generous, varied spread expertly displayed on a large central table, but I'm a creature of habit and just had an American coffee and a chocolate muffin. However, Julio casually walked around the table and tried each dish. By the time he'd completed his third round of brioches, sausages, pineapple, eggs, cake, and bacon, I'm convinced he'd eaten the equivalent of two full meals. When Julio was finally full, he sat down with me and told me about the plan for the day. I was scheduled to meet with Dr. Stefano Terni, who worked at the Italian embassy, and after that we'd head to the administrative office of the Santo Domingo civil hospital.

It was a short walk from the hotel to the embassy, where I then sat and waited in the foyer for Dr. Terni. Fabrizio had warned me that the staff at the embassy wasn't known for being very cooperative, so I was determined not to give anyone the satisfaction of seeing me upset about the wait. Exactly two hours after I arrived, a woman, presumably the secretary, took me to a room so small I thought it was a utility closet, where she left me, saying Dr. Terni would be right with me. I wasn't surprised to discover there was no air conditioning; Dr. Terni was trying to get rid of me as quickly as possible. He arrived about ten minutes later, a good-looking man of about fifty, well dressed in a light-colored suit, sporting a head of gray hair, and smelling of cologne—the stereotypical handsome ambassador. He fixed his charming, powerful smile on his face and apologized for the delay, which he assured me had been caused by the thousand responsibilities he had to deal with. He didn't shake my hand, but began talking before he had even sat down.

"Mr. Ranieri, I'm going to be honest: I really don't see how I can help you. The staff at the *Mattino di Padova* sent me your request for information about the documents that the Padua district attorney requested, but here at the embassy, we have no more news at the moment. Furthermore, we do not feel that it is appropriate to give you, a reporter, any information about a case that is already being handled by the authorities."

I had not flown for eleven hours sandwiched between two disagreeable passengers just to be sent away with my tail between my legs by some shiny-haired bureaucrat, so I replied, "Dr. Terni, I'm going to be honest with you, as well. This case doesn't just matter to the authorities; it matters very much to me personally, given the fact that somebody tried to kill me."

"Yes, I did hear about that, and I'm sorry—"

I didn't give him the chance to start his diplomatic speech but looked him straight in the eye and continued. "Therefore, I'd like to ask you to be a bit more willing to listen and cooperate, if you don't mind."

Terni stiffened, perhaps not used to such an undiplomatic approach. "All right, what can I do?"

"First of all, I suggest that the next time you are unable to be punctual for an appointment, at least inform the person who is wasting their time waiting for you of just how long you're going to be."

"Look, delays cannot always be foreseen, and anyway, I've just—"

I interrupted him again. "Drop it, Dr. Terni. I'm not stupid. It's obvious that I'm not welcome here and that you want to get rid of me as soon as possible. Unfortunately, I'm quite happy here in Santo Domingo, and as the paper I work for is paying for my stay, I have no intention of leaving without the things I came for."

Terni gave me a crafty smile, trying to disguise how irritated he was with me.

"Fine, Mr. Ranieri. What else can I do?"

Despite his words, his attitude clearly showed he had no desire whatsoever to cooperate.

"I want information about the Casati Vitali family."

"Mr. Ranieri, this is not an information office. You can't just turn up here asking questions about somebody."

"In 1992, Countess Casati Vitali died immediately after giving birth, and I'd like to know who was responsible for ascertaining the circumstances of her death," I insisted.

Dr. Terni had to give in despite himself.

"That's easy. At that time, the hospital in Santo Domingo issued a death certificate that the Italian embassy in Santo Domingo gave to the Italian authorities, after which the embassy arranged for her remains to be returned to Italy."

"Yes, I guessed that was the procedure. What I want to know, though, is whether anyone did anything to ascertain whether the information given in the death certificate was true or not."

"Not that I know of."

"Not even the local police?"

"As I said, not that I know of. In that sort of case, the police here just countersign the doctors' report. There's no need for a police investigation every time someone dies."

"Why did the Italian embassy arrange for the countess's remains to be returned instead of Count Alvise Casati Vitali taking care of it himself?"

"Certain procedures have to be performed by the embassy. You can't just load a body onto a plane like normal luggage. You need authorizations that only the embassy can grant."

"Does the embassy have a copy of the hospital report?"

"Unfortunately, no. That's what the Padua district attorney asked for. We sent the request to the hospital and the police authorities in Santo Domingo, and we still haven't gotten anything back from them."

"In your opinion, are hospital or police authorities, or both, being purposely reticent about this?"

"We're talking about pieces of paper dating back twenty years. In my opinion, there's little hope of finding them, whether the hospital and police want to or not."

"OK, another question then: At that time, was Count Alvise Casati Vitali alone or was he accompanied by someone else?"

"What do you mean?"

"I mean, was he seeing other women?"

As I said it, I realized I was thinking out loud and hadn't really intended to ask Terni that. I was so taken with my role as detective that nothing would stop me until he gave me the name of the killer.

"I'm sorry, Ranieri, but are you seriously asking the embassy about some man's illicit affairs?"

I tried to backtrack a little. "What I mean is, is there any way to trace the visas that were issued to other people who may have accompanied the count?"

"Perhaps the flight's passenger list can be traced. You'll have to ask the airline, if it still exists, and if they kept the list. Now, I'm sorry, Ranieri, but I have a lot to do and there are people who actually need my help. So if there's nothing else, I'll say good-bye."

"Dr. Terni, I'm going to talk to the hospital and the airline. Can I call you if I have more questions?"

"Of course."

The temperature had risen above a hundred degrees in the room, and when we shook hands in good-bye, it was like wringing out two sweat-soaked rags.

I found Julio sitting in the foyer where I'd waited earlier. We left the building and headed for the car to go to the clinic at Corazones Unidos, which Julio said was the fanciest hospital in the rich Gazcue district and thus, perhaps, where Arcadio was born and his mother had died.

Once we were in the car, I sent an email asking Fabrizio to find out which airline the count had used back then.

After about twenty minutes, Julio and I reached the clinic, and, from the entrance alone, it was clear that this was a place for the elite. At reception, I was greeted by a smiling woman who asked how she could help. I explained my complicated request, with Julio acting as interpreter. She accompanied us to the general administration office and introduced us to the clerk, Zacarias. After some fruitless digital research accompanied by colorful curses in his native tongue, Zacarias told us he'd have to conduct a manual search for the file, because there was no electronic database for cases from that time. Unfortunately, due to lack of space, the paper archives had been moved to an outbuilding. We would have to wait until somebody looked for the file and brought it to the head office. I tried to ask Zacarias how long it would take, and he gave me a rather confused look, then he turned to Julio and spoke very quietly to him and then to me, but I didn't understand a word.

Julio explained paternally what I should have figured out myself.

"If you want those documents, you'll have to give him a tip."

After lengthy negotiations, we fixed an appointment for the next day, and if Zacarias brought me the documents I had requested, I would pay him fifty dollars.

While I was leaving the hospital, I received Fabrizio's email; he had done an Internet search and found that, in March 1991, the only airline that flew between Milan and Santo Domingo was Alitalia. I sent him another email asking him to check whether the airline could tell him if anyone else was on board with the count and the newborn Arcadio. By now, I was beginning to feel more like a detective than a reporter. However, an email from Piovesan asking me to send him some copy for an article immediately brought me back to why I was really on the island.

Thankful for modern technology, whereby I could write an article without being obliged to stay in the hotel, I asked Julio to take me to a nearby beach, where I could catch the last few hours of sunlight. About half an hour later, we reached Boca Chica, a sandy beach with coconut trees, emerald green sea, and a blinding sun. Sadistically, I emailed Fabrizio a detailed description of that paradise. Strangely, he didn't reply, probably due to company policy forbidding the use of obscene language.

I took my shirt and trousers off since, just by chance, I'd put on my bathing trunks that morning, and then took out my laptop. Julio and I found beach chairs and umbrellas near the kiosk—known locally as a *chiringuito*—closest to the parking lot.

The beauty of the island was distracting, but I finally settled down to write the article for Piovesan and the rest of the clan.

CHAPTER EIGHTEEN

As I didn't have much to work from, I focused on the problems we faced gathering information about past events that could give us insight into the recent homicides. Of course, I didn't hide the fact that the primary source of the problems was the uncooperative officials at the Italian embassy.

When I sent the text to the paper for editing, I knew it wouldn't be enough for the article that Piovesan had in mind. However, there was nothing I could do about it so, like me, he'd just have to wait for the file from Corazones Unidos.

As soon as I'd sent the email, I closed my laptop and looked up at the amazing paradise around me. Again I thought sadistically of Fabrizio, trapped in the office with Piovesan, and then I went into the ocean for a swim. The water was so warm I wondered if there was some sort of hidden thermostat. The only problem was my bandaged hand, which the surgeon had said I couldn't get wet.

I slowly entered the water, enjoying each single magical moment, and waded for about five minutes with my right hand up in the air. Not being able to dive into that crystalline water was like being at the wheel of a Ferrari and not being allowed to go faster than thirty miles per hour.

A little frustrated, I returned to the beach, expecting to see a watchful Julio sitting under the umbrella. From about ten yards away, I realized with horror that my bag was missing and with that sense of panic and impotence we all feel in such moments, I had made a mental list of everything that was missing before I even reached the umbrella. Between my laptop, wallet, all my documents, the company Blackberry, and a thousand dollars I'd changed, I'd lost my whole life.

I looked around for any suspicious characters to chase after, but the faces I saw immediately convinced me that was not a good idea. I imagined that whoever it was had been watching me from the start, so I decided it was pointless to search up and down the two miles of beach.

Near the *chiringuito,* I saw Julio chatting with some girls lying in the sun. I shouted at him furiously and, perhaps due to the shock, spoke in a language that surprised even me. "Bloody hell, Julio! They've cleaned us out!

Seeing as I had always spoken to Julio in Italian, he was equally surprised by my mixture of Spanish, Esperanto, and northern Italian dialect.

Obviously confused, Julio answered in Spanish. "Ricardo, I don't understand . . . What's going on?"

"While you were chatting up those chicks, they nicked my bag! That's what happened. Son of a bitch!"

"Sorry, Riccardo, what does 'nicked' mean?"

"It means we're up to our necks in shit!"

I did nothing to hide my anger, but shouting helped me calm down a bit. I explained to Julio again what had happened, and he was clearly mortified but hoped that we hadn't lost everything. I explained that bag thieves often contacted their victims to try and sell back their documents, and if that happened, I was willing to pay any price to have my laptop and Blackberry back so I wouldn't have to tell Piovesan what had happened.

Thank god Zacarias wasn't giving me the documents until tomorrow. I could just imagine what it would mean asking for duplicates from the embassy when I'd just finished insulting them in the paper.

In a rotten mood and penniless, I decided we should go back to the hotel before anyone stole the wheels off the car, as well.

I collected my keys from reception and told them what had happened on the beach so that, should the thieves try to contact me, the hotel staff would be aware I was willing to negotiate.

When Julio heard me telling reception about it, he nearly doubled over laughing.

"Do you really think the thieves are going to come knocking at reception?"

"How else can they contact me?"

"It's not that difficult to work out, Riccardo. It's us who have to go to them."

"We've got to go to them? How do we know where to find them?"

"There are two or three bars where it's sufficient to say a word, and magically you find everything you're looking for."

Julio's surprising knowledge of the underworld made me suspect that his distraction at the beach might not be a coincidence, and I realized I'd have to be much more cautious and attentive in the future, and also that I'd have to change my attitude and remember that, even though I was in the Caribbean, I wasn't there on holiday, but searching for information about the facts that had led to all the violence back home.

While I was resolving to be as watchful as a tiger hunting in the jungle, Julio was trying to attract my attention with gestures I could not comprehend. At the limit of my patience, I asked what the hell he was trying to say.

Julio calmly replied, "Ricardo, for the love of God, you dropped your room key. You are more absent-minded than a woman in love!"

To the list of resolutions I'd just made, I added waking my brain up. I told Julio to wait for me at reception while I went to my room for a shower.

Apart from washing the saltwater off, the shower helped give me some courage to face the evening, which promised to be rather interesting. I quickly dressed as anonymously as my luggage would allow, in jeans and a white sweater, and then I put my remaining five hundred euros in my pocket and went back down to the lobby.

Julio clearly had doubts about my ability to handle this sort of negotiation and suggested I wait for him at the hotel, as he said it would be easier to find the property without me. There was no way that was going to happen, and I made him understand that not only would I be accompanying him, as I didn't trust anyone anymore, but I would handle the negotiations myself. Obviously offended, Julio took me to a bar so full of thugs it made Alcatraz look like a convent. To be honest, it wasn't so much a bar as a bamboo roof with an old fridge underneath.

There were about ten customers standing around holding beers, leaning against whatever was strong enough to hold them up. When I got out of the car, their eyes felt like an X-ray machine. I tried to look confident, but I don't think I was very convincing. Julio asked one of them if he'd heard anything about a theft that day on the beach. At the same time, a guy the size of an elephant with a scar-lined face and an insolent attitude said something to me in Spanish that I didn't understand. I tried repeating the same words I'd heard Julio use to explain what I was looking for. I probably made some mistakes, though, because the giant just grimaced at me disdainfully.

Overcoming the impulse to thump the oversized Mike Tyson, I tried to simply humiliate him by maintaining the cold, detached attitude I'd learned from my European, middle-class education. I'm not sure whether he was impressed with the lesson in style I gave him, but what I do know is that when he moved toward me, Julio didn't even have to tell me to get in the car; I was already inside with the door closed and my seatbelt tightly fastened.

Julio and I headed to the next thieves' den, any self-confidence I'd formerly felt or feigned now completely gone. I felt myself falling prey to tangible fear and the eternal, unanswered question: What the hell was I doing?

The second bar was quite close to the beach we'd been on that afternoon.

Again, the establishment was little more than a few poles holding up a cane roof. This time, however, we didn't even have to get out of the car. As soon as Julio pulled up in his Peugeot, we were met by two young guys who, to my relief, didn't seem as menacing as the others. In fact, as they were walking over to our car, I sized them up and determined that, if it came to a fight, I might stand a chance.

With newfound courage, if not my former recklessness, I leaned toward Julio to listen to what they were saying. The first kid placed his hands on the car door and leaned over to look inside, greeting Julio with the typical American high five. As he leaned in, I saw an enormous pistol hooked to his belt and my naïve hopes of standing a chance evaporated. I decided it was best to be as diplomatic as possible to avoid the risk of rubbing this armed child the wrong way.

Confirming my worst suspicions, Julio seemed well versed in how to handle the underworld, and the two kids promised us an answer the next day.

Despite the importance of finding everything that had been stolen, I sincerely hoped that Julio didn't want to go to the third bar. He did, of course, and even added that it was the most dangerous of them all. According to him, the second anything was stolen in Santo Domingo, in the Toro bar in Puerto Plata, they already knew what it was and who'd done it.

The name Puerto Plata reminded me that, when Fabrizio researched the count's business in Santo Domingo, he'd found several donations to the orphanage in that *barrio*. It was immediately apparent just how dangerous the area was: absolutely no street lights, just small beacons strategically placed so cars had to perform a slow slalom under the watchful eyes of small groups of armed men, the self-appointed customs officers of the *barrio*.

As we entered an alley, I was surprised and comforted to see a uniformed police officer approach. Strangely, though, he greeted Julio with a high five, as if the police were committed to total informality in that neighborhood.

As we pulled over to the roadside next to one of the makeshift beacons, I realized that what I'd thought was a police officer was just someone wearing a police jacket with a filthy pair of jeans and a dirty button-down shirt. I suddenly had a moment of clarity: here I was risking my neck in this godforsaken place to try to understand why my neck was at risk at home! Brilliant, Riccardo!

The fake cop leaned against my car door to keep his eye on me while talking to Julio. When I realized Julio was talking about me, explaining why on earth I was there, I tried to smile convincingly at the man, despite my innards being knotted in fear. He looked from Julio to me and smiled back, showing an amazing array of about ten teeth, if not fewer. Most likely owing to this defect, every time he spoke, he spat like a camel.

When Julio had finished his explanation, the fake cop, smiling and spitting, gave us the name of the person he thought was on shift for thefts at the Boca Chica beach that day.

I was so busy trying to avoid getting spat on that I almost forgot how afraid I was. At the end of their conversation, I decided to go with my gut feeling and asked our shady companion if he knew the Casati Vitali family by any chance. I spoke in Italian and looked to Julio to translate, but there was no need. As soon as he heard the name Casati Vitali our *barrio* host took of his hat, which had been hiding imminent baldness, and with even more saliva to shower our Peugeot, launched into a soggy profusion of compliments about how generous they were, especially Count Alvise.

Encouraged by his friendly reaction, I asked him what he thought about the count's son, Arcadio. His answer, I confess, didn't surprise me: the boy would have had to grow up a great deal before he earned the same respect as his father. Still encouraged, I asked him if he'd ever known Arcadio's mother, and again his answer came as no surprise as he stated in a funereal tone that nobody had ever really known his mother. I thought it better not to dig any further in case he became suspicious about why I was so interested.

The man clearly thought I'd been dropping the name of the count's family to give him an impression of my importance, because when we asked how I could get my stolen property back, not only did he refuse to discuss money, he even told me I'd get a surprise at my hotel the next morning. We finally said good-bye like old friends, and he made me promise to say hello to the count for him.

On the way back, Julio couldn't compliment me enough for my reckless bravado, and I thought it pointless to tell him the truth.

As we were returning to the hotel, I thought over what he'd said about the Count of Nogaredo. It was obvious that he was widely known in Santo Domingo because he owned several thousand acres of farmland, but that the underworld knew him as well opened a whole new range of ideas that I hadn't considered so far.

The bits of information I was collecting were like X-ray glimpses of an older painting the count had concealed behind a shiny new one.

When we got to the hotel, I paid for some time at an Internet terminal and sent an email to the paper, asking them to forward it to Giulia. I wished I could have spoken to one of her detectives to see if they were making any progress, but it was almost midnight in Santo Domingo and six in the morning in Italy, so I gave up for the day and went to bed.

I spent the night trying to concoct plausible explanations for everything that had happened, but around five in the morning, I decided that not only had the count's wife died during childbirth, but her child wasn't even his.

By then, though, the count must have been so taken with the idea of having an heir to his title that he began to search for a way around the obstacle that fate had placed between him and the continuance of his dynasty.

The donations to the orphanage smelled decidedly like an exchange, and I was willing to bet that an investigation into the count's bank transfers would have revealed many more suspicious "donations" to the local authorities that registered the births. If I was right, the famous certificate that the industrious clerk at Corazones Unidos had promised me the next morning would never arrive, or if it did, it would be as fake as Julio's Rolex.

I still had to figure out the connection between all this and the murders at Frassanelle, though. The most plausible theory was that Massimo had accidentally discovered that the count's blood was incompatible with his son's, which unleashed the fury that had led to his and his wife's deaths. The text he'd sent me in a desperate attempt to save himself and Patty should have been my death sentence, as well. Massimo must have thought that discovering an illegal adoption, despite any pain it could cause, would never be sufficient motive for murder.

No matter how hard I tried, though, the piece I couldn't make fit was Stella's murder. She'd handled all the bank accounts, managed the entire estate, and she was grandmother to Arcadio and mother to Count Alvise, so surely she must have known everything already.

Some missing information would never be found in Santo Domingo, so I decided there and then that as soon as I got my cell phone, computer, and passport back, I'd fly home to Italy.

CHAPTER NINETEEN

On my way to breakfast the next morning, the clerk at the reception desk called me over to tell me there was a package for me.

I took the package and, despite my desire to open it right away, feigned nonchalance and continued to the breakfast room. As soon as I sat down, I ripped it open.

As the fake cop had promised, I was very much surprised. There was no trace of my wallet or the thousand dollars, but there was a handwritten note saying the money would go to the Puerto Plata orphanage. Still, they had returned my Blackberry, computer, and—thank God—my passport.

I turned on my cell phone to see if there were any messages from Italy, and as I stood up to go and get my breakfast, Julio appeared and clapped me on the shoulder and then began his gluttonous ritual, canvassing the buffet and eating more food than a bear on waking up in spring.

I joined him on his second lap and told him I'd decided to go back to Italy as soon as I'd spoken to Zacarias at the hospital. I had an open return, so all I had to do was book a seat on the flight I wanted. Over a roast shank of pork and a jam brioche, Julio expressed his deep regret for my decision, as I was robbing him of such a pleasant companion. He seemed so sincere that I didn't ask if it was the money he was paid to help me that he'd really miss.

After coffee, I turned to my Blackberry and found two unread messages from Fabrizio. The first said Piovesan was furious about my lack of progress at both the embassy and the clinic, but the second message made me sit up. Apparently, Giulia had ordered an arrest warrant for the Count of Nogaredo. I presumed she'd reached the same conclusions I had regarding Count Alvise's illegal actions when his wife died, but I wondered what actual evidence she'd unearthed. Perhaps Giulia was hoping an arrest would put pressure on the count so she could get him to explain how those distant events were linked to the recent murders.

Anxious to wrap things up and get back to Padua, I decided to tell Julio to quit inhaling the buffet and take me to the hospital.

Despite the fact that the sky was still cloudy, it felt even hotter than the day before. Julio and I reached the hospital in less than thirty minutes, but by the time we arrived, I was sweating so much I'd have been a strong contender in a wet T-shirt contest.

Julio asked for Zacarias at the front desk, and, like the first time, we were taken to the administration office. When Zacarias saw us, he came over shaking his head and said what I'd imagined he might: there was no trace of the count's wife's file. It had either never existed, or, more likely, somebody had taken it.

We wasted ten minutes arguing over what I should pay Zacarias, who'd done the job but without the required result. In the end, we settled on twenty-five euros. Unfortunately, not even Mario Draghi could have convinced the man that a euro was worth more than a dollar.

On our way back to the hotel, a storm broke out of nowhere, and within moments it was coming down so hard we couldn't see more than two or three yards ahead of us. The road looked like a carwash. Julio managed to park less than fifteen feet from the hotel, but that was still far enough for me to get soaked to the skin as I ran inside. The stiff bandage, which the equally stiff surgeon had put on my hand, was as soggy as the rest of me. It had been ten days since my surgery, so I figured I'd go to the hospital to have the bandage removed when I got back.

At the hotel reception desk, I asked the clerk who had given me the package earlier if she could find out when the next direct flight to Italy was. She searched the airport website and found that Alitalia flight AZ 697 left Santo Domingo at one fifteen and arrived at Milan Malpensa at six forty-five the following morning. Perfect. I asked her to book a seat in my name and then asked Julio to wait for me in the lobby while I packed. As soon as I reached my room, I tore off my wet clothes, jumped in the shower, and within ten minutes, was back in the lobby. I left the clerk five euros, calculated more or less at Zacarias's exchange rate, for the two bottles of water I had consumed in my room and then headed for the door.

On reaching it, however, Julio and I drew up short. The rain was coming down even harder, and there was a river raging down the sidewalk between us and the Peugeot. It was almost eleven and the airport was about a one-hour drive from the hotel, so there was no time to lose, but we decided to wait a few minutes to see whether the rain would slow down or not.

Watching the downpour in a trance, I couldn't help wondering why I was so useless at getting to the airport. At least I'd be sure to go to the right one this time.

After about ten minutes, I went to ask the receptionist if she had any idea how long the storm would last. With a fatalistic air worthy of a Greek philosopher, she told me the forecasts said it would last about three days, but what really got my goat was that Julio happily confirmed the forecast.

I couldn't help protesting. "Julio, if you already knew it wouldn't stop raining for three days, why have we been waiting?"

"Because you are the boss, obviously!"

I never thought I'd miss Paolo.

Calling on all my self-control, I avoided arguing uselessly with him, and, deciding I shouldn't take anything for granted on that island of nutcases, I told him to run. Under the fury of the black sky, we stoically crossed the fifteen feet that separated us from the car. When we finally got in and closed the doors, we looked as if we'd jumped in the ocean, but at least the car started, and we set off.

Traveling along the main roads in Santo Domingo, you're struck by a strange comfort level with danger. All the traffic seems to travel down the center of the road and constantly invade the opposite lane. Just before each crash, a horn sounds like some sort of primeval sonar, and somebody gets out of the way.

On a number of occasions along the way, I reconsidered my convictions regarding religious faith. Like the most fervent of pagans, I called on the god of the road, of the lampposts, and of the cars coming the other way. I explored new theological horizons by calling on the patron saints of brakes and tire pressure. Finally, I had a real epiphany when the tiny Peugeot suddenly came face-to-face with a semi the size of a mountain, so close we could count the dead flies on the headlights.

At about twelve twenty, I got out of Julio's car and, resisting the temptation to kiss the pavement, entered the airport. As usual, I'd totally broken the rule of checking in for international flights at least two hours beforehand. I'd always found that the risk of missing the plane was offset by the fact that there was never a line at check-in, and the ground staff was anxious to get you through so they could close boarding.

I checked my luggage and went through security without a hitch, after which I had fifteen minutes left: a luxury in my book. I decided to buy two bottles of duty-free rum to drink with my friends at Enrico's restaurant at Frassanelle.

While I was boarding, I realized that, in all the stress of driving with Julio, I'd forgotten to call Fabrizio to tell him I was coming home. As

I stepped onto the plane, I scrolled to his number under the watchful eye of the flight attendant, but I hadn't considered the Italian prefix, so a seductive South American voice asked me to check the number. I tried again with the prefix 039, with the same result, so I sat in my seat and tried again with 0039, but the South American lady was still there. I went back to calling on all the unknown local divinities, cursing that voice even though it was so seductive, looking for the + sign on my Blackberry. I was about to give in to the supernatural powers that keypad symbols have of becoming invisible when you're in a hurry, when it magically appeared at the top right. I dialed the number with +39, and the seductive voice was no more. After two rings, one of the flight attendants began ritually describing the plane's safety measures, heedless of my desperate need to talk to Italy. At the fifth ring, I realized I might be on foot when I got to Malpensa.

When I finally heard Fabrizio's voice, it reassured me that there was some wonderful god out there, after all.

"Ciao, Riccardo. How are things?"

"Fine, Fabrizio. Thanks. Listen, I don't have much time because the plane is taking off. I arrive at six forty-five tomorrow morning at Malpensa. Can you send someone to pick me up? Is there any news about the murders?"

" . . . "

"Fabrizio?"

" . . . "

"Hello, Fabrizio?"

" . . . "

I looked at my dead Blackberry and had a vision of the battery charger in my carry-on, but the flight attendant was already asking passengers to switch off all their electronic devices.

I was still convinced there were certain divinities out there, but they were looking slightly less impressive now.

Resigned to my fate, I leaned back in my seat.

The return flight was just as endless as the outgoing one; this time I wasn't able to sleep due to a horde of so many babies that I imagined a new baby boom was actively underway.

The nursery plane landed on time in Malpensa.

The temperature was much milder there, and the weather was much more pleasant than in the Caribbean.

CHAPTER TWENTY

After picking up my luggage, I went to catch the Malpensa Express from the airport to Milan Cadorna station.

I stopped at a newsstand on the way to buy the *Corriere* and the *Repubblica*. As I imagined, they'd never heard of *Mattino di Padova* in Milan, but I could hardly blame the newsagent for that. When I was first contacted for a job with the *Mattino*, like a typical provincial Milanese, I didn't even know if Padua was before or after Vicenza.

I made it onto the train five minutes before it was due to depart, so I plugged my phone in to recharge it and started reading the *Corriere*. I must admit I opened the paper with mixed emotions, nerves, and burning curiosity, because I knew that the bombshell that had been dropped when the count was arrested would make headlines in the national press, as well. In spite of that, I certainly wasn't prepared for the punch in the guts when I saw the article at the foot of the front page: "Alvise Casati Vitali, Count of Nogaredo, Commits Suicide." I read the headline two or three times in the hope I'd misunderstood it somehow, but the subtitle wiped away all my doubts: "Another victim in the Frassanelle case."

Still suffering from shock, I read the ten lines of the article, which continued inside on page eighteen, while my cell phone came back to life and started twittering louder than an aviary full of canaries. In the typical Italian way, Giulia had informed the count of the impending arrest in advance, and to avoid the dishonor of prison, he'd decided to shoot himself in the head in the cellar at his castle in Montemerlo. The article explained that the warrant for his arrest mainly referred to crimes of false parental authority and illegal adoption. The facts given fit with what I'd learned in Santo Domingo, but there was nothing to be pleased about. I was still firmly convinced that while the count might not have committed the murders, he was the key to finding out who the killer was. You don't have to be Sherlock Holmes to see that the count's death would make the search for the truth even more difficult.

It was seven thirty in the morning when I called Fabrizio, who answered sleepily, "Riccardo, where are you?"

"On the Malpensa Express to Milan Cadorna."

"Great, so you're back in Italy. We've all been trying to contact you for the last two days—Piovesan, Dal Nero. When will you be here?"

"I'll reach Cadorna in half an hour, then I'll take the subway to Central Station and get the first train to Padua. That should put me in the office by this afternoon. What's been going on in the meantime?"

"Have you heard about the count's suicide?"

"Yes, I just read about it in the *Corriere*. Is it true?"

"What do you mean, is it true? You just said you read about it in the *Corriere*."

"No, idiot. I mean, do you think it's true the count committed suicide, or did he get some help?" I probed.

"Oh, got it! No, it seems like a real suicide. Dal Nero sent some officers to his house, and when they got there, he said he wanted to collect a few things, then went down to the cellar and shot himself. Did you discover anything in Santo Domingo?"

"Sure, I discovered who stole my bag with my laptop and Blackberry and a thousand bucks in Boca Chica."

"No, I meant did you discover anything about the case?"

"I know; I just wanted you to understand that if I hadn't gone to Santo Domingo, I would have saved myself time and money, which I didn't get back, by the way."

"Fool. Good luck explaining that to Grandi and Piovesan."

"Ooh, I'm trembling with fear. I did learn one thing, though."

"What?"

"The count had woven an intricate web of relations with the local underworld. He's better known in the poorest *barrio* than in the embassy. What did Dal Nero want me for?"

"Probably because she's crazy about you, and also because she wants to put another of her henchmen on your heels."

"What do I do to women? Listen, Fabrizio, will you be in the office when I get there?"

"If nothing comes up, I should be."

"OK. I'll call Dal Nero now, and then, when I get to the office, you can fill me in. See you later."

"Bye, Ric."

Before calling Giulia, I read the article in the *Repubblica* to see if it gave any more details than the *Corriere*. There was nothing apart from a few statements from Arcadio suggesting the poor interviewer should consider a slightly different and certainly more profitable profession.

Torn between my desire to hear her voice and the anxiety that Paolo had infected me with, I finally decided to call Giulia.

"Giulia? Hi, it's Riccardo. How are things?"

"Hi, Riccardo. Fine, thanks. What about you, are you back from Santo Domingo yet?"

I might have been kidding myself, but I almost got the impression she was happy to hear from me.

"I landed at Malpensa an hour ago, and now I'm on the Malpensa Express for Milan. I should reach Padua about two."

"I suppose you heard about the count?"

"I read it in the *Corriere*. I'm sorry, because I'm convinced he was the key to everything."

"Exactly. Did you find out anything in Santo Domingo?"

"Sure! I discovered they're terrible drivers, and when it rains, if you can't swim like Michael Phelps, you'll drown."

"Riccardo."

"Sorry, Giulia. I found out that the count was better known with the underworld than he was at the Italian embassy."

"Can you come by my office later this afternoon?"

"So you did miss me?"

"Riccardo."

"Yes, as soon as I get to Padua, OK?"

"OK. See you later and . . . Well, yes."

"Well yes. . . what?"

"Well, yes, maybe I did miss you."

"You missed me?"

"No! And no more bullshit! Bye."

"Bye."

When a woman knows you're courting her and wants to lead you on, sometime she just keeps you walking on a tightrope without a safety net for ages.

Luckily, I'm not a starry-eyed teenager, so her little slight rolled right off my manly back.

Who was I kidding? Once I was on the train to Padua, I spent the three-hour journey pointlessly mulling over the meaning of Giulia's joke. I considered it from her point of view over and over again, wondering what she thought and what she thought I thought. I examined it from a totally unbiased standpoint and then from one side and then the other. In the end, I gave up. The only truth that was clear to me was that I was falling helplessly for her. A moment later, I was in Padua.

I caught a taxi to police headquarters, and when I entered, there was Silvia on duty in her usual spot.

"Hi, Silvia, how are you?"

"Welcome back, Riccardo. I'm fine, thanks. And you? I heard you went to Santo Domingo; I'm so jealous!"

"Well, yeah, but it was hardly a holiday."

"Oh, you poor thing! Yeah, I can just imagine how boring it was for you, while we were here enjoying ourselves with a week of nonstop rain!"

"You might not believe it, but going somewhere like that without being able to swim in the ocean because of my hand, and then spending the evenings trying to find the bag someone stole with my whole life in it, is not like a romantic getaway to Club Meditérranée."

"Come off it, Riccà, otherwise I'll pop you one . . . ," Silvia joked. Then, serious again, she said, "Dal Nero is waiting for you in her office."

"I'll go right up. See you later, Silvia."

While I was going up in that elevator that moved slower than a dumbwaiter, I realized that, in my rush to see Giulia, I'd forgotten how I looked. After an eleven-hour flight and three plus hours on trains, I needed a shave, I probably had bags under my eyes, and I felt dirtier than an Italian politician's conscience. What's more, instead of minty-fresh breath, I was exhaling a concentrated mix of nuclear waste—just the right weapon to seduce a woman. It was too late now to go home and freshen up, so all I could do was hope that Giulia liked men with a neglected, or even downtrodden, air.

Giulia's office door was ajar, so I knocked and went in. She was sitting behind her desk and Paolo was sitting in front of her.

Giulia briefly greeted me and invited me in. I went over and shook her hand, still using my left, of course, and kissed her on the cheek, holding my breath in the hope she wouldn't get a whiff. Then I greeted Paolo and sat down in front of her desk.

"Apologies for my appearance, but I haven't had a chance to go home and freshen up yet."

I didn't expect her to say, "Don't worry, I like the Bruce Willis look," but neither did I expect her response.

"Yes, you look really tired."

I bit my lip, but I wasn't going to let her get away with that, and I coolly replied, "Looks as though you've been working hard recently, as well?"

Paolo began fidgeting in his chair.

Giulia held my gaze, then a small smile crept over her lips as she asked, "Did your trip go OK?"

"If you're speaking in strictly travel terms, yes, and on the way back, I even went to the right airport. But if you're talking about digging up good information in Santo Domingo, then I'm afraid not."

"What do you mean?"

"I wasted tons of time at the Italian embassy just to find out that Dr. Terni, the industrious official who works there, suffers from very sweaty hands. At Corazones Unidos Hospital, for the modest sum of twenty-five euros, I found out they've lost the file regarding how the count's wife died during childbirth. The only upside, which cost me a thousand dollars, was having my bag stolen because while I was trying to find it, I spoke to one of the local thugs, who knows the Casati Vitali family better even than Arcadio does."

Before replying, Giulia let out a deep I-told-you-so sigh. She said, "Yeah, I knew it would be a waste of your time. You should know that when we requested certain documents from the Italian embassy, we told their officials that they were sworn to secrecy and weren't authorized to give anybody else information. What's more, we already knew about the local affairs of the Casati Vitali family, and we knew that any document you might unearth would be fake or, shall we say, adapted to the count's needs. Still, the fact that you saw firsthand that the count was well known in the local underworld does confirm my suspicions."

"What about you? Have you learned anything new?"

"To a certain extent, although I hoped I would be able to force the count to tell me the truth so we could solve the case. Everything is much more complicated now."

"But doesn't that famous file you asked the Italian embassy for help us in any way?"

"As you might guess, that famous file is basically his wife's medical case history, and in my opinion, it's totally unreliable, if not completely fake. The people at the embassy told me that finding a report from twenty years ago in a Santo Domingo hospital would probably be as likely as winning the lottery. Strangely enough, though, when we requested the file, it arrived just two days later. I don't believe a single line of what is written on those forms."

"But you said there was some news."

"Yes. We really did win the lottery."

"What do you mean?"

"We did some digging at Monselice Hospital, where Dr. Salvioni worked at the time Countess Maria Teresa died, and do you know what we discovered?"

"What?"

"The countess suffered from a corpus luteum disorder."

"What?"

"She suffered from endocrine sterility."

"What sterility?"

"For God's sake, Riccardo, she couldn't have children!"

I had no answer to that one and asked in confusion, "So, wait, what do you think happened to the countess?"

"I can't exclude the possibility that the count had his wife killed, probably by some hit man from Santo Domingo. In fact, you just confirmed that the count really is connected to the underworld down there, which would explain his extreme gesture of suicide. The crimes I accused him of couldn't have been such an unbearable burden, but there was the chance we'd discover he'd killed his wife."

"But why would he kill the Salvionis and try to kill me?"

"Because with that text message, you were all a threat to his secret. When I realized that Arcadio couldn't be Count Alvise's son, I asked the Santo Domingo police to investigate the death of the countess."

"That's great. You've practically solved the case!"

"Afraid not, Riccardo. There are still too many things that don't fit. For a start, I don't think the count personally killed the Salvionis, because given his age, he wouldn't have been strong enough. What's more, Roncadelle's murder seems pointless."

"Maybe old Stella found out that Arcadio wasn't Alvise's biological son."

"I think she'd always known. However, if the count was strong enough to kill his own adoptive mother, could he really be so weak that he'd kill himself over an arrest warrant?"

"Maybe he was having a bad day?"

"Riccardo."

"I'm sorry, but I thought it was finally falling into place."

"If you want to know what I think, I believe that the count may well have been guilty of numerous crimes, including the murder of his wife, but in this case, he was more the victim."

"So who's the psycho going around killing everyone?"

"Before we can understand who, we've got to determine why."

Paolo, feeling excluded from the conversation, needed to make his presence felt with his usual elegant style. "Good idea, I'll make a note of that."

After looking disdainfully at Paolo, Giulia resumed. "There's something else I can't figure out."

"What's that?"

"If Dr. Salvioni knew Arcadio wasn't the count's son, and maybe even suspected the count had had his wife killed, why did he wait until now to do something?"

"Because Arcadio was such a jerk about beating us at golf!"

"Riccardo."

"Giulia, all joking aside, I know people who really would kill their mother to win a game."

Now it was my turn for her disdainful look.

"The only thing that's certain is that the case isn't closed. Far from it. What's more," she added, looking me straight in the eye, "is that we have no idea how all this new information might affect the *detente* between you and the killer. Therefore, Officer Battiston will remain closer to you than a dead fly on your windscreen."

"Great. I missed having Paolo breathing down my neck . . ."

"Would you prefer the killer?"

"Perhaps I would."

"Get out!"

So the reformed Battiston-Ranieri duo left the DA's office to go to the *Mattino* and face the wrath of Piovesan and company, which would be considerable in light of the cost and poor outcome of my jaunt to the Caribbean.

After defying all laws of physics by managing to park a ten-foot-long car in an eight-foot space, Paolo and I entered the *Mattino* building, to be greeted warmly as always by Giannino.

I left Paolo to keep him company and went up to the editorial office, where Fabrizio and Gibbo were working on the article. Before he even said hello, Piovesan immediately cleared up any doubts as to the generosity of our HR office, telling me I'd only be refunded for my documented expenses. If government offices took such a strict line, nobody there would ever have done any work.

I gave them a detailed account of my trip to Santo Domingo. Both Gibbo and Fabrizio expressed their disappointment when I told them about my attempts at resistance with the two girls in the nightclub. Shaking his head, Gibbo claimed that in those extenuating circumstances, company policy should include an exception to the documented expenses rule.

When I'd finished, they had enough material for a good article. To the great relief of Fabrizio, who said I should go under full-scale decontamination to get rid of the smell of my sweat and breath, I finally decided to go home and get some well-earned rest.

CHAPTER TWENTY-ONE

When we arrived home, Paolo and I had to fight off Mila and Newton's joyful assault.

I stayed under the shower for forty-five minutes and then lay down on the bed without even eating. It was only eight in the evening, but I fell right to sleep and didn't wake up until nine the following morning.

A few minutes later, I found Paolo arguing with the coffee machine in the kitchen.

"I was just thinking about coming to wake you," he said by way of greeting.

"Paolo, I was way behind on my sleep. That was the best I've slept since I was eighteen."

"You might have been behind before, but you've definitely caught up now. Don't you have to go to work?"

"You're worse than Piovesan. No, I've got other plans this morning."

"Really?"

While he was talking, his argument with the coffee machine was taking a turn for the worse as far as my stock of expensive coffee was concerned.

"Paolo, you're trying to squish a wafer into the container that's meant for capsules."

"Really? That's why no coffee comes out. Shit, I've been trying for half an hour!"

"Leave it. I'll do it."

"So?"

"So, what?"

"Are you still asleep, Riccardo? What plans have you got for today?"

"Ah, right . . . I've got to go to the hospital and get my beloved surgeon to take this messed-up bandage off, then I'll celebrate an evening of luxury when I can finally take a shower without it!"

I was washed and rested, and I'd even managed to shave without cutting my throat open, and now at last, I was going to have the damn bandage taken off. If happiness is counted in small things, I was happy right then.

But happiness is the most fleeting of all emotions. In fact, I could never have imagined the excruciating pain I'd be suffering soon after when the surgeon removed the bandage and stitches from my poor hand.

When Paolo and I arrived at the hospital, he insisted on parking in the area reserved for ambulances. After the talking-to he'd received the week before from Giulia about not letting me out of his sight, he wouldn't listen when I tried to explain that the circumstances were completely different and ordered me to get out of the car.

We had to wait an hour before they called me, and when Dr. Migliorini opened the door to her surgery, she recognized me straight away.

She invited me in saying, "So, Mr. . . . um . . . Ranieri, right?"

"Ranieri, right."

"How are you?"

"Fine. My hand doesn't hurt at all, and I can't wait to get this thing off."

"Remind me, when were you operated on?"

"I think it must be about ten days ago."

Pointing to the couch, she said, "Let's try cutting the bandage off. Sit down here."

She procured some scissors and disinfectant and then stood by my side and started cutting the bandage.

"Have you been in the sun, Mr. Ranieri?"

"I just got back from a work trip to Santa Domingo, but I tried to keep out of the sun."

"You didn't go in the water with this hand, did you?"

"No, of course not."

"It can't have been much fun to go to the Dominican Republic without being able to go in the sea or sunbathe."

"Oh, Doctor! You're the first one to understand! When I talk about it, everyone else just laughs at me . . ."

She smiled while still cutting away at my bandage.

"You went to Santo Domingo to look into that family, didn't you?"

Her question was no surprise. Having been overwhelmed by the press and police the day I was admitted, I imagined she'd been following the case.

"Yes, I wanted to understand what's been causing all this chaos."

"Have you figured anything out?"

"Not much, and now that the count has committed suicide, everything the detectives and I have discovered is pretty worthless."

My hand was then finally exposed in all its pale glory. It tingled all over, and I couldn't believe that it was actually attached to my body, seeing as I couldn't so much as wiggle a finger. I told the doctor, who reassured me.

"Don't worry—it's normal. Don't try to force the movements—it'll hurt too much. You'll need to gradually start doing some exercises to restore its mobility. Let me see."

The doctor examined my hand under the lamp to see how it was healing and, satisfied with the results, told me she'd take out the stitches.

"Will it hurt?"

"Nothing to it, don't worry."

I hadn't reached forty years of age without knowing that when a doctor or dentist says there's nothing to it, you'd better come prepared with opiates to treat the pain or hope your neurotransmitters have gone on strike.

I instinctively pulled back my arm. The doctor turned around to look at me. "Ranieri! You're not scared, are you?"

"Do you want me to tell the truth?"

"I don't believe it. Look at you! A grown adult acting like a child."

"It's not that I'm scared, just a bit concerned."

Who knows why, but as the doctor started sharpening and disinfecting her tools of torture, Dal Nero appeared in my mind.

"Concerned about what?"

"Look, Doctor, if it was your hand, then no problem. But unfortunately, it's mine, and though I'm not an expert in medicine, I know that I'm the one who'll feel the pain."

"What pain? Don't be ridiculous! Just a bit of discomfort, it'll only take a moment."

That moment lasted fifteen minutes, during which I found it hard to hold back my tears. I could feel the thread sliding under skin that was sensitive like only the palm and back of your hand can be, and the shooting pain was excruciating. I managed to hold my arm still, but it was a real challenge. I could feel the sweat running down my neck and back, and even being brushed by the doctor's abundant breasts wasn't much help. Still, I managed to resist both the desire to scream and the urge to scoot closer to her.

When it was finally over, I was left with an amazingly white hand, except for the spot where the bullet had passed through, where it was mainly purple with shades of gray. As my torturer had warned me, any movements I tried to make were so painful they took my breath away, so I put my hand in my pocket and swore to leave it there until it returned to normal.

"All finished, Mr. Ranieri. See, wasn't so bad, was it?"

"You want to know something, Doctor?"

"What's that?"

"Speaking from experience, the cure is much worse than the cut, if you get my meaning."

She looked at me rather confused.

"You aren't from the Veneto, are you?"

"I'm from Turin," she replied. "Why do you ask?"

"Sorry, it's just a Veneto saying. You know, like when you have a hole in a sweater, and you darn it up so thickly that it would have been better just to leave the hole?"

There is nothing more embarrassing when talking to a woman than having to explain a joke to her. The second most embarrassing thing is when she smiles pityingly at you, like Dr. Migliorini did before answering, "Ranieri, what a fuss! Now, just remember to call this rehabilitation center. Otherwise, it will take a year to get full use of your hand back. Got it?"

"Thanks for everything. I hope to see you in happier circumstances, Doctor."

"Good-bye, Mr. Ranieri. Don't get shot again, OK?"

Paolo was waiting for me with the look of someone who's been laughing his socks off and finding it hard to stop.

"What's up?" I asked.

"What a hero! I could hear everything through the door. Show me your hand."

"I can assure you the bullet hurt a lot less than what the doctor just did."

"You don't even know what real pain is."

"And you do?"

With the face of John Wayne facing down Indians, Paolo replied, "In my line of work, we're used to living with pain."

When somebody answers a straight question evasively, I usually suspect they're full of it, and in Paolo's case, I was certain.

"In your job, sure, but I was asking about you. Have you ever felt real pain?"

"Once I was clubbed on the head and I can assure you—"

I didn't let him finish. "Paolo, if I tell an officer of the law to fuck off, is it a crime?"

With the air of someone who knows his back is covered, he retorted, "Oh, yes."

"Well, do you know what?"

Not quite so sure of himself now, he said, "No, what?"

"Fuck off!"

On our way out of the hospital, Paolo and I passed the newsstand, and I bought the latest *Corriere* and *Mattino*. The count had killed himself two days before and was no longer front-page news, not even in the *Mattino*. I thought back to what Giulia had said the day Massimo was found, that time was of the essence. In fact, 90 percent of cases that are solved are solved within three days. In this case, however, after three days, the assassin still hadn't stopped killing. At least the paper had sold a few more copies than usual.

I'd told Fabrizio I wouldn't be in the office until that evening, because I hadn't known how long it'd take to get the stitches out, so I still had five or six hours free. I decided to hit the club and play around with my putter awhile, as I really wanted to play and see my friends. And who knows, maybe I'd find out who the killer was.

Paolo and I reached the club around lunchtime, and he strongly protested the idea of a quick sandwich at the bar and forced me to sit down in the restaurant. Rather than watch Paolo as he worked his way through an appetizer, entrée, and dessert, as soon as I'd finished my sliced cured beef, I decided to mingle with the other tables and say hello to the folks I knew. An air of sadness and concern had been hanging over Frassanelle for about ten days now; not only did the members not feel like smiling, but I had the impression that my being there was cause for suspicion. As I couldn't prevent them from thinking I had something to do with the deaths of their friends, I decided to go back to my table and wait for Paolo to finish his light snack. After forty minutes, I couldn't stand it any longer, so I convinced him at least to get up and have coffee at the bar.

Once again, Francesca jumped when she saw me.

"Francesca, you've got to get used to seeing me. If you jump like that every time, you're going to give yourself a heart attack," I calmly said.

"Sorry, Ranieri . . . All these deaths, you know, you can't get used to it."

Her reaction reminded me that I'd forgotten to tell Giulia about Francesca going to Bastia to ask around about me after the attempted homicide.

When I'd finished my coffee, I went to the parking lot, found a spot with reception, and called Giulia's number.

"Giulia, how are you? Can you talk?"

"Hello, Riccardo. Sure, no problem. What did you want to tell me?"

"It's probably nothing, but a few days ago one of the restaurant owners in Bastia told me that Francesca, one of the two bartenders at the Frassanelle Golf Club, had being asking about me in town."

"Normal curiosity given the circumstances, don't you think?"

"Perhaps, but not for Francesca. She's one of the shyest people around, so going around asking questions about me is really weird. Believe me, even the fact she was out is strange."

"OK, I'll ask a few questions. What's the name of the restaurant?"

"Trattoria da Aldo. Ask the owner—her name is Lucia."

"I'll let you know. Wait, are you still there?"

"Yes."

"I just spoke with the police, and you've still got Battiston until this evening, but after that you're free and an easy target again. Happy?"

"About time. They clearly don't think I'm a target anymore."

"Riccardo, all they think about is what it costs. They couldn't care less about your safety."

"That's OK. Between you and me, if the assassin wanted to kill me, he would manage it even with Paolo there."

"When I assigned Battiston to you, I knew he wouldn't stop a bullet, but he was a deterrent because the assassin wouldn't want to kill you with a witness around. He wasn't an escort as much as an extra set of eyes."

"Oh, got it . . . Do you want to talk to Paolo now?"

"No. They'll call him from the station with new orders. Tomorrow afternoon, I've got to talk to President Galli at Frassanelle. Can you be there, as well, please?"

"You don't give up, do you?"

"Give up? What?"

"Trying to seduce me!"

"Riccardo."

"OK, what time?"

"Three o'clock. Bye."

I went back into the club to break the news to Paolo.

"The party's over."

"What do you mean?"

"You've got to go back to work tomorrow."

"Like this is a party. Why? What did she say?"

"That you're with me until this evening, then they'll call you from the station to assign you to a new job."

"OK, maybe I'll call them myself."

I wanted to try out my newly free hand, so I went to the bag room, where I found Carlo and asked him for my putter.

"You got the bandage off, then?"

"That's right, but I can't play with any other irons yet, so I'll just have to make do with the putter."

"Well done. To make money, you need to play short."

"To make money I ought to go to work."

Who knows why, but every time I met Carlo I felt obliged to make trivial remarks as he quoted tired golfing clichés.

Once again, Carlo felt he had to accompany me to the putting green to watch my attempts, or probably to casually try and find out something about the case. Five minutes in, I realized there was nothing casual about it: Carlo was brazenly submitting me to a real inquisition, and when he asked me if I'd figured out who the killer was, I decided to put an end to the conversation, even at the risk of seeming rude.

"Look, I'm sorry, Carlo, but even if I had figured that out, I wouldn't tell you, and besides that, I came here to relax for a while and get my mind of all the stress this case is causing me. If you keep asking questions, I won't even manage to hit a ball, let alone relax."

"No, of course not. Sorry . . . I was just curious, you know, just chatting. You're right. Now show me how you hit it."

So leaving me alone wasn't an option.

One of the worst things about the practice green is that, even though you might try to choose a time when there's nobody else around, within a few minutes, you find yourself surrounded by players who just can't resist giving you advice. Nine times out of ten, the aim of their advice is to make them feel like they are golfology teachers, and you're the poor idiot who doesn't have a clue what he's doing.

I tried not to think about Carlo and concentrated on gripping my putter without ruining Dr. Migliorini's work. I managed to position my hand on the grip, but there was no way I could tighten it. Still, my disability wasn't that important. One of the many paradoxes of golf is that right-handed players have to guide their swing with their left, and the right hand just accompanies the movement. It's more complicated for left-handed players. In theory, the opposite is the case: the right moves and the left accompanies. However, as the majority of golf club manufacturers were concerned with limiting costs, they don't provide left-hand irons, and the instructors try to convince players that they'll be better off playing righty.

Maybe because I'd been dying to play, or because my injured hand meant that my grip was much more gentle, but I found myself doing really well. In fact, from a yard, all the balls went in the hole, and from ten yards, they all came close. Even Carlo couldn't find anything to criticize, so he abandoned his self-appointed role as teacher, dropping his last pearl of wisdom on the way.

"Good, Ranieri, very good. But remember: a long ball is never short."

Christ! No matter how hard I tried, I couldn't stop thinking about that stupid comment, like the first song you hear when you wake up in the morning. In spite of it being absolutely devoid of logic, it played in my head like a broken record.

There could only be one moral here: on the putting green, spectators are willing to spout any manner of bullshit just to mess with you.

CHAPTER TWENTY-TWO

Coming off the green, I was hot and sweaty, but I couldn't bring myself to go down to the locker room for a shower.

I knew I'd have to face my demons there sooner or later, but I just wasn't ready. At about four o'clock, Paolo and I got back in the car to go to Padua, and when we pulled out of the club, our phones began ringing at the same time.

"Hi, Fabrizio, missing me?"

"Hi, Ric. Yeah, just a bit, but I wanted to tell you we've got some news."

"You mean you didn't call me just to hear my voice? Never mind, what's up?"

"ADN-Kronos has just broadcast the news that two officials from the Italian embassy in Santo Domingo, who worked there at the time of Countess Maria Teresa's death, have been arrested. Apparently, they've been accused of hiding the murder of the dead count's dead wife."

"Murder, eh? I must confess I'm not real surprised."

"Wait, that's not all. According to the report, which mentions various witnesses, the countess wasn't even pregnant!"

"That's no revelation either."

"Why?"

"Because Dal Nero told me yesterday."

"Shit, Riccardo, how about you telling me something once in a while?"

I knew he was right, and I explained. "It's not that I didn't want to, Fabrizio, but Dal Nero swore me to secrecy. What could I do? Besides, every time I think I've figured out who the killer is, something happens that turns everything upside down."

"You thought the count's dead wife was the killer?"

"His wife, no, but his biological son, yes. Think about it. All the signs were there: the motive, the strength, given that the presumed son would be about twenty years old, and the grudge against the family. Really, the biological son was my favorite suspect. Now that's out, as well."

"Are you coming in?"

"Yes, I'll be there in half an hour."

Paolo was hanging up with his superiors, who'd told him to report to the station at eight the next morning for his new assignment. He couldn't hide the fact that he was pleased. From his point of view, the fact that I hadn't gotten injured any further meant he'd done his job successfully. And although he didn't mention it, I'm sure that a good part of his relief came from not having to see Giulia again.

I, on the other hand, was totally let down. If the count had no biological son and legitimate heir, it meant we were no closer to figuring out who the killer was. What's more, the idea that maybe there was more than one really bummed me out.

If, after fifteen days since the Salvionis had been murdered, there was still no real list of suspects, it meant that everybody must have taken the wrong approach to the investigation. Maybe we'd focused too much on the motive, while the psychology of a man able to commit those sorts of murders probably follows no sort of rationale. Or maybe we'd focused too much on the count's family and had overlooked other possibilities. I decided that after spending an hour with Fabrizio, I would go over everything that had happened from the moment I first found Massimo's body through my trip to Santo Domingo.

When I got to the office, I asked Paolo to wait at the entrance as usual, and I went up.

Grandi was with Fabrizio and said, "Ah, Ranieri! Have you heard the news?"

"Are you talking about the Italian embassy officials in Santo Domingo?"

"Yes, that, but also the fact that the countess wasn't pregnant."

"Sure"—I decided not to tell him I'd known since the day before—"but if nothing else, it means the count had a good reason to commit suicide."

"What do you mean if nothing else?" Fabrizio asked. "Is there another suspect?"

"No, it's just that of all the ideas I've gone over, I was convinced the killer was Count Alvise's unacknowledged son."

"Man. Instead of unwinding, the plot is even tighter now."

"Seriously. I'm meeting with DA Dal Nero at Frassanelle tomorrow. We'll see what she thinks."

"How's your hand, Ranieri?" Grandi asked, changing the subject.

"Fine. They took the stitches out this morning. I still can't move my fingers properly, but it should return to normal eventually."

"Do you have to keep going to the hospital?"

"Theoretically, yes, for rehabilitation, but I think I can manage without."

"Are you sure?"

"No, but the idea of someone in a white coat getting close to me again is more frightening than being left with a useless hand."

"Well, it's your hand. I'll see you guys later."

Fabrizio looked up and said, "Happy, Ric? Back on the front page tomorrow!"

"Funny. I've been hopping between the front and fifth page for ten days now. All that's left is the entertainment section, and I'll have made a tour of the whole paper."

"You never know. How are you at burlesque?"

"Fuck off. Is the article ready yet?"

"Yes, you can read the draft in our shared folder."

I read the article, fascinated by how Fabrizio had managed to describe the situation, weaving in hints from my trip to Santo Domingo, as well. He had perfectly balanced the facts with the way things work in Santo Domingo, a city that seems to continually fall victim to the influence of the rich and powerful. I thought he deserved praise.

"It's not much, but at least it's presentable. If I had time, I'd correct it from start to finish. Still, it's OK for the *Mattino*."

"Thank you. I was afraid the leading critic of the Literary Academy would reject my work. What a relief."

"Do you know what, though?"

"What?"

"I still can't figure any of it out, really. We keep finding victims, but there's no trace of the guilty parties."

"Luckily, the count killed himself, because if we had to wait for you . . ."

"I mean it, I'm not kidding. Do you know something? I think the answer must be much simpler than we've been thinking. We've been digging around in all the family dirt and making ourselves crazy trying to understand what sort of conspiracies the count and his friends were in on. Salvioni sends a mysterious message. Stella Roncadelle is more powerful than Barack Obama. In the end, I bet it turns out that the killer is someone pissed off about a parking ticket."

"Shit, that must have been a steep ticket!"

"Do you know what I'm going to do?"

"Um, I'm afraid so."

"Do you know that feeling when you get an idea, but can't fully get it in focus, but you know it's the right one?"

"My ideas are never the right ones."

"I'm going back to where it all started and work forward until I find that bastard."

"Yeah, that's what I was afraid of."

"I'm heading out. I'll see you tomorrow after I've spoken to Dal Nero."

"OK, Ric, one last question."

"What?"

"Who are you leaving your cigar cutter to?"

"Hell no, Fabrizio! If you want the inheritance, you've got to kill someone first."

I asked Paolo to take me home so I could pick up my own car and he could finally go back to his life. I needed time to be alone and think—like a killer, if I could.

I thought that if I stopped trying to fit all the pieces of the puzzle together logically, maybe I'd manage to get a fresh perspective on the whole thing. The more I cleared my mind of all the assumptions that analyzing the facts had led us to, the more I'd feel like I was on the right track. First I'd thought the assassin had had something to gain, but now I couldn't help wondering if it was all some sort of self-punishment. If the assassin's mind was twisted, then I'd have to make my mind twisted, too.

Prey to my investigative delirium, I left Paolo and his protection in front of my house. I bade him farewell until the next murder, then I went to fill the dogs' bowls. Finally, I got into my own car and went straight back to Frassanelle. Alone.

When I got there at about seven thirty, three other cars were in the lot, and one was Enrico's. Clearly, the members had all left, and only a few employees were still around. I headed for the clubhouse and walked past the unattended bar. There was no one around, and I kept moving fast so my fear wouldn't get the better of me and make me turn back. I went downstairs and stopped at the same point where, on the day Massimo's body was found, I'd bumped into Officers Costanzo and Cipolla, together with Galli and the two secretaries.

I paused for a moment to try to remember what had been said, then I went past the secretaries' office to the locker room. The silence was disturbed only by the buzzing of the tired fluorescent lights and the sound of a dripping showerhead. I knew the lights were programmed to automatically turn off at eight, so I still had twenty minutes to look around.

Fear rushed over me as I entered the locker room, but I didn't care; just the opposite—it gave me an adrenaline rush that helped me stop thinking and, instead, just relive the sensations of what had happened. I sat down in the same place on the bench where Costanzo had grabbed me, and I remembered his questions—the typical "What are you up to?"—and his reproach at my clarifying the right word for the sauna— "There's a murdered man in there, and you're arguing with me about whether it's a Turkish bath?"—while we were waiting for Giulia.

It's strange. I'm not normally that pedantic . . . So why did I say that? Something didn't fit. Hell, why wasn't it a Turkish bath? What actually made it a sauna? What difference did it make? I shook my head and tried not to think about it. I needed to feel, not think.

I stood up and walked past my locker. Everything was talking to me; I felt like I'd been hypnotized. I was perceiving with my senses instead of thinking with my mind. I saw the empty basket for the dirty towels, which Carlo had been collecting that day for the laundry, and my eyes caught something that didn't fit. My mind was unable to decode the message, but my instinct was enough.

I stood stock-still to try to crystallize the sensation and took the time to metabolize each single perception. I moved toward the sauna, my heart beating faster. I closed my eyes for a moment and heard steps coming down the stairs. But it didn't matter. In that moment, I went back to that day like I was in a time machine, like I was really back there when I saw the sauna door and its porthole window. The feeling of alarm was as strong now as it was then, and everything was telling me the killer was behind me. He'd always been there. I'd seen him, touched him, and he'd never run away or hidden. I was overcome with a pain that took my breath away, and I leaned against the sauna door and bent my head to drink from the cup of truth. I'd always known who it was; my eyes had seen, but my mind hadn't understood. I looked clearly through the window at the spot where Massimo had just been a fuzzy stain. I heard the steps very close to me again, turned around, and saw the killer standing before me.

When he met my eye, he realized that I knew.

"I couldn't let him destroy my son's life."

"Arcadio is your son?"

"You still don't get it, do you? You're all so caught up in your golf, all you care about is putting that fucking ball in the hole, then you drink champagne and have dinner together, right? None of you give a fuck about real life. When he said those words, I had to destroy him. That's what your friend Salvioni wanted, right?"

I let him talk without interrupting, hoping that someone would arrive in the meantime. I'd left my trance because now I needed my brain to work—and fast. In a physical confrontation with Carlo, I wouldn't stand a chance. Even if my right hand had been working, his muscles had been sculpted by routine hard work, and if that weren't enough, he had a golf club in his hand and murder in his eyes.

"Why did you leave your son to the count? Why didn't you bring him up?"

"What sort of life could I have given him? I didn't even have the money to buy food. I was eighteen and nobody would give me a job. But what the fuck do you know about it? You've always had everything. What do you know about having to tell the mother of your child that she can't keep him? Do you know what it means not even having clothes to be able to go out in public? I earned a little doing odd jobs around the count's castle, but it wasn't enough even to feed myself, much less a family. Then one day, the count turned up and said he'd heard about the pregnancy, and offered to take my son in exchange for money. Do you know what it means for a parent to hand their son over to another person so he can have a future? Then after all the sacrifice and pain, you three come along and decide that Arcadio isn't Count Alvise's son, and do you know where that piece of shit doctor decided to have his little chat with the count? In the club bag room! And not only did he complain about Arcadio's behavior, no! Salvioni had to ruin everyone's lives and throw the truth in the count's face when anyone can understand it should have been kept secret. He told the count he knew that Arcadio wasn't his son. I followed Salvioni to the bag room and hid, so I could hear everything. When I couldn't take it anymore and confronted him, do you know what that prick did? He pulled out his phone and wrote you a text. Do you know what he said to me? If I stay calm, he won't send the message, but if I raise my fist, then he will—but the bastard was already sending it to you, and the count saw it all! Then he told me that he'd sent it to you because you were a reporter and curious as shit and would do anything to discover the truth. I killed him with my own hands while the count stood there paralyzed with fear, and in the end, he ran off. Now I'm going to do the same to you!"

"Apart from the fact you already tried and failed."

"I wasn't certain you were a threat to my family. I told you that if you'd just behave properly, the killer would leave you alone. Don't you remember that day you came to practice your pathetic putting? You didn't understand anything I was telling you, did you? I even stitched Salvioni's mouth shut so you'd see you had to keep quiet, and I put him in the sauna as a warning for all of you."

"You killed Arcadio's grandmother, you psycho!"

"What grandmother? The nasty old woman was so afraid that she wanted to give her toy back to me and go confess everything to the police."

Despite my frantic efforts to find a solution, fear prevented me from thinking clearly. All I could think of was how to buy a little more time and piss him off, something I'm an expert at, until I forced him to lose control.

When Carlo made a move, I raised my arm like a traffic cop, and shouted. "Hey, hey! Wait a minute. It's just you and me here, and you don't have time to call for backup."

My brazen attempt to turn the tables worked, throwing Carlo off balance enough that I was able to go on. "Before I send you to your maker, I want to tell you a couple things. You're right when you say I don't give a fuck about your useless life, but what did you expect, you idiot? That I'd start crying and beg for mercy? From a prick like you? My friend Massimo is dead, do you not get that—"

Carlo leapt forward, but I'd achieved my goal: just then, the eight o'clock timer triggered all the switches and plunged the locker room into darkness.

I leapt forward, too, to shorten the distance between us and avoid getting hit by the golf club. I tried to rotate my hip so as to absorb the blow with my shoulder, but I didn't have time, and then we were pressed right up against each other. Luckily, Carlo never imagined that I'd attack him. His stance was better suited to a running lunge than a face-to-face fight. I jumped up with my head down so my forehead slammed him full in the face, stunning him for a few moments. We both fell. Still on the ground, I rolled onto my side and jumped back up. I knew I still had the advantage of a few fractions of a second, so I pulled back my right leg, kicked toward where I thought his head was, and hit the mark. This helped me maintain my small edge. I tried running toward the door, but after a couple of steps, I banged into the wall. I started moving again, feeling my way along the wall, trying to make as little noise as possible so Carlo couldn't detect where I was, but then he let out a shout of inhuman fury. My ploy to piss him off had certainly worked, but now I thought I might have overdone it.

I kept on scurrying along the wall, confident I'd found the best way to get through the dark, but I forgot to hold one hand out in front of me to feel for any obstacles, and I ran right into the first locker in the row. The blow was so hard it knocked me backward, causing me to lose my balance and contact with the wall.

In the meantime, Carlo had realized that, while it was liberating to scream at the top of his voice, it wasn't the best tactic under these circumstances. He'd obviously heard me collide with the locker and worked out where I was. I couldn't stop now, so I just began walking in any direction with my arms out in front like a sleepwalker, and without realizing it, I was back at the sauna. Carlo was moving fast, swinging the club willy-nilly, hoping he'd be lucky and hit me, but the iron whistled through the air as it moved, and, in addition to giving me goose bumps, it helped me track where he was. I guessed there were about fifteen or twenty feet between us, but I couldn't play cat and mouse all night, and the ferocious beast was between me and the exit.

When I touched the wood wall in the sauna, I recognized it by its rough surface and the heat it still gave off. I knew there was a metal ladle in there that we used to pour water onto the stones, so I opened the door and groped around for it. It wasn't a golf club, but it was something. I knew Carlo must have heard the sauna door, but I didn't realize how close he'd gotten.

I heard his voice just a step away, threatening me, making me back into the sauna in surprise.

"I'm gonna kill you, Ranieri!"

I heard the whistle of the iron and felt a searing pain in my side. Instinctively, I bent over and reacted by swinging out the ladle. Carlo didn't expect me to have a weapon and I hit him full in the face. In the surprise, he stumbled backward, and I hit him some more with all the strength I had. As I raised the ladle, I whacked something attached to the wall so hard that I heard an awful metallic tearing sound, and when I hit Carlo again, the impact felt different, somehow softer. His cry of pain sounded suffocated, and a spurt of blood hit me. I didn't know what had happened, but I didn't stop, and prey to frenzy, I continued hitting his body. His moans of pain got weaker with each blow, and finally I had no more strength to lift my arms.

It was utter exhaustion that stopped me at last. I dropped the ladle on the floor and bent over my knees to catch my breath, then I stepped out of the sauna and was blinded by sudden light.

I heard somebody shout from outside the locker room and I turned around to look into the now-lit sauna: Carlo was on the floor in a pool of blood, his throat wide open. I collapsed against the locker room wall and waited for someone to come.

After a few minutes, or maybe an eternity, Marshal Costanzo and Enrico were standing in front of me.

The marshal spoke first. "Start talking, Ranieri."

I looked at him, but no words came, so I pointed to the sauna door.

Enrico looked in and saw Carlo's body.

"Holy shit, what the fuck happened?" he exclaimed in horror.

Marshal Costanzo went to the sauna, turning pale at the sight of the body.

"He tried to kill me! He killed Massimo . . ."

Costanzo spoke firmly and decisively. "Enrico, go and call District Attorney Dal Nero and ask her to come immediately. Call an ambulance. Oh! And call Cipolla and ask him to come as well."

My arms were shaking and my legs felt weak; I slid down and sat on the floor with my back against the wall.

The marshal was towering over me. I noticed he'd pulled out his gun, but I didn't particularly care.

"Is he dead?"

"Almost, Ranieri."

My hands were covered with blood: the left with Carlo's, the right probably mine because I could feel the pain where I'd been operated on.

Cipolla arrived, and he was as horrified as Enrico. Costanzo was clearly torn between wanting to interrogate me and fear of getting pulled into this mess, so he just kept looking at me with something approaching respect. A few minutes later, I heard the very familiar sound of the ambulance and police sirens, and soon the sauna was filled with paramedics. I looked for the giant paramedic who'd assisted me in the past, but I couldn't see him. Then the police arrived, and while the officers were still standing around me, I saw the medics lift Carlo's dying body, place him on the stretcher, and carry him out. A few minutes later, I heard the sound of the ambulance siren leaving, but then another arrived for me.

I looked at my right hand. The blood was coagulating on the old wound, but it still hurt a lot, then I felt my forehead where I found a bump where I'd head-butted Carlo, or maybe it was from hitting the locker. I looked down at the ground and was overcome by a sense of fatigue like I'd never felt before. Finally, I took my cigar case out of my pocket, put a cigar in my mouth, and lit it.

Costanzo complained, "Hey, Ranieri, what do you think you're doing? You can't smoke here."

I looked at him without speaking, shrugged my shoulders, and took a drag of my cigar.

"Ah, Ranieri! You again, I knew it. This is a record!"

Delighted at finding his favorite patient in rough shape once again, the giant paramedic knelt down beside me in his orange jacket with its white fluorescent stripes.

"What happened this time?"

"I hurt all over."

"Let's see your hands."

"The blood on the left hand isn't mine."

Then I saw Giulia behind him. She knelt down, too, and asked, full of concern, "What happened, Riccardo? What can you tell me?"

While the paramedic was tending to my hand, I told Giulia and Marshal Costanzo everything that had happened.

"But how did you know it was him?" Giulia asked at the end.

"It was something I said to Marshal Costanzo."

Hearing he'd somehow helped solve the case, the marshal proudly stuck out his chest.

"When I found Salvioni's body in the sauna, the marshal called it a Turkish bath, and I corrected him, saying it's a sauna."

"So?"

"It wasn't until today that I realized why I corrected him. When I saw Salvioni's body through the window, I had to go inside to see it properly because the window was steamed up. But unlike a Turkish bath, a sauna doesn't fill with steam, so the glass never steams up. So that meant that somebody had held the sauna door open for a long time, or at least long enough to drag the body in there and then kill him. Then I remembered that I'd seen Carlo before I took a shower that day, while he was collecting the dirty towels, and I figured he was getting them ready for the laundry, but this evening, when I saw the laundry baskets, I remembered that the cleaners collect the towels—not the caddies. So that morning, Carlo must have been cleaning Salvioni's blood off himself!"

Giulia bent over and rested her hand on my knee, saying with affectionate respect, "Bravo, Riccardo. You've been as good as you were crazy."

Then she turned to the paramedic and asked, "Do you think we should take Mr. Ranieri to the hospital?"

"Ranieri, let's go and check out that bump on your head, OK?"

"Now, look, my friend—"

Giulia broke in, "Friend? Do you know each other?"

"Know each other? We go together like peas and carrots! Anyway, I have no intention of getting in an ambulance again or going back to that hospital. Just one last thing, though."

"What?"

"Just so we're clear—I'm a carrot!"

EPILOGUE

For some reason I didn't understand, I was taken to the Abano police station.

Giulia stayed with me, peppering me with questions, making me repeat at least ten times everything Carlo had said.

When we entered the station, Giulia and I were informed that Carlo was dead. In the sauna, I'd caught the ladle on the metal grill over a light, which broke the ladle and turned it into a very sharp hook, and with my next blows, I'd cut open Carlo's throat.

Two police officers took me into a room and sat me down at a table, where I'd make my statement with Giulia present. There was also a plainclothes officer with us who introduced himself, but in my confused state, I didn't understand who he was.

I'd killed a man. I wanted to take a moment to try to understand how I felt about that, but the police didn't give me time, asking thousands of questions, asking me to remember everything Carlo and I had said. When I'd finished my detailed report, they asked me to start again from the beginning. When the officer asked his opening question again for the millionth time, I'd had enough.

"Listen, I know you have to be certain I'm not making things up, and I realize that when a man's dead you have to follow certain procedures, but if you make me tell the story yet again, then I'll probably change something so it doesn't sound so monotonous."

Neither they nor Giulia laughed. Instead, they made me repeat everything three more times over. After the sixth, they were finally satisfied.

After leaving me alone in the room for twenty minutes, Giulia came back to tell me they'd already located some blood-stained towels hidden in the bag room, and I was free to go or, perhaps, be accompanied home.

I looked her in the eyes and asked, "It's all over, right?"

She smiled and looked warmly at me.

"I wish it was all over, but I'm afraid there's still something missing."

"What?"

"Riccardo, we're convinced that Carlo didn't kill Patty Salvioni."

"Do you have any idea who did?"

"Yes, I think we finally do."

"Can you tell me?"

"Arcadio's mother."

Still in shock from everything that had happened, it hadn't yet dawned on me that, if Carlo was Arcadio's father, his mother was probably Italian and not from Santo Domingo as I'd imagined.

"Do you know who she is?"

"Unfortunately, no, but we should be able to work that out pretty quickly. Given the danger, you do realize that we can't leave you at home alone, don't you?"

"Sure, another cop on my heels, then?"

"Paolo again, and he's on his way here now. And until we've arrested Arcadio's mother, there'll be a police car stationed in front of your gate."

I was so infamous in Bastia at this point that having a police car in front of my house could hardly make things worse.

Paolo arrived five minutes later, seeming more rattled than I was. Panting, he asked me what had happened.

"Paolo, don't get me wrong . . . but please don't ask me that. If I have to repeat it one more time, I'll kill myself."

Giulia filled him in, then I said good-bye to her, and we arranged to meet late the next morning at Frassanelle.

As Paolo was driving me home, I called Piovesan.

"Riccardo, what happened? Fabrizio went to the Frassanelle Golf Club because we heard there'd been some kind of argument between you and a club employee!"

"I wouldn't call it an argument. Carlo, the head caddy, tried to kill me because I realized he killed Massimo Salvioni. And Mrs. Roncadelle."

"Shit! So you discovered who the killer was, then!"

"Yes, one of them."

"What? Do you mean there are others?"

"Salvioni's wife was killed by a woman."

"Do you know who?"

"The investigators have an idea. I can't say any more, because if that woman reads the papers tomorrow and tries to run, then I'll have to run, too, because Dal Nero wouldn't be very forgiving."

I decided it was time to change the topic.

"Gibbo, I'm going home. Tell Fabrizio to come by my place so we can link my computer to the office and send the article as soon as it's ready."

"I'll call him now. Well done, Ricky! See, I was right to bring you to breaking news. Good job, damn it, good job!"

When Paolo and I reached the gate to my house, Fabrizio was already there chatting with Giuseppe and his wife. I greeted them hastily, and then we rushed into the house to connect to the editing office.

As it was already after midnight by now, Romeo Sottil, the printing manager, gave us thirty minutes at most to completely rework the front page and insert the entire article. We worked feverishly and managed to put together a piece that the other papers couldn't get for at least another day. I kept strictly to the facts and didn't reveal anything that Carlo had confessed to me, but hinted that the main motives were found not only in serious poverty, but also in the folly of a father who had to give up his son to give him a better life.

"This man, he wasn't normal, though!"

I was so absorbed in writing the article that only then did I realize that Giuseppe had crept into my house and was listening to our conversation.

I started to offer everyone a drink, but then the weight of the day's events overwhelmed me. Throwing hospitality to the wind, I said good night, took a quick shower, and went to bed.

Despite my exhaustion, I didn't sleep a wink that night.

I tried not to think about it, but my fight with Carlo kept replaying before my eyes. I thought of all the implications of what he'd said: a life spent living so close to, but impossibly separated from, his son, a lifetime of suffering, just to give that boy a new identity. I was certain now that Arcadio knew nothing about any of it, and when he learned the truth, it would be a real blow; first he wasn't Count Alvise's real son, now he was the killer's. I knew nothing about Carlo's private life, if he was married or had a partner. I hoped Giulia would tell me the next morning.

At about seven, fed up with turning around and around like a spit over the fire, I couldn't stay in bed any longer. I got up, dressed quickly, woke Paolo, and after a quick breakfast, we headed off to Frassanelle.

When we arrived, there were three police cars outside the club, and I assumed they'd come to talk to Galli. A police officer was blocking the entrance to members and, above all, the press, but Paolo didn't even need to show his badge—the officer recognized me and waved us in.

Once inside, everyone there was standing at the bar. I caught Francesca's eye for a moment, and, once again, there was that strong sensation, totally separate from logical thought. I replayed the words

Carlo shouted at me during his confession. That day when Massimo and I had complained about Arcadio, Francesca was behind the bar. She was Arcadio's real mother.

In the middle of the group of police officers, Giulia was watching me, and when I caught her eye and nodded toward Francesca, she nodded back.

Like a sequence in a mirror, everything finished where it had started.

With Galli there, Giulia told me that she and the investigators had figured out who Arcadio's mother was after I'd told her about Francesca asking about me in Bastia. She also told me how she'd told Arcadio everything and how upset he was. She said he would need a long time to gather up the remnants of his existence after so much shock. I was so upset about having killed a man that it took a little while to fully comprehend that it wasn't just Salvioni who'd opened the horrific can of worms with his complaints in front of the bartender, but me, too.

Galli was called away by one of his secretaries, so I was left alone for a moment with Giulia. We looked at each other without speaking, and I thought her expression seemed slightly embarrassed, even shy. As if to escape the awkwardness, she told me about Francesca's confession.

"Patty Salvioni heard some suspicious noises in her husband's study, so she went to the door armed with a golf club that he kept at home, and she saw Francesca. Francesca, panicking about being caught stealing the documents from the medical files, grabbed the club from Patty's hand and hit her with it repeatedly."

I was speechless, but again I felt a certain tension between Giulia and me.

We looked at each other without speaking. I drew closer to her face, sensing that the inevitable moment had arrived. Her look betrayed the full storm of emotions she was feeling, but I wasn't going to let the moment pass, so without giving her time to think, I caressed her lips with my finger and kissed her tenderly on the cheek. Then I moved my mouth close to her ear and whispered sincerely and reassuringly to her,

"Giulia, don't be afraid. I don't want to hurt you. When you feel ready, please call me."

We looked into each other's eyes again and, in hers, I read a serene complicity that gave me great hope for my, our, future.

It was two months before I wanted to go back to playing golf.

I'm a pretty average player, so if I want to have a shot, I have to follow my routine methodically and persistently.

So, in an effort to reestablish that routine, the first time I went to play at the club, I stopped at the bar.

"Welcome back, Riccardo."

"Thank you, Luisa. How are you?"

"Fine. Do you want your usual espresso in a mug?"

"Yes, please."

"Riccardo, can I ask you . . . Why do you always order a single shot in a big mug?"

I had no more patience for mysteries, so I answered, "Luisa, the price is the same, isn't it?"

"Yes, but . . ."

"So why risk being sold short?"

ACKNOWLEDGMENTS

I wrote this book to fulfill a dream that I'd always kept hidden, not even confessing it to myself at times.

But no matter how strong my desire to write, the book would never have come to life without the tireless encouragement of certain people. In strict alphabetic and chronological disorder, I thank Goralda (no printing error, that's her name), Erica, Antonella, Nicoletta, Gianni, and Chiara—whom I cruelly left hanging at chapter eight—as well as Luca and Daniela. Without the individual help of each of them, *Murder on the 18th Green* would have been nothing more than a fussy order at the bar.

If the book is legible and error free, thanks go to the expertise of Tiziana Cappellini, whose skill is equaled only by her patience.

While the characters in the book are all fictitious, I must point out certain facts: the caddies at the Frassanelle Golf Club are not in the habit of killing the club members. What's more, Massimo, the real caddy master, is a close friend and also the loving father of one of the most polite and smartest boys I know. To further remove any doubt as to my inspiration, Massimo is an excellent golf player, unlike Carlo Buonafiore, who is purely the fruit of my imagination.

My real neighbors are wonderful people (and very reserved!), and without them, my garden would resemble an unexplored jungle, and I'd never have discovered that I had jujube trees!

Although the land where the golf course stands is effectively owned by a count, the character of Alvise Casati Vitali di Nogaredo in my book only took shape in my mind—after the third glass of Cabernet I was drinking at dinner with friends.

All the businesses and their relative managers and owners are invented, except Enrico, who runs the restaurant at the golf club. He really does exist, as does his excellent cooking. In fact, if you're ever in the Veneto, I strongly recommend you go for a meal there—it really is worth it.

I used poetic license to create the caricature of Marshal Costanzo, but recently I met the real marshal in Bastia: a very serious, reliable, and efficient man. Given how different he is, I feel it superfluous to deny all other references to reality.

Finally, and running the risk of a lawsuit for slander, I must reveal that two key characters whom I described in minute detail really do exist: Mila and Newton, my beloved German shepherds.

ABOUT THE AUTHOR

Federico Maria Rivalta was born in Milan in 1959. A graduate in economics and commerce, he is a director at one of Italy's leading private companies. *Murder on the 18th Green* is his first novel.

ABOUT THE TRANSLATOR

Elizabeth Pollard is an Italian-to-English literary translator working with Centro Studi Ateneo.